Carson Spade

A Fake Wife for the Cowboy Billionaire

by Sophie Devon

Morgan Spade by Sophie Devon. Published by Thady Publishing. Copyright © 2022 Sophie Devon. This is a work of fiction. Names, characters, places and incidents are either the products of the author's imagination or are used fictitiously. Any resemblance to actual persons, living or dead, business, companies, events or locales are entirely coincidental. All rights reserved. No portion of this book may be reproduced in any form without permission from the publisher, except as permitted by U.S. copyright law.

Chapter One

"Come on down to Big Clem's Baby Barn and pick out a new bassinet for your little cowboy," a hearty voice burbled through the car radio.

"The first 100 mothers get a free pack of diapers!"

Carson Spade switched off the car radio to cut off the obnoxious voice mid-bawl. He adjusted one shoulder, loosened his collar, and pulled his gleaming Jaguar off the highway and curved up the off ramp outside the Dallas-Fort Worth Airport. To his dismay, even the billboards flashing past on the side of the road were screaming *baby, baby, baby.*

Hey you there buddy, why aren't you married yet?

Most guys have at least one kid by your age, Jack.

Having a hard time holding on to a woman?

Carson ran a hand through his head of sleek black hair, and slowly the exit ramp signs reverted to their normal look. It was just possible that he might be interpreting the toy store and amusement park billboards through the filter of his irritation.

He was the third Spade brother, and the oldest who was still single. Still, he hadn't expected that his two older brothers getting married would result in all eyes turning to *him* after. He was surprised by how fast it happened, too.

It seemed he was the only one around the ranch who wasn't worried about him settling down.

Carson, my cousin's going to be in town this weekend. Will you help me show her the sights?

Hey Carson, I saw Janine O'Leary at the post office yesterday. Didn't you and her use to date in high school?

How old are you now, Carson?

Carson grumbled under his breath and shifted into second gear. He didn't share Buck and Morgan's religious faith, but he was almost tempted to cross himself when he imagined what they were plotting for him.

It was time for a vacation from the family.

He stopped at the light and flicked his turning signal. When he searched his own heart, he could truthfully say that he was glad that Buck and Morgan were happy. Marriage seemed to suit them. He was fond of his nieces and nephews. They were good kids.

But it was nevertheless true that things had changed.

Radically.

Carson turned onto the main drag outside the airport and moved into the right hand lane. Only a few short years ago the Seven ranch house had been a comfortable, if not always civilized bachelor cave. It was perfect for parties, and he'd thrown quite a few that had lasted into the wee hours of the morning. Not one of his brothers had opened his mouth to complain, even though some of them hadn't approved.

His privacy had been near-total. He'd stayed gone as often as he'd stayed home, and only Buck had the nerve to quiz him about where he'd been. Even that had only been because Buck thought it was his job to know everything that was going on with the family.

Carson sighed. Now, if he ducked out for even a day or two, his new sisters-in-law would be sure to tease the whole story out of him after. It was likely just female curiosity; but still.

There had been a time when he could walk downstairs wearing nothing but a highball glass, free of any worry about who he might meet on the stairs.

Not anymore.

Now he wrapped up in a housecoat even when he went to the kitchen for a midnight snack, because his sisters-in-law and his little niece were in the house, too. And his legendary all-night parties were a thing of the past, as well. There were two kids and one newborn across the hall, and the fastest way to get Buck pounding on his door was to wake his baby after ten at night.

Considering all of those things, there had never been a better time for him to get out of Dodge. He sent the sleek Jaguar zooming down the parking lot lane, blew past the entry gates, and moved into the express lane.

Twenty minutes later Carson found himself comfortably ensconced in the VIP lounge outside his boarding gate. He had a first-class ticket to bluegrass country in his pocket, a steaming espresso in his hand, and a made-to-order reason for skipping town: The fall thoroughbred yearling auction in Lexington, Kentucky.

But if he was honest with himself, he would've grabbed any plausible excuse to get out of that house, where his mere existence was a challenge to every matchmaker in his family. Carson took a long, deliberative sip of coffee and stared into space. For the moment, he'd thrown his sisters-in-law off his trail by sacrificing his unsuspecting brother Luke.

Kate had a friend in town who apparently needed a husband.

Carson shook with silent laughter as he imagined Luke's outraged face. His only regret was that he couldn't be there to see the awful truth dawn on his younger brother: that he was the entree for Kate's husband-hungry guest.

Carson's phone vibrated in his jacket, and he chuckled and took another sip of coffee before picking it up.

"Hello?"

To his surprise, Morgan's voice answered. His silent second brother wasn't one for unnecessary gab, and a flick of worry branched over him.

"Hey Carson, it's Morgan."

"Well, I can't remember the last time you called me," Carson teased. "Is everything all right?"

To his relief, his brother's voice was jubilant. "Better than all right," he replied, and Carson could hear an ear-to-ear smile in his voice. "I just thought I'd tell you before you heard it from somebody else. We found out today that Heather's having triplets!"

The news struck the smile right off Carson's face, and his first thought was, *You poor devil;* but of course his brother was delighted, and Carson tried to be delighted for him.

"Why...that's amazing, Morg," he stammered. "Congratulations to you and Heather!"

"We still don't know what they all are," Morgan went on, "but we kinda hope they're a mix of boys and girls."

Carson boggled as he imagined the ranch house after three more babies in it, and he reached for his pack of cigarettes and shook out a paper cylinder. "Well, Mom had twin sisters, so I guess multiples run in the family," he mumbled.

"Hey, that's right," Morgan laughed, "I'd forgotten about Aunt Marlene and Irene. Guess that gene just skipped a generation."

"Well, I'm glad for you and Heather, Morg," Carson said, and he meant it; but the inevitable inrush of Heather's female friends that was sure to follow made him doubly glad he was on his way out of state. "I'm glad you called!"

"Yeah, I just couldn't keep it to myself," Morgan mumbled happily; then added, "Oh yeah, I almost forgot. Luke said to tell you that he wants to see you when you get back."

Carson lit his cigarette and sputtered smoke and laughter into the air. "Oh? What about?"

"He didn't tell. He just said you'd know."

"Well, it must have something to do with that dinner he had at Kate and Buck's," Carson replied softly. "I think he met a friend of Kate's. She and Luke must've hit it off."

"Oh?" Morgan rumbled. "I didn't know that Luke was seeing a friend of Kate's."

"Oh yeah," Carson replied, and struggled to keep his voice even. "Probably *real* taken with her. Why else would he call me to talk about it?"

"Yeah, you're likely right," Morgan mumbled. "I'll have to see if Heather and Kate can fix something up for them, then."

"I know he'll be grateful," Carson replied, with closed eyes and a wavering voice. "Look, Morg, my plane is boarding, so I have to go. But I'm over the moon about your news. Give Heather a kiss for me!"

"I'll do it," Morgan rumbled. "Talk to you later."

"Bye, Morg."

Carson pressed the red button and took a last sip of coffee before rising to board the plane. But his laughter faded as the grim reality gripped him:

Multiples run in the family.

One more reason I'm not getting married, he thought with a shudder, and took one last drag on his cigarette before the gate attendant made him throw it away.

Chapter Two

"Here we are, Mr. Spade. I hope you have a pleasant stay."

The limo driver smiled at Carson over the opened car door, and Carson climbed out of the limo's plush back seat. His afternoon flight to Lexington had been smooth and pleasant, and he was looking forward to a nice filet mignon and a glass of fine bourbon at his club. He stood up and tugged his navy jacket straight.

The Turf Club was the most exclusive resort within a hundred miles of Lexington. The immaculately-manicured campus was well outside the city, tucked away in rolling green hills behind tall security gates that only its employees and its well-heeled guests ever passed. There was a five-acre lake with a massive fountain just beyond the entrance, and the long, flat, cobbled main drive rolled through Kentucky horse pastures for two miles before the hotel even crept into view.

The main club house was a beautiful old white-columned mansion with three stories and a wraparound porch. The house was surrounded by ancient oaks whose massive branches and clouds of leaves threw a pleasant, dappled shade over the gardens and grounds.

The main house was connected to its matching white outbuildings by vine-shaded, covered walkways: the long, low restaurant, the gym, the pool, the tennis courts. Further on, the pleasant green grounds were dotted with antebellum-style bungalows for guests who desired more privacy.

Beyond those were a huge complex of resort stables and pastures for the club horses.

Carson adjusted his cuffs and launched off the edge of the curving drive, down the short path, up the porch steps, and up to the glittering, beveled front door. A beaming doorman opened it for him.

"Welcome back, Mr. Spade. We've been expecting you. Your room is ready."

"Thanks, Wilson," Carson murmured, and stepped into the lobby. The gleaming windows of the big room were ceiling high, and the polished wooden floors creaked softly under his shoes as he drifted to the huge front desk. An antique painting of Aristides, the first race horse to win the Kentucky Derby, hung in a golden frame on the wall behind the clerk's head.

"Good afternoon, Mr. Spade!" the young woman chirped brightly, and handed him a key.

"Lunch is just served in the restaurant, but perhaps you'd prefer it to be brought to your room?"

Carson took the key and smiled, "I'm good. I'll have a filet mignon, the house salad, and a glass of Pappy Van Winkle to start—neat, with a drop of water."

"I'll phone your order into the kitchen, Mr. Spade. Your lunch will be ready at the restaurant in twenty minutes at your usual table."

"Thanks."

Carson turned to skip up the gleaming stairway on the right side of the big room, and he hummed to himself as he went. He'd been dreaming of that steak all the way from Dallas, and twenty minutes gave him just enough time to get a quick shower and shave before his meal.

He sauntered down the thickly-carpeted upstairs hall and jingled the room keys in his hand. He always got the same room, the Secretariat Suite at the very end of the hall, because it was huge and comfortable and had a particularly fine view of the grounds from the bedroom balcony.

There was a frosted transom window over the polished wooden door, and when Carson opened it, he walked into a perfectly-reproduced antebellum bedroom. The wooden floors gleamed, the cherry wood furniture was period and elegant, and the big windows opposite the door were thrown open to reveal the garden outside drowsing under a mellow, early-autumn sun. The afternoon breeze was flowing in through those open doors, and it made the whole suite smell of fresh air, pressed linen, and mown grass.

Carson closed the suite door behind him and loosened his collar. He drifted across the floor to the balcony doorway and out into the soft, shaded afternoon. The scent of autumn leaves whispered to him from the big oak directly opposite his balcony, and as he watched, a pair of squirrels went scrambling over one of its massive branches. His glance moved to the gaps in the oak's sun-dappled leaves. Through them, far in the distance, he could see sleek thoroughbreds galloping across a green meadow.

Carson stuck his hands in his trouser pockets and exhaled a long, slow, satisfied breath.

Yes, the Turf Club was just the sort of place he liked: civilized, old-money elegant, and full of potential buyers for the Seven yearlings. Carson stood still and silent for a minute and watched as the sleek thoroughbreds pranced in the distance.

He had three beauties of his own on the way: champion-level yearlings that deserved to get top dollar, all sired by Lickety Split, a Preakness winner that they'd bought for stud duty. Their current crop of yearlings were all sleek, fast colts by Lickety Split and three of their best fillies. They'd named them Seven Bells, Blue Streak, and High Spade. They were all a rich red-brown, just like the bourbon awaiting him in the restaurant; and like it, they were smooth as silk.

The best of them, in his opinion, was High Spade. The year-old colt was a beautiful specimen, long and lean, quick, full of fire. But all of them were worth upwards of a million dollars.

With luck, High Spade might fetch twice the money of the other two colts: and he was determined to get as much for their beautiful yearlings as he could.

Carson's phone disrupted his reverie with a shrill, insistent alarm. He dug it out of his pocket and saw that he had a curt text from home. It was from Luke, and it was right to the point. It read:

I hate you, man.

I'm coming for you.

Carson chuckled under his breath and tapped out a reply.

Just thinking of your happiness, buddy.

Let us know if there's good news.

He pressed the send button and sauntered off to the bathroom, laughing to himself.

Yes, everything was going very conveniently so far.

Smooth as silk.

Chapter Three

"Donna, Mr. Spade's arrived and he wants a glass of Pappy Van Winkle with his lunch in fifteen minutes."

Donna Bouchet balanced her phone between her ear and her shoulder, unlocked a tiny drawer on her 100-year-old desk, and fished a key out. "I'll be right down. Thanks, Vicky."

"Sure."

Donna stood up, smoothed out her white blouse and linen skirt, and walked briskly out of her office and down the big staircase of the main house. As the general manager of the Turf Club, she was responsible not just for the day to day operations of the resort, but the security of its most expensive assets.

And 25-year-old Pappy Van Winkle *was* expensive. It was one of the rarest, finest, most sought-after bourbons in Kentucky, and every bottle in their inventory was worth $40,000.

She hurried to the back porch of the mansion, descended its well worn brick steps, and breezed through the walkway that connected it to the elegant, plantation-style restaurant a hundred yards across the manicured lawn. She had to make Mr. Spade's drink personally, because the owners of the club didn't trust even vetted bartenders with a $40,000 bottle of liquor. A bottle of stolen Pappy would be snapped up, no questions asked, by any number of eager buyers.

Donna opened the brass-trimmed door of The Coach House Restaurant, turned right in the cobbled foyer, opened a locked door, and descended a dark, narrow flight of stairs. Their select liquors were kept in the wine cellar underneath the restaurant in a special locked room. The club possessed four precious bottles of the rare, 25-year-old Pappys, and they were lucky to have them.

It was a point of pride for Donna that none of those bottles, or anything else entrusted to her care, had ever been damaged or gone missing.

She fished out the key and opened the metal door at the bottom of the stairs. The restaurant manager was the only other person to have the key to the wine cellar, a cool, dimly-lit, brick-lined room with racks of bottles on every wall. It was the storehouse for the everyday wines and liquors, and the most expensive of them cost no more than a few thousand dollars.

But the door at the far end of the cellar guarded the real treasure cave. It could only be opened by her own thumb on the biometric lock, and it held bottles of top-shelf liquor that were up to fifty years old; aged, handcrafted cigars; exotic pipe tobaccos; and even imported teas. Most of these rare, artisan labels were known only to connoisseurs and all were breathtakingly expensive. Their combined value was in the millions of dollars, and a theft would be devastating to the club.

Donna pressed her thumb to the biometric lock with a little smile. She sometimes fantasized that she was a cat burglar, complete with mask and black bag, come to clean out that little room. It gave a mundane task a furtive little tingle of excitement.

A cat burglar was almost the only thing she hadn't yet been in her varied career. In her short life she'd already lived on four continents and worked in a wide variety of jobs. At the moment, it was high-end hospitality, but she'd been a chorus girl on Broadway, an Australian flight attendant, a designer for a small fashion house in Paris, and an apprentice bobby in London.

She had a restless foot and it was beginning to tingle again, which might explain why she was fantasizing about cleaning out the little store room and disappearing into the blue.

Her life at the club, pleasant as it was, had become stale. Predictable. She'd been the manager for three years already, and she knew her routine so well she could recite it in her sleep. That feeling usually preceded a letter of resignation and a plane trip to another part of the world.

She had a far higher tolerance for risk, than for boredom.

Donna reached for the bottle of bourbon, pressed it securely against her body, and closed the door of the little room behind her.

She hurried through the wine cellar and climbed up the stairs at a good clip, because she couldn't keep Mr. Spade waiting. He was a lifetime member of the Turf Club, one of the richest men in their rarefied clientele, and one of the most respected names in thoroughbred breeding circles.

She turned at the top of the stairs to lock the outer cellar door. Carson Spade came to the club almost exclusively to attend the fall yearling sale at Keeneland, and to rub elbows with buyers beforehand. He was a tall, gorgeous, thirtyish Texan. He was single and had no children or ex wives. He had refined tastes in food, clothes, and drink; he sometimes attended polo tournaments while in town; and he never attended any two of them with the same woman on his arm.

That was the extent of her file on Mr. Spade. She had one for every member of the club. It was her job to know their guests' personalities and preferences, because she was expected to anticipate their requests.

She paused on the threshold of the elegant dining room, took a deep breath, and launched out to Mr. Spade's table by the big southern windows. He was already there, and Donna raised an eyebrow as she threaded a careful path through the linen-draped tables.

She'd forgotten how handsome he was. He looked like a model sitting at that window table, with the light glancing off his ink-black, precisely cut hair and strong, perfectly-shaved profile. His clothes were designer label and flawlessly pressed, and as she approached, she learned that he was slightly fragrant of some heavenly cologne. She tilted her head as she neared. She was almost sure it was Clive Christian—probably 1872.

That, too, was a connoisseur label, and she gave the fellow a twinkling glance as she paused beside his table.

Well, aren't you just the dashing devil, she thought wryly, but pasted a big, professional smile on her face.

"Here we are, Mr. Spade." She set the bottle of bourbon down on the tablecloth and opened it deftly. The waiter had already set a Glencairn glass there for her, and she poured out two fingers of caramel-colored alcohol, carefully stoppered the bottle, and pinched a speck of water into his drink from a glass dropper lying on the linen tablecloth.

She waited, as she was required to do, and watched as Carson Spade lifted the glass to his lips, took a deliberative pull, closed his eyes, and sighed.

"Satisfactory?" she inquired brightly.

He nodded, his eyes still closed. "Very."

"Would you like me to leave the bottle with you, Mr. Spade?"

He opened a pair of ice-blue eyes and nodded. "Yes, thank you."

"Is there anything else I can do to make your meal memorable, Mr. Spade?"

He glanced up at her, and the flick of those pale eyes sent a weird thrill through her nervous system. He smiled just a tiny bit, and his voice sounded faintly amused.

"Everything's wonderful, thank you very much, Miss..." "Bouchet," she answered. "Donna Bouchet."

"Delighted, Miss Bouchet," he replied in a deep, big-cat purr.

"Very good. Enjoy your meal, Mr. Spade."

Donna turned on her heel and marched out of the dining room, but she could feel Carson Spade's eyes on her back every step of the way.

And on the off chance that he really was watching, she smiled and tossed her head just enough to send a shining wave of red-blonde hair rippling over her shoulder.

Chapter Four

Carson watched as his svelte hostess placed the bottle of bourbon on the table in front of him. He didn't intend to drink it himself—he found that one glass at a sitting was just enough.

No, that bottle of Pappy was a business investment. It was meant for the biggest of his big-fish prospects, and it was probably the most pleasant lure on the planet.

Carson lifted his glass to his lips, but was momentarily distracted by the departure of the sleek blonde whose hair was a gleaming blend of copper and gold. She flicked her shining mane over one shoulder as she sashayed out.

I may have to hang around for a few days after the sale, he thought to himself. *That is one gorgeous woman.*

His eyes followed her until she disappeared around the corner of the doorway. She had a long, glorious waterfall of hair, beautiful tapering eyes, delicate, smiling lips, and a figure that would make a showgirl jealous. Her tailored white blouse and linen sheath skirt weren't exactly revealing, but they couldn't hide her curves, either.

Carson's eyes returned to his glass. A woman like her was probably involved, though. Possibly married.

But he might take the trouble to find out.

The smiling waiter arrived just then and placed a sizzling filet mignon in front of him. It was thick, juicy, fragrant, and nestled between herbed potatoes on an antique china plate.

"*Bon appetit,* Mr. Spade."

Carson shook out his napkin. "Thank you," he murmured and reached for his knife and fork. The first bite of hot, buttery, succulent steak confirmed for him that the club still had a world-class chef, and that he'd chosen the most comfortable base possible from which to drum up sales.

His eyes skimmed the room. He didn't see anyone he recognized as a top buyer, though the other diners were likely there for the same reason he was: to attend the auction.

He was in town early for the yearling auction, but his most important work was done at the Turf Club and at the many pre-sale parties around town. The personal touch was essential to making big sales, and he was good at pressing the flesh. He always made sure the buyers knew all about the Seven yearlings long before they arrived at Keeneland.

Motion in the dining room doorway made Carson look up, then look again. The sun broke through the clouds, and his dim sales prospects were suddenly dazzlingly bright.

Well I'll be hanged, he thought in dawning astonishment. *It's old Blandings at last.*

There was a white-haired man standing in the doorway. He was tall, distinguished, and impeccably groomed with his snowy hair combed back from his brow and his moustache neatly trimmed. He was wearing a double-breasted navy jacket with gold buttons, he had a large gold signet ring on his left hand, and his sharp trousers and gleaming shoes had clearly been tailored to him.

He was flanked by the waiter and the smiling restaurant manager, who had appeared like magic to hail such a joyous arrival. Both of them beamed at the old man like he was a long-lost relative. They escorted Blandings to a table across the room, helped him settle in, offered him a cigar, and lit it for him.

Carson watched in growing excitement. Bertrand Blandings was one of the richest men in America and a fanatical racing enthusiast. He owned the Flying B Stables in Wyoming and some of his horses had showed and placed in the Kentucky Derby and other high stakes, high profile races in America and Europe.

Blandings was always on the lookout for promising yearlings, and he was in town solely to spend his money on horses.

Just the kind of prospect he was there to cultivate.

Carson's eyes slid to the smiling manager. The fellow was bowing and scraping and rolling out the red carpet because the club had been trying to snag Blandings for years. The old man was an icon in racing circles, and if he joined the club, a flood of others would be sure to follow.

Not that the Turf Club was short of members, or had unlimited room; but he could see them adding a new wing or two for such a whale.

Carson chuckled under his breath at that mental image and raised a hand to snag a passing waiter. The boy leaned over his table and looked a question.

"I'd like you to send a message to the older man over there," Carson murmured, and nodded toward Blandings. "After the others leave his table. Tell him that I'd like to offer him a drink."

"Certainly, Mr. Spade."

Carson raised his glass to his lips and watched the manager and the waiter over the rim. The two hovered over Blandings' table for a few moments more, then carried themselves off at last. He watched as his waiter walked over and leaned down to whisper his message into Blandings' ear. The white-haired man looked up and made eye contact with him across the room.

Carson smiled and raised his glass slightly, and he saw the old man nod.

Carson's heart rate quickened as the elderly newcomer rose slowly from his chair, flicked a speck off the sleeve of his jacket, and sauntered across the room to his table.

Carson flashed his best, brightest, most welcoming smile and motioned to the opposite chair. "Sit down and have some bourbon with me, Mr. Blandings. I do hate to drink alone."

He watched in some amusement as Blandings' eyes flicked to the label on the bourbon bottle. The old man's whole face brightened at what he saw.

"Well, I won't lie, I love a good glass of Kentucky bourbon," the older man confessed, and lowered himself into the chair, slowly and with a sigh. "How's the world treating you, Spade? I haven't seen you in two years, I think."

Carson reached for the bottle and tipped it just enough to pour caramel-colored liquor into the glass Blandings lifted. "Three. We've missed you at Keeneland."

The older man lifted the glass of bourbon to his moustached lips. He took a long sip, closed his eyes appreciatively, and exhaled in deep appreciation.

He shook himself back to the present and replied: "I've had some family drama that sidelined me, but I'm back now. My wife wanted a villa in Venice, and the red tape and repair work we had to go through almost drove me crazy. We're only just now starting to enjoy the place."

Carson chuckled and reached into his jacket for cigarettes. He extended the elegant pewter case to his companion, and the older man shook his head.

Carson stuck a cigarette into his mouth and bent his head to light up. He blew a gentle spiral of smoke up into the air.

"Well, Mr. Blandings, you'll find a good lineup this year," he promised. "The Seven has three fast yearlings at the auction, all by Lickety Split."

The elderly man's eyes glinted keenly over his glass. "That was a fine racehorse," he agreed. "Preakness winner, wasn't he?"

"That's right. Each foal is out of a different dam, all of them purse winners."

"I'll have to take a look," Blandings drawled, and settled more comfortably in his chair. "Are they here yet?"

Carson waved his cigarette hand lazily. "Not yet. They're coming up in a few days, and I'm stabling them at Keeneland. I'll be happy to show them to you if you want a private viewing."

"I'd like that," Blandings replied slowly. "I'm here at the club for a couple of weeks, so you can let me know when they arrive. Are you going to the Breeders' Party at the Continental?"

Carson flashed a smile. "Oh yes, all of them. The Breeders' Association always throws great bashes."

The older man raised his brows and his glass. "That's true, but I'm not looking forward to it," he confessed. "Your neighbor has been in my hair for the last month, nagging me to attend," he sighed. "He's a stubborn man. He must be on some kind of committee."

Carson's hand froze in the act of lifting his glass. His eyes moved to his companion's.

"What neighbor?" he asked mildly, but his heart jerked in dread, because he already knew what neighbor.

"Somebody with a funny name," Blandings sighed. "Chester, or Duster, or something like that."

"Buster," Carson echoed grimly, and took a deep pull of bourbon. "Buster Hogan."

"Yes, that's it," Blandings agreed. "Buster. He's probably called me every day for the last two weeks." He lifted his head and glanced around the dining room suddenly.

"He's not a member of *this* club, is he?"

"No, thank heaven," Carson muttered into his drink. "If he was, I wouldn't be here. Buster lives next door to us back home. I've done my time with him."

"Yes, poor devil," Blandings muttered, and shot him a sympathetic look. "That must be trying."

Carson shook his head and laughed. "Oh, I could tell you stories that you wouldn't believe."

"Still," the older man sighed, "he raises fine thoroughbreds. A horse auction isn't a personality contest between the owners, after all."

Carson raised his eyes. "True enough. It's about the yearlings, and Buster's aren't as fine as ours," he countered with a smile. "His foals this year are sired by a horse that placed fifth in the Breeder's Cup, and nowhere else. Not all that promising. Genetics are everything, and we spare no expense on our studs."

"So I've heard," Blandings replied softly. "I'll have to come by and see your yearlings." He drained his glass and rose slowly from the table.

"Thank you for the excellent bourbon, Spade. I look forward to seeing those beauties of yours."

"I look forward to showing them to you," Carson smiled, and raised his glass. "Enjoy the club."

The older man raised a hand in parting and ambled back to his own table. Carson watched him go, then took another, more brooding sip from his glass.

Buster was going to be stiff competition at the auction, if only on the strength of his nagging and his connections. He usually was, of course; but this time Buster had evidently wangled some kind of official post with the Breeder's Association.

It gave him slightly better access to the buyers, and the wheels in Carson's head were already turning, to figure out ways to counter it.

Chapter Five

Donna Bouchet opened the door of her apartment, kicked off her shoes, and flicked on the radio. It was the end of the day, and she was ready to relax.

A woman's voice wailed over a driving beat, and Donna raised her arms, mouthed the words, and swayed in the hall. She hadn't gone out dancing in a while, and she was in the mood for it.

She closed her eyes and whirled in a circle, then whirled again, her blonde hair whipping behind her like a golden banner. She loved to dance, and she'd been told she was good at it. The only problem was, she didn't have a man to dance with.

"Dance with me, baby," she sang to the jangling radio. "Groove with me all night long, yeah."

She padded into the kitchen, opened the refrigerator, and pulled out a wine spritzer and a plate of grapes and cheese. It was a leftover from a wine and cheese event at the restaurant, and it was all she had for dinner.

Donna drifted into the little living room and flicked on the television. She wasn't a big t.v. watcher, but she didn't have much else to do at home alone.

Donna sank down onto her pink leather couch and popped a grape into her mouth with a dissatisfied expression. The program on the screen was a celebrity dance contest.

I wish I had a star to go out dancing with, she thought wryly.

But she didn't have a star. She didn't even have a boyfriend at the moment. Her last steady had been Maxim in Paris, and they'd broken up over her plans to move to London. Maxim had been adamant that English cuisine would kill him, and she'd gotten bored with her life as a designer.

She'd been ready for a change; and so she moved to London, and Maxim had stayed in France.

Donna settled into the couch and unscrewed the bottle top. It wasn't like she didn't have men at the club hitting on her all day, every day. Most were rich, and some were charming, but all of them were over sixty.

I don't care how rich they are, she thought. *I refuse to go out with a man old enough to be my father.*

She took a refreshing sip of the spritzer and watched as a couple whirled together on the stage. She sighed and picked a square of Brie off her plate.

She knew what her trouble was. She was bored again.

She slapped her plate down on the couch and drifted through the apartment to the balcony doors. She opened them to gaze out over the soft, rolling meadows of the Turf Club back pastures.

As the manager, the club had given her a bungalow on premises to live in. It was in the newest, least desirable addition to the fabulous complex, but even the least desirable lodging was breathtaking. The two-story bungalow resembled a townhouse in New Orleans, with its white brick walls and black wrought-iron railings.

On the inside, it was like a luxury hotel suite, complete with a Jacuzzi tub, a full-body shower, luxury appliances and a breathtaking master bedroom suite with a canopy bed and a big balcony overlooking rolling green pastureland. It was easily the most elegant, comfortable house she'd ever lived in.

And she was *itching* to leave it.

Donna took another drink of spritzer. It had been growing on her, the urge to move on to a new place and a new adventure. Her stint at the Turf Club had been a lush, pleasant experience, but it was getting a little too routine.

Borderline boring.

It might be time for a change. Maybe she'd take a job as the manager of a ski resort in Taos, or even in Switzerland. Maybe she'd parlay her fashion design experience to a job as a costume designer for a movie. She'd gotten a call from an old friend who was putting one together.

The movie was being shot in India, and it would be a year's commitment at least.

Her business phone abruptly interrupted her reverie, and Donna reached for it with a sigh. She had a new text.

To her surprise, it was from Carson Spade. That dark, handsome guy who looked like he'd just stepped off a runway in Milan.

Urgent question, it read.

And that was it.

Donna frowned at the screen. *What urgent question,* she thought dryly. *And how urgent? Does he need the answer right now, tonight, tomorrow?*

She glanced at the time stamp. The message had just been sent.

She tapped out an answering text. *What's your question, Mr. Spade? I'll be happy to answer it if I can.*

She stood stock-still in the middle of her apartment, waiting for a reply, but to her exasperation, there was none.

What on earth, she thought.

There was no further explanation, and she had no choice but to go looking for her shoes. Donna sighed and went padding back through her apartment. She slipped her feet into her low-heeled flats, found her keys, and skipped down the stairs.

She was expected to deliver over the top, 110 percent customer service, and if that meant schlepping across the grounds after hours to answer a single question, she was obliged to do it.

She descended the brick steps of her condo. It was a glorious early evening: the setting sun painted the tops of the trees an antique gold and deepened the fall colors that were just beginning to peep out: bright lemons, deep oranges, vibrant reds.

It was a beautiful hour for a stroll, cool with just a nip of fall in the air, and the pleasant surroundings helped blunt her exasperation. But Donna pulled her hair back into a ponytail as she walked, thinking that this was just one more reason she needed to move on.

Her manager's job sometimes required her to behave almost like a nanny, and she'd never been a hand-holder.

She skirted the new complex of bungalows, crossed the big mowed meadow that separated it from the restaurant, and breezed up the walkway to the main house. If she remembered correctly, Mr. Spade was on the second floor, in the Secretariat suite.

She entered the back door, shouldered past groups of laughing club members to gain the main staircase, and hurried up. The carpeted upstairs hall was beginning to buzz with rich clientele who were either going down to the restaurant, or out for the evening. She smiled at them as she passed and drove right down to the big wooden door at the end of the hall.

Donna paused outside, took a deep breath, and rapped softly. "Mr. Spade? This is Donna Bouchet, the manager. I'm here to answer your text."

There was a soft, pleasant sound from inside, something that sounded faintly like humming, and after a moment the door opened. Carson Spade stood just inside, immaculately dressed, scrubbed, fragrant, and shiny. Donna inhaled, and her eyes flicked over him for a split-second. His perfectly-pressed, pale blue dress shirt was open three buttons, revealing the beginnings of a smooth, muscular chest.

Just the kind she liked.

His tanned face split into a beautiful white smile. "Good evening, Miss Bouchet. Won't you come in?"

He stepped back to let her enter, but Donna smiled, tilted her head, and replied smoothly: "I'm sorry, Mr. Spade, but I'm not allowed to enter a guest's room. How can I help you?"

He raised his arm and buttoned one cuff. "I understand completely, Miss Bouchet. I was hoping to take advantage of your knowledge of the area."

Donna clasped her hands at her waist. "I'll be happy to help you if I can."

He raised his glacial eyes to hers, and Donna inhaled slightly. Those beautiful eyes practically glowed, they were mesmerizing: and she blinked to avoid being snared by them.

"What's the best, most exciting club in this town?" he demanded.

Donna glanced away and considered. "For food, I'd say the Excalibur; for live shows, the Music Box; and for dancing, I'd say 201."

"Where's this 201?"

Donna raised her eyes to his face, and her pulse quickened. "It's in the heart of downtown," she answered softly, with a mixture of exasperation and amusement. "About a 30 minute cab ride from here."

"Good," he sighed, and looked up from his cuff. "I want you to show me."

Donna almost laughed aloud. She didn't know whether to be annoyed or charmed by his nerve; but she didn't yet have a replacement job lined up, so she replied, smoothly and professionally.

"I'm afraid I don't understand."

Carson Spade sauntered to the doorway, his eyes on hers. The setting sun streamed down the floor behind him and outlined his tall, sleek silhouette with a golden finger. He looked like the leading man in some romantic movie.

"I want you to come dancing with me," he replied softly, and reached out for her hand.

"It's a lovely night to go dancing, and I'd bet a thousand dollars you're a beautiful dancer. Will you come with me?"

Donna raised an eyebrow. She wasn't supposed to date club members, it was an ironclad rule; but on the other hand, she couldn't remember the last time she'd been dancing with a handsome man, and it *was* a beautiful evening.

She didn't plan to be there much longer anyway.

The edge of her mouth curled up ever so slightly, and after a long moment, she took the hand he offered. Carson's smile deepened, and Donna noticed that he seemed genuinely delighted.

He rubbed her palm with his thumb to show it, too, and Donna looked away. She wasn't sixteen years old, but that slow caress still sent such electricity up her spine that she had to pull her hand back.

"Give me thirty minutes to change," she murmured, but Carson's light eyes flicked over her.

"You look perfect," he replied with a shrug and a grin. "Let's go."

Donna allowed him to slip an arm around her waist and lead her down the hall. One of the other employees passing by shot her a startled glance, and Donna was reminded that she didn't yet have a replacement job.

Why the blazes did I agree to this, she wondered suddenly; but Carson only winked at her and tightened his fingers on her waist as he squired her down the stairs.

Chapter Six

"This is it."

The limousine glided to a stop on the curb of a dark, dingy backstreet in downtown Lexington. Donna nodded through the limo window at a battered metal door in the side of an old brick warehouse.

Carson frowned faintly in disbelief. "This?" He gestured toward the door. The only identification there was the street number over the door—201— and a tattered 'For Rent' sign on the side of the building.

Donna smiled at him as she set her glass of champagne down on a little tray in the back seat. "They don't advertise. It's a very hush-hush club. Exclusive."

Carson shook his head and smiled. "Okay, I'm game." He pushed his door open, climbed out, and walked around the car to open the door for his companion. He was rewarded by the sight of a long, sleek leg as Donna slid out of the back seat.

Carson's eye moved appreciatively over that elegant stem, and he smiled to himself. No man had ever been more pleased than he was to discover Donna Bouchet was free. He held out his hand, and she took it as she emerged from the limo.

He led her to the door, but to his surprise, she put a hand on his arm when he raised it to knock.

"When they ask, you have to give a password," she smiled. "It's a speakeasy."

One side of his mouth curved up. "What is it?"

Donna leaned in and whispered in his ear, and Carson rolled his head back and shouted with laughter.

"I'm not kidding," she assured him. "That's really it."

Carson shook his head, and as he watched a small square in the door opened and a pair of eyes stared out.

Carson rubbed his nose. "Um..." He stepped up to the square and mumbled under his breath.

"Welcome to 201," a deep voice replied, and the door opened to throw a golden arc of light across the dark sidewalk. Carson slipped his arm around Donna's waist and let her enter the dimly-lit hall beyond the door.

A prickle ran down his neck as they followed the big doorman. The hall was grimy and dark, and he couldn't see a door on the other end. He was starting to wonder if he was going to have to fight somebody when the doorman raised a beefy hand and waved it over a metal box on the wall.

A door-shaped rectangle slowly appeared in one side wall, and as they watched it slowly swung out to reveal another dimly-lit hall. The doorman nodded toward it.

"Enjoy your evening," the big man mumbled, and Carson shot him a wary glance, took Donna's hand, and took the lead through the doorway.

The new hall was as elegant as the outer one had been grimy. It was carpeted and wood-paneled, with soft lights illuminating mirrored shelves of odd items: old lipstick tubes, a man's dress shoe, a leather cigarette case.

He paused to stare at them, and then shot Donna a questioning look.

"They're spy paraphernalia," she laughed. "Genuine, too. Old cold war stuff." She nodded toward the lipstick tube, and Carson noticed a small plaque under it.

Soviet one-bullet gun, 1961.

His eyes moved to the man's shoe. The plaque under it read, *American, hollow heel, 1942.*

A slow smile spread across his face. "Slick," he approved, and looked up. "I'm sure I'm slow, but I don't see a way out of here. Do we have to be spies to get into the club?"

Donna shot him a mischievous glance. "Try. I bet you can figure it out."

Carson raised his brows and scanned the hall. There was no visible door besides the one they'd just used. Just two long, glass cases full of historical artifacts.

Carson slowly paced the hall, scanning the shelves for knobs, drawers, or handles. There were none.

He glanced up at the ceiling. It was ornate sculpted plaster, but the lights were recessed. No dangling chains, no wall plates.

His eyes sank to the floor. It was completely carpeted except for a narrow metal floor vent the size and shape of a pedal. He drifted over to stare down at it, and then back at Donna. She was standing there with her arms crossed, but there was a twinkle in her eye.

He pressed his foot to the grill, and the whole wall suddenly swung back like a giant door to reveal a huge room full of low lights and beautiful people and throbbing music. Carson laughed to see it, and Donna joined in as she moved up to put a hand on his arm.

"See?" she teased, and the laughter in her gold-brown eyes made Carson catch his breath. She looked like a spy herself, there in the dim club lights, a sleek *femme fatale*.

She made him very glad he'd come to town.

He extended an arm, and she took it as they swayed through the crowd. "What would you like to do first?" he asked with a smile. "Eat dinner, or dance?"

Donna's smile deepened, and she drawled, "Oh, I came to dance," and twined her arms around his neck. The throbbing music suddenly ended, and the band eased into a slow, sweet, romantic song. Carson smiled down into Donna's golden eyes as he slid his hands around her waist and eased her out onto the dance floor.

"You smell wonderful," he murmured in her ear as they swayed. Her body felt light and graceful in his arms, and her softly spiced perfume drugged his senses in a faint, pleasant way.

She smiled up into his eyes, and his hands tightened around her waist. Carson swirled her around suddenly in his arms, and he laughed a long, low, delighted laugh.

The evening unfolding before him promised to be very pleasant indeed.

Chapter Seven

Bennie Macardle, the top hand in the Seven Ranch's thoroughbred stable, raised his head off his chest and sat up straight in his chair. He peered down the long center aisle of the barn.

It was two o'clock in the morning, and cold as a brass toilet outside; but something had roused him up from a light drowse.

He stood up slowly, his eyes still on the stable door. Most of the horses were asleep, but one or two had their heads poking out over the stall doors, ears pricked up.

He hadn't imagined it. They'd heard it, too. Something had made a noise.

Bennie reached for a pitchfork propped up against one wall and held it out in front of him as he advanced. His eyes swept the big barn, left to right and back again.

He swallowed and told himself that it was probably just the barn cat chasing a mouse, or that one of the horses had bumped against the stall walls; but the skin was prickling on the back of his neck.

There wasn't a horse in that barn that wasn't worth two million dollars at least; and there were three yearlings in it about to be shipped to Kentucky for sale.

He stopped in the middle of the barn and went dead quiet, listening, for a long few minutes; but he heard nothing but the gentle breathing of sleeping horses.

Aw, it's nothing.

He told himself that a prowler would have to kill a state-of-the-art alarm system to get into the stable yard undetected. The whole county would hear that, if it went off. Stadium lights would flood the complex with a blinding white glare, and a silent alarm would alert the main house and call the local police.

Bennie let the pitchfork droop in his hands, and he finally propped it against the wall. There was no one in that barn but him and those horses.

Or at least, that was what he very much hoped: but when the horses at the stall doors pricked their ears and turned to look behind him, a thrill of fear snaked up his spine. He turned slowly, wide eyed and with a pounding heart: but he saw no prowler.

I'm going loco, he thought in disgust. *Maybe that creepy movie I watched the other night is messing with me.*

He sighed, shuffled back to his chair, and sank down into the seat. He crossed his hands on his chest and settled in more comfortably, but he couldn't drop off again.

He was on edge now, watching the horses. They looked nervous. They rolled their eyes back and forth and listened for sounds with their ears held high.

Bennie shifted his weight nervously. *Maybe I should have a look around,* he told himself. *If anything happens to these fancy horses, I'll be out of a job.*

He rose slowly, sighed, and walked back down the aisle to pick up the pitchfork again; but his fingers had no sooner curled around the handle than a low, clear sound made his head jerk up.

The sound of the locked barn door lock being jiggled from outside.

The horses snorted and danced, and a thrill of terror flicked up Bennie's spine. He gripped the pitchfork, then came to his senses.

A man his age wasn't being paid to fight rustlers. They had the best security system in the world, and it was time to use it.

He hurried to a big metal box mounted on a wooden beam, flicked it open, and mashed the red button inside. Instantly the world lit up like Friday night football, with blinding light streaming in through every crack in the wooden barn. The horses snorted and danced inside their stalls in fear, but Bennie's ear was cocked to the outside. To his relief, there was a scrambling sound across the gravel outside.

The sound of frantic retreat.

A second later his phone rang, and he dug it out of his jeans pocket. He knew who it was even before he lifted it to his ear.

Buck Spade's voice jumped through the line. "What's going on down there?" he demanded sharply, and Bennie gasped, "Somebody's trying to get into the barn. The alarm didn't trip until they were messing with the door. I had to hit the panic button!"

"I'm coming down," Buck yelped, and the line went dead.

Bennie returned the phone to his jeans pocket, closed his eyes, and pressed his brow against the wall. He was pretty sure that the would-be rustler, whoever it was, was long gone; but he wasn't going to open the barn door to anybody but his boss.

Buck was going to show up with a shotgun, and that was what they needed.

Ten minutes later there came the sound of a truck roaring up outside, and Bennie hurried to the barn door. Buck's voice yelled out, "Bennie, are you alright in there?"

"I'm all right," he sang back, and hurried to open the door. As soon as he opened it, four shadows rushed in, backlit by the garish glare outside. The first three were men carrying shotguns, and the fourth was smaller and unarmed.

Buck stalked to the alarm box, switched off the security lights, and turned to demand: "Are the horses hurt?"

"No. Nobody got in," Bennie replied as Morgan moved from stall to stall, shotgun in hand. He glanced in every opening, then moved into the office and unused rooms to check for intruders.

Luke turned at the door to stand guard with a sawed off, and Morgan's wife Heather set a black bag on the barn floor and began checking the skittish thoroughbreds. She was wearing a long pink housecoat and slippers.

"I don't see anybody in here," Morgan mumbled, and Buck stuck a hand on his hip in disgust.

"Well, the police are on their way, so we'll just wait until they roll up," he grumbled. "But I wanna know how that rattler got around a $100,000 perimeter alarm. We got buried cables, and backup power, and he still knocked it out long enough to get to the barn door!"

He turned his head to call to Luke. "You see anybody out there?"

His younger brother shook his blonde head. "Nah. He's probably halfway to Dallas by now."

Bennie staggered to his chair and sank down into it with a shuddering gasp. His heart was galloping. Morgan ambled up and grunted: "You sure you're okay?"

Bennie nodded. "Just shook up, is all. I never thought anybody could get past that alarm!" His gaze moved past Morgan to his little wife, who was soothing one of the geldings. He jerked a thumb toward her and looked up into her husband's face.

"What's she doing here?"

Morgan lifted one shoulder in a fatalistic gesture. "She told me that if I didn't bring her along, she was coming on her own," he rumbled.

Heather moved to another stall, where a frightened mare was snorting and thrashing. She called over her shoulder, "I think I'll give this pretty girl a little sedative. She's not having any of it."

Buck turned to Bennie and asked, "Which of these beauts are Carson's yearlings?"

Bennie wiped his mouth on his shoulder and pointed to three consecutive stalls in the middle of the barn. "Eight, nine, and ten," he replied, and Buck stalked over to inspect them.

"I need to call Carson and tell him about this," he murmured, half to himself. "I wish I didn't have to bother him, but he'll want to know."

Heather glanced at him over her shoulder. "Can't it wait until morning?" she objected, and Buck shrugged and reached for his phone. "He'll be up."

Chapter Eight

"Happy days."

Carson touched his champagne glass to Donna's with a faint *ting* and raised it to his lips. After a good half hour of dancing she was ready to eat, and they were seated at a dimly-lit corner table tucked away in the restaurant two rooms behind the dance floor.

Its throbbing music was completely shut out. The only sound in the little restaurant was the soft, unintelligible hum of jazz in the background, the tinkle of silverware, and the soft, distant voices of the other shadowed diners.

"I don't know very much about you," Donna was saying, with a soft, teasing smile. "Just that you're here to sell horses at Keeneland, and that you live in Texas, isn't that right?"

Carson smiled at her over the flickering candle. "That's right. Our ranch is the Seven Spades."

"*Our* ranch?" she echoed, and made a face. "Please don't tell me you're married."

He sputtered, "No, I'm not married, I promise you. I was talking about my family. I have six brothers."

She raised laughing eyes to his. "All in the same place?"

His smile shrank into a grimace. "All in the same place."

"That sounds a little cramped."

Carson tilted his head. "Not the way we do it. I'll admit, it can get annoying at times, but it's mostly very comfortable."

She raised her brows over her drink, and a waiter came by and set a platter of exquisite canapes on the table, each one a jewel-like work of art: red caviar on toast, dates stuffed with cream cheese and wrapped in bacon, cucumber sandwiches.

"Enjoy."

Carson took one and popped it into his mouth, then blotted his mouth with his napkin. He was just about to ask Donna about herself when his phone buzzed in his jacket. He pulled it out discreetly and glanced down at the number.

To his surprise, it was Buck, at two in the morning. Buck, who went to bed at sunset and got up before dawn.

Something was wrong.

His brows twitched together, but he looked up to give his companion an apologetic smile. "Excuse me. I have a call. I won't be a minute."

"Sure."

Carson stood up and walked through the dim restaurant to a little nook on the far end of the room. He slipped into an antique telephone booth and closed the glass door behind him.

"Hello?"

Buck's agitated voice boomed on the other end. "Hey Carson. I'm sorry to bust in on you at this hour, but we just had somebody try to break into the stable where your yearlings are."

Carson jerked bolt upright in alarm. "Are they okay?"

"They ain't hurt, just a little spooked. Some scumbag beat the alarm and was trying to pick the lock on the door when Bennie hit the red button. The bum had run off by the time we got there."

Carson pulled his hand over his mouth and was silent for a long moment.

"Are you there?"

"Yeah, I'm here." Carson took a deep breath to calm himself, but suspicion flared in him in spite of that. They had lots of competitors at the upcoming auction, but only one was close enough to try to mess with their horses.

"It was one of Buster's hands," he growled, "I know it!"

"That's what I said," Buck agreed angrily. "He wants to beat us out at the auction, and he knows the only way he can do it is to kick us out of the running somehow. Leave it to that skunk to cheat. It's the only way he knows!"

Carson bit his mouth into a straight line and calculated. "Are you sure the yearlings are all right?"

"Yeah, they're okay. Heather checked 'em, and she says their vitals are fine. They settled down pretty quick, but Luke and Morgan are spending the night in the barn, just in case that guy tries to come back."

Carson nodded grimly. "I want you to send those horses up here right away," he replied. "Keeneland has security that'll be harder to beat than ours, and I'm going to hire a private guard. I'm trying to reel in Bertrand Blandings, and I'm off to a good start. I'm not going to let Buster Hogan ruin my sale."

There was a short pause on the other end. "Who's Bertrand Blandings?"

Carson frowned and closed his eyes. "Never mind."

Buck's voice gathered strength. "Don't worry about those horses, I'll take a few hands and bring 'em up myself. Are you still staying at the Turf Club?"

"That's right."

"Well I'll meet you at Keeneland tomorrow afternoon with the horses. We'll get 'em checked in and stabled up, and then I'll drop by the club for dinner before catching a flight back."

"Thanks," Carson sighed gratefully and rubbed the back of his neck. That was one of the best things about his oldest brother. Buck always came in clutch when it mattered.

On the other hand, he was going to have to hope they didn't run into Buster Hogan at Keeneland, because if Buck caught sight of their cheating neighbor, there was going to be a fist fight.

Maybe Buck wouldn't be the only one swinging punches at Buster, either.

"I'll see you tomorrow," Buck promised. "I'll call you when we get into town."

"Sounds good. Thanks for calling."

"Yep," Buck muttered, then added, with a tinge of curiosity in his voice: "What are you doing up at two in the morning anyway, boy?"

"Good night, Buck," Carson drawled, and hung up the phone.

He slipped the phone back into his jacket, took a deep breath, and walked out of the little booth. He walked soundlessly across the restaurant to the little table and slipped back into his seat.

"Sorry about that," he smiled. "Where were we?"

Donna's glowing eyes met his, held them. A speculative look flitted over her face and she tilted her head as she considered him.

"You're upset," she observed softly.

Carson shot her a startled glance, then instantly pasted on a smile. "Nonsense! The night is young. Let's dance."

But she didn't take the hand he extended to her. "No, I don't think so," she murmured, and set her drink down. "It's been fun, but I can see that something bad has happened. You're somewhere else."

Carson stared at her, temporarily speechless, but finally smiled and admitted: "I must be losing my touch. And you're right, I did get annoying news, but it doesn't have to spoil our evening."

She returned his smile and shrugged. "I'm paid to read people. And it's alright if we call it a night, really. I understand. Life happens."

Carson nodded in amusement. "Yes, it does. Well, pretty lady, I'm sorry for that, but if that's your decision, I'll take you back home. Maybe we can do this again later this week."

"That would be nice."

Carson tossed down a hundred dollar bill, stood, and helped Donna out of her seat. He escorted her through the dim restaurant, and down a long side hall that skirted the dance floor and the thrashing crowd. He found himself facing another dead end, and he turned to Donna and looked a question.

She laughed under her breath, then reached out and twisted the fire alarm box on the wall.

A bookcase swung out for them, and they walked through it and out into the night.

Chapter Nine

"Thank you for coming out with me tonight," Carson whispered. Donna glanced up at him. They were standing on the stoop of her condo, and the lantern over the door cast Carson mostly into shadow; but its golden glow glanced off his eyes and sent a delicious little shudder down her spine.

It was almost four in the morning, and chilly, and the profound silence of a country night surrounded them. Carson leaned down slightly to press his lips to hers in a goodbye kiss, but Donna turned her head slightly to one side.

If he was disappointed, he didn't show it. "Good night, beautiful," he murmured, and took her chin in his hand. "Can I call you?"

Donna looked up and smiled. "You can call me."

He gazed down at her for a long moment, as if he was thinking of kissing her again; but he smiled, stepped back, and raised his hand in a jaunty wave.

"Sleep tight."

He turned and walked off into the darkness, and Donna entered the house.

She sighed, tossed her bag on a chair in the foyer, and shook her hair free. She wasn't sure if she was going out with Carson Spade again. He was gorgeous, he was disastrously charming, he was rich, and he'd be fun to go out with a few times before she moved on. But if she saw much more of him, she was going to get snagged by those jeweled eyes.

She wasn't going to let him hypnotize her. She was leaving.

She walked upstairs to her bedroom, flopped down on her bed, and reached for the phone on the nightstand. She tapped out a number and waited.

A man's recorded voice announced, "This is Tim, I'm not here right now. Leave a message at the beep and I'll get back to you."

Donna rolled over on her stomach and murmured, "Tim, this is Donna. If you still need a costume designer for that movie of yours, call me. Bye."

She sighed and hung up the phone. India would be a big change for her, but even a night of dancing hadn't tamed that restless foot of hers.

She was ready for a challenge.

She glanced ruefully at the bedside clock. She had to get up at seven to be at work by eight.

Three hours of sleep, if she was lucky.

She pulled herself off the bed, threw back the downy covers, and climbed in without bothering to change. She'd change in the morning.

She was going to be a zombie in the morning, but her lovely evening made it worth the cost. She couldn't remember the last time she'd had such a magical evening with such a pleasant man.

She wasn't at all unwilling to enjoy a few more of them before she left town, or Carson did.

But when she snuggled into her pillow and drifted off to sleep, Carson Spade's sparkling eyes still smiled at her; and she sighed and snuggled in tighter before drifting into deeper, and even more pleasant dreams.

The jangling of her alarm clock dragged her back up to consciousness three hours later. Donna sighed, stretched, yawned, and slipped out of bed on the way to the bathroom and a nice, long, hot shower.

Twenty minutes later she emerged from the bathroom in a puff of steam, wrapped up to her ears in a fluffy white terrycloth robe.

She shuffled off to the kitchen, pulled an instant breakfast out of the fridge, and popped it into the microwave. It was light outside, but it felt brutally early.

The microwave beeped, Donna pulled the plastic tray out of the microwave, and fished a plastic fork out of a drawer. She drifted out to her balcony, and she opened the door to let in the fresh morning air. Her balcony overlooked a tranquil pasture swathed in a gray blanket of morning mist. A handful of beautiful thoroughbreds were grazing peacefully halfway across it, and none so much as lifted their heads at the distant sound of her door opening.

Donna smiled to herself. Her condo was the last one in the little street, so she wouldn't be shocking anyone but the horses if she ate her breakfast on her balcony, in her housecoat.

Donna settled down in her patio chair and dug her fork into a mound of scrambled eggs. In spite of the lovely view, it definitely felt as if she was Cinderella after the night of the ball.

It was time to suit up in her sensible top and skirt and go back to humoring the fabulously wealthy.

That's one thing I'll be glad to get back if I change jobs, she thought to herself. *The freedom to tell somebody to go boil their head.*

I'll just have to learn how to do it in Hindi.

The sound of a clear, soft beep from inside her bedroom made her turn her head. She could hear someone leaving a message on her phone through the open balcony door.

A man's voice mumbled, "Hi Donna, this is Tim. I was glad to get your message. I'd love you to be our costume designer, but like I said, I want you to come out on location with us. We're flying out next month to Bombay. If you're interested, let me know and we can work out the details."

A slow smile curled Donna's lips. That settled that.

The job was hers if she wanted it, and she had a few weeks to decide.

She crossed her legs and addressed her breakfast in a more leisurely fashion. She had just enough time to put in her two weeks' notice, buy an online course to learn how to speak basic Hindi, and buy the kit she needed for a yearlong stay in a tropical country.

If she decided to go.

Donna licked her fork and stared absently into the distance. It would be hard to give up the luxury of living in an American resort; not to mention other first-world comforts that she mostly took for granted.

But a chance like this might never come again.

The bedside alarm jangled loudly, this time to warn her that she had only a half-hour to dress and get to her office. Donna stood up and hurried back into the house, shouldering out of her housecoat as she went.

Until she was sure of her choice, she was going to play it cool.

Chapter Ten

"Here she comes."

Donna frowned slightly as she walked into the clubhouse lobby. The two girls at the front desk stopped talking and stared at her in open curiosity as she walked in.

She tilted her head and smiled quizzically. "Good morning."

"Morning."

They leaned out to stare at her as she passed. Donna could tell that they were barely repressing giggles, and she sputtered to herself as she passed. It looked as if word had gotten out that she'd flouted the club laws last night, and she could probably look forward to a heart to heart with her boss.

That was another thing she wouldn't miss, if she moved on: the club's stuffy rules about workplace romance. The owners were against it, and it had been made clear to her that their clientele was off limits to employees.

It had amused her, because evidently they had seen her as a woman likely to break that rule.

Donna turned into the little hall behind the main staircase, then through the door of her office. She was arrested in the doorway by the sight of a gorgeous bouquet of pale blue roses on her desk.

A ghost of a smile dawned across her lips, and she drifted to the desk to pick a little card out of the spray. It read:

Thanks for a beautiful evening. You dance like a dream.

Carson

Donna smiled and tapped her hand with the little card, thinking, *You're going to make me sorry to leave, Carson Spade.*

The phone on her desk trilled, and she leaned over to pick up the receiver with her eyes still on the perfect blooms.

"Good morning, Turf Club, Donna Bouchet."

Her boss' muddy voice intoned: "Good morning, Donna. Could you step up to my office for a few minutes?"

Donna swallowed an irritated sigh but replied, "Of course, I'll be right up, Mr. Tolliver."

The line clicked off, and Donna replaced the receiver. She reached out to caress the velvety rose petals, smiled again, and turned to report to her boss' office.

She was about to get chewed, and she wanted to take that pleasant mental image with her.

"Please sit down, Donna."

Mr. Tolliver gestured to a leather chair opposite his big desk, and she closed the door behind her and took a seat. She crossed her legs, clasped her hands together across them, and gave him a quizzical look.

Her boss was a big man whose love of cigars had given him a deep, thick voice. He was always dressed to the nines, and he wore a gold signet ring on one big finger.

He was a nice man, and easy to work with usually; and she felt a bit sorry for him, because she could see he was very uncomfortable.

He cleared his throat. "Donna, this is somewhat awkward for me," he began, "I hesitate to get involved in my employee's personal lives; but I have been told that you may have gone out with one of our club members last night. Is that true?"

Donna nodded pleasantly. "It is true."

Mr. Tolliver picked up a pen and fidgeted with it. "I see. Then I have to remind you that we have a policy against club employees dating guests."

Donna shrugged her shoulders. "Mr. Spade asked me to show him one of the clubs in town," she smiled. "It would have been rude to refuse."

Her boss cleared his throat again and looked uncomfortable. "Well, I hope you will not make a habit of seeing Mr. Spade socially," he replied. "He'll be gone after the Keeneland auction. I am trusting you to be busy until then."

Donna shot him a mischievous look. "What if he doesn't want me to be busy?"

Her boss shot her an exasperated look. "The Turf Club maintains a no-fraternization policy for the protection of our employees," he replied. "I know a young woman like you has had occasion to explain it to our guests before now."

Donna bowed her head in amused acknowledgement. *That part is true enough,* she thought dryly. *But I can protect myself just fine, thank you.*

Her boss stared at her as if she was an unruly daughter. "Well, I've said my piece, Donna. The club policy is clear, and our employees are expected to follow it. I hope there will be no need to speak of it again."

So do I, Donna agreed in secret amusement, and was tempted to tell him she was tendering her resignation; but she wanted to give Tim's offer more thought before she decided, and so she held her peace.

Then too, she liked her boss, and she preferred to say goodbye on a less awkward occasion. She tilted her head and gave him a bland smile.

"It won't be a problem, I promise."

And that's true enough, she thought to herself, *because I don't expect to see Carson Spade again.*

The pinched look on his face cleared, and her boss relaxed visibly. "Thank you, Donna. I appreciate it."

Chapter Eleven

Carson stared absently into the mirror and adjusted his tie. It was the last touch he was giving his appearance before he left the club to go over to meet Buck at Keeneland; but his mind wasn't on business.

It was odd. He was worried about the yearlings, he was focused on his goal to sell them all to Bertrand Blandings; but all that had been abruptly shoved to the back of his mind.

Ever since he first met her at the club restaurant, all he could think about was Donna Bouchet.

He'd speculated about how it would feel to hold her in his arms, if her long coppery hair felt as silky as it looked.

He wondered how her lips tasted.

And now that he'd spent a night out in her company, he could confirm that she was sleek and graceful and exciting, that her gold-brown eyes glowed like topaz over a candlelit table, that she moved as softly and smoothly as swirling water when she danced.

He knew little about her, but she'd let it fall that she'd lived and worked in Paris before she came to the club. Something about fashion design.

That much wasn't all that different from any number of other women he'd dated, but for some reason, Donna danced in his head like a recurring dream. That faint, spicy cologne of hers haunted him.

He gave his tie a sharp tug, gave himself a bemused look, and turned away from the mirror.

He'd no sooner stepped out of his rental car and handed the keys to the valet than he spotted Buck waiting for him in the big outdoor pavilion outside the main entrance of the Keeneland complex. To his relief, Buck had conformed to the dress code and had left his jeans and plain white shirt at home. His big older brother was wearing a tailored linen jacket, a string tie, and a pair of dress slacks; but boots were peeking out from under them.

Buck didn't look happy or comfortable; and Carson judged it wise to start smoothing him down.

"Well, Buck! Thanks for coming up. Let's go see where those yearlings are stabled."

Buck's face brightened slightly to see him, but his voice was glum as he answered, "I hate to go back. Those stables are busier than Dallas at rush hour, and it took awhile to get our horses all checked in and over to the right barn. I didn't know this place had *dozens* of 'em!"

Carson slapped Buck on the back. "Welcome to the world of thoroughbred racing," he grinned. "It isn't all glitz and glamor. Admit it now, Buck, you don't think I do any work up here. You think I come up here to party."

Buck shot him a straight look. "You weren't in your bed last night when I called you, I know that," he retorted. "Unless you had twenty people in it."

Carson laughed and took his arm. "I'm not straight-laced like you and Morgan, Buck," he teased. "I believe in enjoying life."

To his relief, Buck let that crack slide. Maybe it was because he was tired, but Buck didn't argue with him or tell him he needed prayer; he just jerked a thumb toward a golf cart parked on the drive.

"Come on, I'll drive you over to the barn. These are new boots, and I don't feel like walking all the way back over there again."

Carson laughed and climbed into the cart, and Buck slid in beside him and sent it puttering down the drive. "The horses did good on the flight," he muttered, "and on the way over here. Least, two of 'em did. High Spade kicked up a little sand."

"He's high strung," Carson agreed. "But that can be a good thing. He's got fire. I think we could get twice for him what the others will bring, and I've got a big prospect on my line already. I'm going to bring him over to see the yearlings tomorrow if I can work it out."

"Well, good hunting," Buck muttered. "For what we spend on these horses, we could use some money coming back for a change."

"Now, now, grandma. You sound like Miss Annie."

Buck gave him an exasperated look. "She had a lot more sense than you do, boy."

Ten minutes later Buck pulled the golf cart up to Barn Number One, and they climbed out to walk in. A security guard met them at the entrance, and Carson sighed and flashed his ID card.

He put a hand on Buck's shoulder. "This is my brother," he explained. "We've come to see our horses."

The guard stepped aside. "Come right in, gentlemen. Your horses are in stalls eight, nine, and ten."

Carson stuck his hands in his pockets and drifted down the center aisle of the bright, spotless barn. The competition was already there in force: gleaming dapple-gray fillies from the legendary Oak Tree Stables in Lexington, elegant black colts from the

Diamond Dan Stables in Colorado, and magnificent palomino-blonde geldings from the Flamingo Ranch in Florida.

They sauntered past them all to where their own yearlings were housed, and Buck walked up and stroked Blue Streak on the nose. "Here's our boys," he murmured with an indulgent smile. "They're pretty things, I got to admit."

The horse nuzzled his chest, and Buck chuckled and rubbed its ears.

Carson sighed and enjoyed a pretty picture. The Seven yearlings were exceptionally fine that year: they were the topaz brown of aged whiskey, with long, lean bodies and elegant, tapering legs. Heather had pronounced them vibrantly healthy, they had a sterling pedigree, and they were smart.

They had every chance of becoming famous in the racing world, and he believed they were worth every penny the family was asking.

And they were asking for a lot of pennies: but he was a pretty good judge of horse flesh, and High Spade was the best yearling they'd had since the legendary Ace of Spades, the blazing yearling they'd sold for a million dollars that had gone on to win the Belmont in America and place second by a hair at the One Thousand Guineas race in the UK.

Carson reached out to caress High Spade's silky muzzle, and the young colt tossed its proud head and snorted.

"That's right, that's right," Carson smiled, and shook his head. "You're the king and you know it."

Buck strolled over to consider the horse. "You think we can get our asking on this fellow?" he wondered aloud.

"Oh yeah," Carson murmured with a smile. "He's got it. This boy gives me a chill down my back. We might actually get more than our target price for this one."

He glanced up at Buck. "I'm going to bring my prospect over so he can see these beauties up close. He's got the cash to spend, and this is his first year back to Keeneland after a long absence. I think he's hungry."

They fell silent as they surveyed the three young horses; and in that pause, a distant and familiar voice blared out from the barn next door. They both frowned and stared at one another.

"I know that voice," Buck growled. "That better not be Buster Hogan, cause if I catch him here I'll beat his eyes together for trying to steal our horses!"

Carson gathered his startled wits and almost prayed. He grabbed Buck's arm and stammered, "It can't be Buster. I heard one of the buyers say that he's not coming up until Friday!"

Carson held Buck's eye. He'd just lied through his teeth, it was Buster's voice all right, but he couldn't let his fiery brother go over there and mop the floor with their main competitor.

To Carson's relief, Buck relaxed slightly and paused in doubt; but just when he thought he'd dodged a bullet, that loud, obnoxious voice brayed out again.

"That's right, these are the strongest horses at Keeneland this year. They're all sound as a bell, and they'll leave these other show horses in the dust!"

Buck's face darkened, and his hands curled into fists. "That *is* Buster!" he growled, and Carson scrambled to block the way. He glared into his brother's face and hissed, "You can't go over there and start a fight. We'll get thrown out!"

Buster's grating laugh made them both wince, and Carson glanced back over his shoulder. To his dismay, they both saw Buster Hogan appear outside and go walking past with another man.

Carson's brows crept together in dawning outrage. The other man was *Bertrand Blandings*.

His hands drifted down from Buck's arms as he stared in disbelief. Buster Hogan had beaten him to the punch.

Buster was trying to *steal his best prospect*.

Buck surged past him, and Carson grabbed him again. "No, Buck, calm down! That's our most promising buyer with him," he gasped. "If you deck Buster I'll lose the sale!"

Buck glared at their neighbor as he passed by. "Look at him," he growled, "grinning like a mule eating briars! All right," he added, and shook Carson's hands off, "I won't pound him! But I want you to get in there and beat him, Carson. Go and steal that old man out from under his nose. Hook him like a catfish! Because Buster deserves to come back to Sandy Creek with his tail dragging between his legs.

"Make him come in last—that lying, cheating snake!"

Chapter Twelve

Carson dragged into his suite at the club that night with a limp collar and bedraggled hair. He'd just put Buck in a cab and seen him off, and he was exhausted.

He tossed his keys down on a table and drifted wearily to the paneled study of the suite. He didn't have the energy to go out again, or to touch base with the lovely Donna Bouchet, or even to plan his next day's strategy.

He half-fell into a leather chair, rolled his head back on the cushions, and stared up at the ceiling.

Buck was hard to manage at the best of times, and when he got mad, it was next to impossible. So he supposed it *was* something that he'd kept Buck from attacking Buster in front of Bertrand Blandings; but it was the only thing he'd accomplished that day.

Carson fumbled in his jacket for his cigarettes and lit one with an unsteady hand. He exhaled smoke, closed his eyes, and let the cigarette send a lazy white spiral up from his nerveless fingers.

He had to admit, seeing Bertrand with Buster had felt like a punch to the gut; but he never lingered on setbacks. Tomorrow he was going to call Bertrand and see if he couldn't get him to look at their horses.

He was confident that the old gentleman would see the difference between Seven and Lazy H horses at once. Buster's horses were always strong, but relatively scruffy. They were healthy, but had a lower pedigree than the Seven thoroughbreds. Buster was too cheap to spend on top-drawer studs, but he always crossed his fingers and hoped for an undeserved miracle.

He usually didn't get one; and the nighttime raid on their stables told him that Buster didn't have much confidence in his most recent crop of yearlings.

Carson lifted the cigarette to his lips. Buck was right. Buster was a cheating reptile who deserved to lose; but if his career in racing had taught him anything, it was that Lady Luck was fickle. She didn't always give a man what he deserved.

So this time, he was going to do his best to help her out.

He'd figure out how tomorrow.

Carson's eyes drifted to the window. It was just sunset, and the last dying rays of daylight painted the side of the wall. It was the time of day that he usually started getting ready to go out, but tonight he was staying in.

He took another drag on his cigarette. For some reason his big, beautiful suite felt a bit empty that evening; and his thoughts returned to Donna.

She was still there, a copper-colored dancer whirling in his mind; just at the forefront instead of the shadows. They'd only spent one evening together, but for some reason he couldn't shake her out of his head.

It wasn't because she hadn't let him kiss her, or more than kiss her. He wasn't the kind of man who chased quick conquests.

He much preferred to let a relationship develop slowly and lusciously, and he'd been told he was good at it.

So he wasn't exactly sure why Donna's eyes haunted him. True, they were a lovely and heavily-lashed pair of topaz gems, they slanted up slightly at the ends, and they gave her a faintly otherworldly look, as if she'd been cast as an elf or a genie in a play. Her hair was like a golden banner, rippling silk that he longed to caress; and her body was sleek and lissome and altogether lovely.

But she had that in common with any number of other women he'd known in his life.

Maybe it was her mysterious air; her familiarity with that sketchy speakeasy, that she ordered a cherry brandy champagne cocktail off the secret menu, that she'd lived in SoHo and the Left Bank and that he'd glimpsed a book titled *Learn to Speak Hindi* tucked in her bag.

She was clearly a woman with an interesting life story, and he wanted to hear it.

Carson sputtered smoke into the air. He'd meant the bouquet of roses to smooth the way for another pleasant evening with Donna, but he was too tired to ask her out that night. He wanted to plan their next outing somewhat more carefully than the first one.

He found that he had a ridiculous ambition to impress her.

Carson snuffed out the cigarette and rose from his chair. He tilted his head back and closed his eyes for a long, silent moment, then slowly leaned out into the air, turned, and swayed as if he was hearing music, and had an unseen woman in his arms.

Chapter Thirteen

"I'm so glad you could come today, Mr. Blandings," Carson beamed, and put on his best and most winsome smile. He'd called Bertrand Blandings, and to his relief, the old gentleman had agreed to meet him at the Keeneland stables. It was a warm, sunny day for September, there wasn't a cloud in the sky, the stables and the horses were beautiful, and he was about to wind up his best pitch.

"Please, call me Bertrand," his guest murmured, and blew a ribbon of cigar smoke into the air as they strolled across the stable grounds. "Everyone else does."

Carson's smile deepened. "Bertrand." He led his guest into the barn, then down the spotless main aisle. "Our yearlings are over here. I believe I told you that they're all out of Lickety

Split, each by a different mare. All winners on the track, of course, and beautiful specimens. We spare no expense on genetics."

The old man stuck his hands in his pockets and stared at the three caramel-colored yearlings with a smile. "Well, I must say, yours is no idle boast," he replied softly. "They're beauties, all right." He reached out to stroke the nearest muzzle, and the young colt tossed its head.

"I looked them up in the sales catalog," he went on. "Very impressive pedigrees."

"Yes," Carson murmured, and rubbed his nose. "Some of our competitors fall short in that area, but blood will tell every time."

The old man nodded. "That's what I believe." He looked up to pin Carson with a keen look from his faded blue eyes. "Can I see you put them through their paces out in the yard? Naturally our inspection team will give them a thorough exam, but I always like to see them for myself."

"Of course."

Carson opened the stall, took Blue Streak by the halter, and led him out of the barn as his prospect trailed behind. The elderly man watched keenly as Carson stroked the horse's twitching mane, then slowly walked him up and down the yard.

"All of our yearlings are in excellent health," Carson told him as he walked. "They have no scars or bumps, and they've got perfect conformation. This boy has a great temperament, too. We call him Mr. Frosty. Nothing gets to him."

The older man watched the yearling's legs as they approached him. "He has a beautiful gait."

"They all do."

"Impressive," Bertrand murmured. "Let's see the other two."

Carson walked Blue Streak back into his stall, closed it up carefully, and opened the next one down to retrieve Seven Bells. He glanced at the older man as he stood waiting out in the yard.

He'd weighed his strategy in his mind as he'd sat in his room the night before: whether to go wide and pitch as many buyers as he could, or to hone in on one or two hot prospects. Both ways had worked for him in the past, but this time, he was putting most all his chips on Bertrand Blandings.

The old fellow was hungry, he could feel it: he'd been away from the track for three long years, and now he was back in the game and flush with cash, like a champion poker player rolling into Vegas.

Buying a racing thoroughbred *was* a bit like poker. It was a high-stakes game with no guarantees; but Carson's conscience was clear. He and his brothers had made sure those yearlings were as close to a sure thing as was humanly possible. The Seven thoroughbreds were the best of the best, and he was going to get top dollar for them.

"This fellow is Seven Bells," Carson announced as he walked the yearling out into the sunshine. "He's named after a racing sailboat my father once owned, and like it, he's trim and fast and completely yar."

Bertrand grunted to acknowledge the joke, and tilted his head as Carson turned the yearling in the yard. He lifted the cigar to his lips and watched as the colt pranced.

"Got a bit of a strut, doesn't he?"

Carson glanced up at the colt's eyes and smiled. "He knows he's handsome, yes."

"Well, I'll have to agree that your horses this year are fine, Carson."

Carson smiled at his companion as he led the colt back into the barn. "You haven't seen the last one. I think he's the best of the lot. High Spade."

"Well by all means, let's have a look at him."

Carson tucked Seven Bells securely into his stall and quickly led High Spade out to the barn yard.

Bertrand Blandings' bushy brows rose as he led the proud young colt out into the sunlight. "My, my," he breathed, and stepped up to run a wondering hand over the horse's glossy flanks. "You've been holding out on us, Carson."

Carson gave the yearling a satisfied glance. "Yes, he's the best horse we've had in years, in my opinion."

The elderly man shook his head in wonder. "I must say, when I saw your asking price for this fellow, I thought it was outrageous, and I still do. But not as outrageous as before I saw this horse."

Carson smiled up at him. "The best is always expensive," he replied simply. "And High Spade is the best horse here. He has the best pedigree, the best conformation, the best health, the best instincts."

"Let me see you walk him."

Carson cracked a smile. "Certainly." He took the colt by the halter and let it walk slowly and proudly across the barn yard. The colt snorted and yanked against his hand, switched its long tail, and strutted like a peacock. Carson kept his back and shoulders ramrod-straight as he paced, knowing that he, too, was part of the effect. He could feel the old man's eyes on the horse walking away. He was close to clinching the sale, he could practically taste it.

He turned to lead the horse back toward his guest, and the old man's keen eyes followed the colt's every move. He said nothing, but the look on his face told Carson everything.

I've got him, he thought jubilantly. *He's going to buy High Spade at least, and maybe the others, too.*

The only question left is for how much.

The old man raised his eyes to Carson's. "Well, I'll say this, Carson: you've got some knockout horses there. I'm giving them serious consideration."

Carson gave him a confident smile as he walked High Spade up to his guest. Bertrand reached out to stroke the horse's silken neck.

"I'll have my inspection team come by in a day or two to check them, and then we'll talk."

"I look forward to it," Carson replied instantly. "Let me put him up again, and we'll have lunch."

The older man's face brightened. "Got any more of that bottle of Pappy?" he ventured with a twinkle in his eye.

"You're in luck," Carson shot over his shoulder.

Chapter Fourteen

"*Namaste*," Donna murmured into the pages of her book on Hindi. "*Mera naam Dona hai.*"

She was lying on the couch in her condo, and she turned the page from the 'Introductions' section to the 'Ordering Out' section of the book. *Most restaurants in Indian cities serve vegetarian fare*, it read. *Travelers should adopt an adventurous attitude to enjoy the many flavors of Indian cuisine.*

She flipped the page and skimmed the other sections. She was trying to concentrate, but to her annoyance, she was having trouble. She had one ear cocked for her phone, and it kept not ringing.

This is ridiculous, she told herself in exasperation. *Carson Spade isn't going to call back. He wanted an evening out on the town, I gave it to him, and now it's over. He's leaving after the auction, I may be leaving the country soon, so it hardly matters that he hasn't called me back.*

She told herself that she was thinking like a teenager, although she couldn't remember having such silly expectations even when she had been a teen. She flipped the page of her book.

Telling time.

"*Samay kya hua?*" she murmured; but the sound of her phone trilling made her toss the book aside and reach for her cell.

"Hello?"

To her astonishment, a computerized voice intoned, "Have you protected your car with an extended warranty?"

"Bah!"

Donna scowled and jammed the red button. *How do they always get my number,* she thought angrily; then turned back to her book with a sigh. But as soon as she started to concentrate, the words always seemed to melt away into Carson's Spade face. After another ten minutes she threw the book across the room in disgust.

It was true, Carson looked like a model for Ralph Lauren, he was witty, charming, and as lusciously smooth as a bowl of *creme-fraiche*. It was indisputable that he was the best-looking man she'd seen in...well, that she'd probably ever seen.

Her irritated glance flicked to the bouquet of pale blue roses on her living room table. They were still lovely.

But it would be crazy to risk her opportunity to work on a movie set and live in India just for a pair of laughing blue eyes. Tim was going to want an answer soon.

She didn't have time to wait around for that gorgeous playboy to call her back.

She stood up impatiently and drifted out onto the balcony, her arms crossed against the cool fall air. Sleek horses gamboled in the pastures rolling away to the line of trees in the distance.

And it occurred to her then, that the white fences that hemmed then in were beautiful, but they were still fences. Those well-tended horses weren't free to sail over the topmost rails and go flying off into the blue.

But she was. There was no feeling like it.

Donna raised her chin. She'd never yet met a man who'd convinced her to give up her freedom for him, and she probably never would. Not Maxim in Paris, not Tommy in London, not Albert in Sydney.

Tall, dark, handsome Carson would surely prove to be just like them, if she was fool enough to hang around for him.

She rubbed one arm and frowned into the distance; but the sudden trill of her cell phone made her turn quickly back into the room.

She lifted the phone to her ear. "Hello?"

To her own annoyance, her heart jumped to hear Carson's smiling voice on the other end of the line. "Hello, pretty lady," he murmured.

Donna kept her tone light and disinterested. She refused to let herself slip into a pointless flirtation with Carson Spade.

"Thank you for the roses, Carson. They're beautiful."

"I'm glad you enjoyed them," he replied smoothly. "It's a beautiful day. I was hoping you'd come with me to Churchill Downs to have lunch and catch a race. "

Donna tucked a sprig of hair behind one ear. It was a beautiful day, and she was off work. She glanced over her shoulder at the sunny sky outside her balcony doors.

Her boss had warned her against going out with Carson again; she herself had other and probably better plans; and he was due to go back to Texas in a matter of weeks. Nothing but a polite refusal made any sense.

But on the other hand, she was young and free, he was gorgeous, and it was a delicious fall day outside.

"Yes, it is a lovely day," she agreed.

"How does a private table at the trackside clubhouse sound for lunch?"

Donna looked up at the ceiling and bit her lip, but she ended up replying, "It sounds nice, Carson."

His tone brightened. "I'll come by to pick you up. Is thirty minutes good?"

"It's fine."

His voice softened to a deep purr. "I'll see you then."

"Goodbye, Carson."

Donna pressed the red button on her phone with a sigh of defeat. *What did I just do?* she thought. *We're bound to be seen walking out of here together.*

But as she went to get dressed, she found that she was less concerned about her boss, than she was with the question of whether to wear the sundress with a huge hat, or the sleek Armani pantsuit with three-inch heels.

A half-hour later she emerged from her condo in a pale yellow linen sundress under a huge black Dior hat and black heels. She slung a little strappy bag over a bare shoulder and skipped down the steps to meet Carson, who was just walking up to meet her.

His brown face split into a white smile, and he held out his hand.

"Why, I came for Donna Bouchet," he teased. "But I find a starlet instead! What have you done with her?"

"Silly," she laughed, and he joined in with her.

They walked across the sun-dappled grounds together, and Carson opened the back door of the main clubhouse for her. Donna bit her lip as she slipped in, knowing that she was most likely burning her bridges, but she was in a reckless mood. A jolt of adrenalin swirled pleasantly in her veins as she wondered if she'd lose her job over Carson Spade; but for the moment at least, she didn't care.

They breezed through the clubhouse and Carson put a hand on her arm briefly. They paused in the lobby, right in front of the main desk, and Donna saw one of the girls behind it raise an eyebrow and smirk at the sight of her.

Carson stepped up and murmured, "Limo ready?"

The girl beamed at him. "Right outside, Mr. Spade."

Donna felt her mouth dropping open as he turned to rejoin her. He slipped a hand smoothly under her elbow and piloted her out the front doors and down the steps. Sure enough, a sleek black limousine was parked outside. The uniformed driver stepped to the back door and opened it as they approached.

Carson waited for her to slide in, and Donna slipped into the buttery soft leather seat. The driver closed the door behind her, and Carson slid in beside her on the other side of the car.

To Donna's surprise and delight, the spacious back seats faced a small but exquisite inlaid wooden counter. It held a slender silver vase with one red rose, two champagne glasses, and a silver bucket filled with ice and an uncorked champagne bottle.

The front door closed, and the driver's grinning face appeared briefly in the connecting window.

"Where to, folks?"

Donna felt a flush of embarrassment, because she knew what that grin meant. She knew the driver well, she worked with him often, and she could expect some serious ribbing when she saw him again without the elegant Carson Spade at her elbow.

Assuming she still worked at the Turf Club that long, of course.

"Churchill Downs," Carson replied, and to Donna's relief, the little window slid shut. Carson reached for the champagne bottle and turned to her with a smile.

"Let me see that glass," he murmured, and she smiled and handed it to him.

Chapter Fifteen

"Tell me all about yourself," Carson smiled. He was strolling down the sunny sidewalks of Churchill Downs with Donna's hand on his elbow, and he was in an optimistic mood.

They'd just finished enjoying an elegant lunch at the clubhouse restaurant: white wine, lobster salad, and a perfect creme brulee crowned with glazed fruit for dessert. They'd strolled out of the restaurant into the sunshine to see the magnificent Churchill Downs racetrack stretching out before them. It was a perfect fall day, with manicured lawns, white railings, and blue sky the backdrop to their conversation.

Carson led Donna down to the stands, helped her into one of the reserved box seats at the track's fabled finish line, then settled in beside her. "You'll have to bare your soul. I'm very curious about a woman who knows all the secret clubs in town and is learning to speak Hindi."

Donna laughed freely for the first time since he'd met her, and that low trill of laughter went right up his spine.

"What do you want to know?"

He loosened his collar and stretched an arm across the back of her chair. "Well, where did you grow up, for starters? Are you a native of Kentucky?"

She shook her head. "No. I wasn't even born in America. I was born on a little island in the Persian Gulf. Very pretty place. Lots of blue water and white buildings."

Carson tried to picture the countries around the Persian Gulf. The only one he could think of was Iraq, and so he smiled and looked a question.

"I was born in a little island country called Bahrain. My father was an oil executive and a distant relative of the king. He met my mother on a business trip to Sweden. She was a fairly successful actress there, and they met at a party at the Bahraini Embassy in Stockholm. It was a whirlwind romance. They married just three months after they met."

Carson raised an eyebrow and smiled. "Are you considered a member of the royal family, then?"

Donna sputtered into her champagne glass. "Technically, if you have the patience to count that far outwards. I grew up on a very nice estate in Manama, but I was always closer to my mother than to my father, and he died five years ago."

"I'm sorry."

Donna shrugged. "I haven't been back home since. I'm in disgrace with his family. They call me a 'rebellious woman.' My father wanted to arrange a marriage for me to his second cousin when I was eighteen, and I caught a flight to New York the same night he announced it." She smiled and shook her head. "My mother was able to wangle me a spot in the chorus line on an off-off Broadway musical, and that was my first job. Lucky I'd had private lessons to learn how to sing and dance."

Carson leaned backward in his chair. "What were you in?"

She smiled and looked away. "Oh, nothing that you've ever heard of," she sputtered. "Mostly forgettable dramas or 'tribute' ripoffs of popular plays." She shook her head. "It was an education, but it was fun while it lasted."

"Did your father try to bring you back to Bahrain?"

"A few times," Donna sighed. "He called me a lot at first, and even came to visit a few times, but there was no way I was going to marry his second cousin. I'd never even seen the man," she sighed, and her expressive eyes flashed.

"My father was a good man, you understand," she added. "Just old-fashioned and more than a bit stubborn. He really believed his cousin would be good for me."

"I see. Where did you go from there?"

"To Sydney. Partly to disappear," she sighed. "I snagged a job as a flight attendant, and that was a lot of fun. I love travel and variety. I'd had a very privileged, sheltered childhood, but I found that I much preferred freedom."

Carson looked down, rubbed his nose, then glanced up into her eyes with a smile.

"Is *any* of what you just told me true?"

She held his eye, dimpled, and leaned in close to whisper: "Not a word of it."

Carson threw his head back and laughed. "You're in the wrong profession, then. You're wasted in hospitality. You should be in advertising," he twinkled.

"Maybe I will be someday."

A strong male voice suddenly blared over the outdoor loudspeakers. "Ladies and gentlemen, welcome to Churchill Downs! We hope you enjoy this lovely afternoon at the races."

Carson turned his gaze from Donna's laughing eyes to the smooth green sweep of the legendary track. There was an afternoon race in the offing: he could see uniformed jockeys lazily urging their thoroughbreds toward the starting gate.

The announcer's voice went on: "The next race will be the Downs Dash. The field is made up of two-year-old fillies and includes Cold Snap, Terrible Daisy, Battle Cat, Cleo's Secret,

Mind Your Business, Urban Legend, Beautiful Dreamer, Tell Ya Grandma, Romance Novel, and Juicy Rumor."

Carson consulted his program and murmured, "I'm sorry, I didn't even think to ask if you wanted to place a bet."

Donna shrugged a smooth, bare shoulder. "It's all right, I don't gamble. I'm not religious, but I was raised in a religious home, and that particular taboo stuck with me. I don't know why."

Carson nodded. "I can relate. My grandfather had an almost religious objection to flashing money around." He fell silent and considered for a moment. "That teaching hit my other brothers right between the eyes, but it seemed to miss me."

Donna laughed softly as the announcer proclaimed, "Horses to the starting gate."

Carson turned his head suddenly and smiled, "Look here. What if I propose a little white wager? Nothing to do with money," he added quickly, as she raised an eyebrow. "I wouldn't want to be responsible for corrupting you," he teased.

"What do you have in mind?"

Carson used the program to point to the horses walking toward the starting gate. "I'll choose a horse, and you choose a horse. The one whose horse finishes fastest wins."

Donna's lips curled up. "And what are the stakes?"

Carson turned to her, pinned her eyes with his own. "If you win, I'll do whatever you want. You decide. If I win, you have to let me kiss you," he smiled, "and of course, go out with me again."

Donna gave him a look between laughter and dismay. "Don't you think that's a little open-ended? What if I win and ask you for a million dollars?"

Carson shrugged and smiled. "I'm good for it."

Donna straightened up in her seat. "All right," she replied briskly, "I'll choose a horse. I like the look of the dun in the middle of the line. Number 6. Which one is that?"

Carson consulted the program. "That's Urban Legend."

"Urban Legend, then," she told him, and folded her hands in her lap. "And you'd better hope she loses. There's no knowing what I might ask."

Carson shot her a quick glance and caught his breath at the mischievous look in those golden eyes. To his delight, she was flirting with him.

"I aim to please," he replied softly; and when she dropped her gaze, he returned to the program, slowly and reluctantly.

"Hurry," she urged him softly. "They're in the gate!"

Carson glanced at the loaded starting gate and took his best shot. "I like the black on the end," he announced, and glanced at the program. "Number 10. Juicy Rumor."

The words had no sooner left his lips than the buzzer sounded, the gates flew open, and the announcer cried, "*Aaaaand* they're off!"

Carson crossed his legs, leaned back in his chair, and watched in amusement as the fillies exploded out of the gate and went flying smoothly down the track. The announcer's voice proclaimed, "Battle Cat takes the early lead with Cleo's Secret a close second and Tell Ya Grandma in third."

Carson turned to give Donna a rueful glance as both their horses fell instantly to the back of the pack. She giggled and murmured, "It looks like we're in trouble."

The announcer barked, "Coming around the first turn, it's Battle Cat and Cleo's Secret, with Terrible Daisy and Juicy Gossip making a move on the inside!"

Carson lounged in his chair, smiling at the distant figures on the far side of the track as they rounded the far curve and came flying down the stretch. Donna frowned and raised a tiny pair of binoculars to her eyes.

"Which number was your horse again?" she asked faintly.

"Number ten."

She frowned and pursed her lips. "Hm. It seems to be moving up. I don't see Number Six."

Carson crossed his arms across his chest. "It's the horse at the back."

Donna raised an eyebrow and turned to give him a wry look. "I have the feeling I've been wangled somehow," she murmured, and raised the binoculars again. Carson followed the fast-moving figures as they came thundering down the flat toward the finish line.

"And Juicy Gossip's charging up the inside! She's left Terrible Daisy in the dust and is moving up on Cleo's Secret!" His voice jumped to a joyous shriek. "It's Juicy Gossip and Battle Cat battling for the lead! And here comes Juicy Gossip for one last burst—Juicy Gossip wins by a nose!"

Carson folded his hands in his lap and looked up at the sky, and then over at Donna. The huge hat hid her face, but the little binoculars slowly drifted down to her lap. Carson waited in pleasant anticipation as she slowly took off the huge hat, set it on the chair beside her, turned, and took his face in two perfectly manicured hands.

He smiled as her golden eyes moved closer, then closed his own to savor a long, soft, sensuous kiss that ended far too soon.

When he exhaled faintly and opened his eyes, he found her reapplying her lipstick as she stared into a little compact.

"That one doesn't count," he informed her, and she turned to stare at him as she put her mirror away. "That one was volunteered."

She giggled softly, and he laughed and reached out for her hand. "I won the wager, so now I'm collecting my winnings. I want you to come with me to the Breeders' Party at the Continental. It's Saturday at noon."

He noticed that Donna's soft lips parted slightly, and waited for what they would say. She paused for an instant, then smiled:

"I'd be delighted. It'll give me a chance to see you in action. I'm assuming this party is as much business as pleasure, yes?"

"Much more pleasure this time," he told her, and gave her hand a brief kiss before releasing it.

Chapter Sixteen

The big limousine pulled back up to the Turf Club entrance well after midnight, and Donna felt Carson's arm go around her shoulder and pull her to his chest. She closed her eyes and yielded up to a long, slow, deliberate kiss that sent a delicate frisson of delight right through her.

Carson's hand cupped her cheek as he smiled down at her. "I'll walk you back to your condo." He gave her another quick peck before climbing out of the car and walking around to her side of the car.

Donna stifled a sigh of regret as the door opened. She looked up to see Carson's sharp white smile and his hand reaching down for hers.

She slid out of the seat and stepped out into the chilly night air, hat in hand. Carson helped her out of the car, shrugged out of his coat, and draped it over her bare shoulders against the cool night air.

It was a chilly night, but a clear one with a big full moon, and the clubhouse and the grounds were almost as visible as in the daytime. The clubhouse was open for the convenience of its guests, but Donna didn't feel like facing the knowing smile of the night clerk, so she murmured, "Let's just walk through the grounds. It's a beautiful night."

Carson slipped an arm around her waist. "It is that," he agreed, and so they skirted the big mansion. They sauntered down the paved path through the magnolia trees, then out into the open past a bank of azalea bushes, and on through the moon-mottled darkness.

Donna felt almost giddy, and surprised at herself for it; but then, it wasn't every day that a girl had a magical day out at Churchill Downs with a gorgeous billionaire.

She could be forgiven for feeling like Cinderella, even if she was hardly a waif. She could be pardoned for forgetting that she'd been around the world and had plenty of jazz of her own.

For feeling a bit swept away.

Carson's hand slipped from her waist to her fingers, and he clasped them warmly as they walked along; but suddenly he raised her arm and turned her just as if they were on a dance floor; and she giggled as she whirled through the friendly darkness, then back into the protection of his arm around her shoulder.

She smiled up into his shadowed face. "I've had a wonderful time," she murmured. "Thank you, Carson."

"It was my pleasure," he murmured, and the fingers around her shoulder tightened.

A big, smiling harvest moon peeped at them through the branches of the pines, and leaves danced past them on the breath of a chilly breeze. They drifted down the manicured sidewalk that skirted the dark Coach House restaurant, past the tidy outdoor patio and restaurant grounds, and on to the smallish cluster of condominiums on the other side of a long, pleasant walk through a meadow fragrant of sweet grass and fallen leaves.

They strolled up to her front steps hand in hand and paused in the little puddle of light over her front door. Carson took her by the shoulders and leaned in for a sweet, soft, good night kiss.

"Sweet dreams, *bella*."

Donna smiled up into his eyes. "Good night."

She slipped reluctantly from his arms, skipped up the steps, turned to give him one last glance over her shoulder, and then slipped inside.

Donna closed the door behind her, closed her eyes, and leaned against it with a smile. She'd never enjoyed a date more in her life—if *date* was what you could call an afternoon between two people who were about to part ways.

She tossed her hat onto a rack by the door and drifted up to her bedroom, humming softly. It almost made her sorry that she was going to be leaving; but that was all but a certainly now.

She'd thumbed her nose to the club in a very public way, but she was still under the spell of Carson's laughing eyes, and at the moment, she didn't care at all that she was most likely going to lose her job over him.

She usually chose excitement over safety, and she was willing to pay the fare for her choices.

She drifted into her bedroom and tossed her bag onto a chair. It was long past midnight, but she was off the next day, so she could afford to be leisurely.

She sank down onto her bed and slipped off her high heels. She stared into space for a moment, replaying the lovely afternoon; but she seemed to remember less about the details of their outing, than the details of Carson's eyes. She smiled and shook her head. They were as clear and ice-blue as a glacial lake, but they were most often alight with laughter. Carson seemed to find the world amusing, sometimes ironic; but he saluted it with affection, and she liked that very much.

She shook her hair free. She found that the more she saw of Carson, the better she liked him. He was wicked smart, that had been clear from the first; but unlike some other rich and intelligent men she'd met, Carson didn't seem to be mean-spirited. She hadn't heard him make a joke at another person's expense, he didn't seem to need to prove anything, and he didn't brag.

He let his results talk, and she liked that, too.

Donna fell back onto her bed, raised her arms above her head, and stared at the ceiling. She especially liked his manners. There was something so courtly about Carson Spade, something experienced and yet a bit old-fashioned. He was smooth as silk, he certainly hadn't hesitated to take her hand or slip an arm around her shoulder or kiss her, but he hadn't tried to seduce her, not even by implication.

It was sweet, and she was intrigued.

After spending a day with him, she had the tingling sense that Carson was a bit of a romantic. Maybe she might stick around for a little while to find out.

She might even postpone her trip to India. Temporarily.

After all, her goal in life was the pursuit of intrigue and adventure; and at the moment, she was having too much fun to move on immediately.

Chapter Seventeen

"I'm not paying you for excuses!"

Buster Hogan rounded on a small group of men muddying up the oriental carpet in his luxurious den. One of them had a wad of chew in one cheek, and Buster stared at it in disgust.

They hadn't had any better sense to show up at his hotel suite, where there was a security camera in every hall, and it made him twice as mad as he'd been. He jabbed a short, straight finger at their noses and barked:

"You told me you knew how to get past a security system. I gave you more than enough money to do it. There was nobody guarding that barn but one old man. It should've been easy!"

The spokesman for the group, a tall, broad-shouldered man with a hard face, raised his eyes to his employer's.

"We did get past the outside alarm. It was just bad luck that the old man got spooked and hit the manual alarm from inside. The only way we could've stopped him would be to kill him, and you didn't pay us near enough for that."

"Bah!"

Buster turned away from them in contempt and threw his cigar down onto the floor. "You screwed up the job, and now Carson Spade's all set to eat my lunch at that horse auction. I've got millions of dollars sunk into those horses, and if I don't sell 'em I'll have to eat the loss! The competition's getting more cutthroat every year, and those Seven horses are the ones to beat."

One of the other men stepped up and ventured, "Spade only has three horses up, don't he, and there's lots of buyers at a place like that. Why are you so worried?"

Buster turned slowly, and the look in his eye made the man step back again and shut his mouth. Buster's face went red.

"Because none of 'em have to buy *anything*," he replied softly; and then his voice jumped to a shout.

"Get out of here, all of you! I should've known better than to work with cons. You're gun shy. Afraid of going back in!"

The foremost man frowned but countered, "We're game enough, if the money's right. That other guy hasn't sold his horses yet. We can still get 'em."

"If the money's right!" Buster roared. "You're lucky I'm even talking to you. I won't throw good money after bad, I'll tell you that! You've botched what should've been the easiest job in the world. If the three of you can't get past one old man, I'm not sending you to the Keeneland stables to get caught by security guards!"

"I tell you, we can do it," the man replied earnestly. "You don't want to steal the horses, do you? Getting rid of 'em's easy as long as you don't want 'em alive."

Buster scowled at him. "I suppose you think you're just going to go in there and shoot them! Get out of here!"

"No, we didn't plan to shoot 'em," the man frowned. "There are other ways, and lots quieter. Get us some ID badges that'll get us into the stable area, and we'll take your competition out. Problem solved!"

Buster's eyes narrowed. "I'm on a Breeder's Association Committee. I'm moving in some important circles. I can't afford to have my name linked to a crime at the biggest thoroughbred auction house in the country."

"You won't be," the other man assured him. "Give us another chance, you won't be sorry."

Buster crossed his arms and tilted his head back. "How do you plan to kill three horses at a guarded track stable?" he scoffed.

The tall man leaned in and smiled. "Just a handful of yew leaves will kill a horse," he whispered. "It's toxic as all fire, just a little bit'll kill a horse within minutes. No cure."

Buster frowned, but was silent, and the man added, "It's just leaves. Easy to smuggle in, easy to deliver, works quick, never fails. Even a tiny bit would make the horse too sick to be sold, if that's all you want."

"They'll know the horses were poisoned," Buster objected, in a softer tone.

"Not if it's mixed in with their feed," the man replied. "Could be an accident."

Buster fell silent. "I'd have to get you out quick," he muttered. "And have you hole up someplace for a long time after."

The man straightened up and stared at Buster through half-closed eyes. "We got no objection to that. Long as it's a decent place to hole up. Plenty of food and booze."

Buster glanced up at him. "I'll think about it," he muttered. "You three have hardly covered yourselves in glory, and I have an important meeting this afternoon. Go back and wait at the hotel. I'll call you if I need you.

"And one more thing," he added coldly. "If you turn on me, if you mention my name to anyone, it'll be the last thing you ever do!"

Buster watched as the three scowling men nodded and shuffled out of his hotel suite; and he cursed under his breath as the gilded suite door snicked shut after them.

"Blockheads," he muttered to himself. "Getting so a man can't find good help any more."

The words had hardly passed his lips when a small, pale, pudgy woman with a cheerful face and a perfectly coiffed head of blonde hair walked into the room. She raised a heavily ringed hand to smooth one eyebrow and chirped, "Did you call me, puddin'?"

Buster sighed and shot his wife an exasperated glance. "No, Martha Sue. And how many times do I have to tell you not to bust in on my business meetings?"

Martha Sue's face clouded like a baby's. She pulled her lips down into a pout and hunched a round shoulder. "You know I never listen to your business, Buster," she objected. "It's so boring. When are you going to take me to all those parties that you promised? We've been in Kentucky almost a week, and I'm tired of this hotel."

Buster nodded grimly. "We're about to," he told her, and her round face brightened.

"When?"

"This afternoon. We're going to the Continental for the Breeder's Party," he replied, and his little wife gasped.

"This afternoon? Why didn't you tell me, Buster? I have to go get ready!"

"It's not for two hours," he told her, but she gave a little scream and hurried out of the room, swaying on her precarious heels. He watched her with an expression of baffled dismay, then walked to a sideboard and poured himself a generous glass of gin.

His thoughts returned to the party. Bertrand Blandings was likely going to be there, and it was a chance to buttonhole him again, to talk up the Lazy H yearlings. Buster sighed and took a big slug of gin. He was going to try to pitch every big buyer he saw there, of course; but Blandings was the big prize. He had the deepest pockets, and he'd been gone for a long time.

He was likely ready to buy; and maybe so ready that he'd take even a few second-tier horses, if Carson Spade didn't grab all the available money. The Spades had all the dumb luck in the world. They always ended up with the finest horses, and they always demanded every dollar of what those horses were worth.

If Blandings bought all three of the Spade horses, he might not have anything left in his budget for the Lazy H yearlings. Buster's eyes narrowed as he lifted his glass to his lips. He wasn't going to let that happen.

Not even if he had to send somebody into the Keeneland stables with fake ID and a handful of poison. It wasn't going to be the three losers who'd just let him down and got caught on camera walking to his hotel room, he'd already decided that; but all the rest was on the table.

His wife's voice drifted out to him from their bedroom. "Buster, should I wear my red dress or my black dress to the party?"

Buster grimaced, but called back, "The red one. It'll draw attention to us."

Martha Sue's laughter drifted through the open bedroom door like bubbles. "Oh, you're sweet, puddin'.'"

Buster looked up from his drink, shook his head, and took another slug.

He'd promised to bring Martha Sue on this trip, but he was already beginning to regret keeping his word. Martha Sue had already hit every shop in Keeneland and was branching out.

He was afraid to check her card balance.

"Look at my new hat, Buster!" she called, and he glanced up just in time to be transfixed by his short, pudgy wife half-hidden under a monstrous red hat.

It made her look like a mushroom, but he knew better than to say so.

"Isn't it just the cleverest thing?" she laughed, and turned her head back and forth. "You can't go to a party around here without a hat!"

She disappeared into the bedroom, and Buster exhaled in a long, painful sigh. The only thing that was going to make his ordeal worthwhile, would be to sell his yearlings to Bertrand Blandings right under Carson Spade's stuck-up nose.

And then to go back to Sandy Creek, and rub it in Buck Spade's big one.

Chapter Eighteen

"This is a crazy idea, John," an anxious-looking man hissed. "You heard what Buster said in that hotel room. He told us to wait, not go bustin' ahead without his okay." He rubbed his face and added, "And all this hay dust is getting up my nose. It's making me sneeze!"

The tallest of the three men turned to scowl at his companion. They were all in the back of a delivery truck, sitting on the floor, and it was a dark night and cold. They all three were jostled by the movement of the truck as it approached the Keeneland stable complex.

"Buster'll change his tune when we get those Spade horses, you'll see," he assured the other two. "It's an easy job, and once it's done we'll get that twenty thousand he promised. Don't you have any ambition?"

"Buster was right about one thing," the third man grumbled. "I don't want to go back in for this, that's for sure."

"Ah, you two are chicken-hearted," the first man grumbled. "Chicken headed, too, if we're gonna be honest! All you got to do is take these leaves and stick your hand out in front of the horse's nose. All they got to do is eat a little. Easy!"

"What about us?" the second man objected. "If this stuff will kill a horse, it can't be good for us, either!"

"Well, you ain't gonna eat it, are you? Trust you two to complicate something that's as simple as falling down. We'll never have an easier chance to make twenty grand, and I'm going for it!"

"What about the guard?" the first man parried, and tugged on a laminated card dangling from a lanyard around his neck. "What if he sees this ID ain't the real thing?"

"Just relax, Carl. We got these baseball hats to throw off the security cameras, we got the fake IDs. We'll wait until the guard walks off or falls asleep, and it's over in five minutes."

"What if he never walks off?"

"Yeah, what if he doesn't fall asleep?"

The tall man shook his head and pulled his mouth down in disgust. "You boys don't deserve to be called cons," he told them. "A con sees his chance and takes it. He doesn't whine and cry like a little kid!"

The truck slowed, then slowly lumbered to a stop with a screech of the brakes. The truck sat there for a long moment, its heavy engine idling loudly.

The men knelt there, listening, as the truck driver produced his identification to the perimeter guards. "Delivery for the stables."

The guard's voice mumbled, "What's in the back?"

"Hay and feed."

"Unlock the back door so I can have a look."

The three men glanced at one another, then scrambled against the back wall of the truck to hide behind the last row of hay bales.

There was the sound of heavy footsteps walking past outside, then the door lock clanged loudly, and the back doors screeched open. The guard climbed up into the back of the truck, and the white glare of a flashlight flicked over the interior.

The guard gave the load a once-over, flicked the flashlight across it again, then turned to climb down. The three men crouched in the darkness as the doors clanged shut again.

"Okay, you're good to go," the guard called, and the engine revved slightly as the big truck slowly lurched past the delivery gate.

"We're in," John told the others jubilantly. "I told you this would be easy! Now all we got to do is wait until the driver parks the truck. We'll wait for him to open the door."

"I don't like it, John. If he brings a bunch of guys in to start unloading right away, we won't be able to do anything except look at 'em. How we getting out of this truck?"

"I'm getting into position now," their leader announced, and grabbed a hay bale to pull himself to his feet. He swayed back and forth as the truck moved along, and his companions watched him with goggling eyes.

"Are you gonna jump the driver?"

The first man paid no attention to them, but kept moving to the back of the cargo area. He crouched down behind a line of bales near the truck doors, and after a minute the truck came to a slow, shuddering stop.

The two men in back raised their heads up over the line of bales just enough to watch as the cab door opened and the sound of approaching footsteps grew louder. There was a loud, grinding noise, then the clank of the back doors being thrown open and locked into position.

It was black night outside, but the square at the other end of the truck revealed the stable loading area, dimly lit at that hour of the morning. The black silhouette of the driver appeared briefly in it as he climbed up into the truck and stepped in a few paces; then there was suddenly a dark blur, a shout, and a heavy thud.

They scrambled out from behind their hiding place and hurried to the door. They found John kneeling beside the unconscious driver. He tore the ID off his neck as they watched, lifted his cap, and looped it over his own neck before crouching to the edge of the doors and jumping down.

They climbed down after him and followed him through the dark loading bay, across an open alley, and on to the first barn of the many in the complex.

The first man moved toward it boldly, and the other two hung back warily as John approached the security guard with a wave and a smile.

"Hello, mister," he grinned. "I just brought in a load of feed and I'm looking for somebody to help me deliver it to the right place."

The uniformed guard stood up and approached him slowly. "Let me see your ID," he muttered, and his hands drifted down to his sides.

John's smile deepened. "Right here." He tugged at the stolen ID on his neck, and the guard glanced at it, and then at his shadowed face.

"This is my first run to this place," John explained with a shamefaced smile. "I'm a little turned around."

The guard nodded. "You're going in the wrong direction. The loading dock is back the way you came, not this way." He turned briefly to gesture toward the stables. "This way is the bar—"

John slammed his fist into the guard's jaw the instant he turned away, and the blow dropped the man to the ground like a rock. John knelt down on the ground, snatched the guard's gun and his key ring, and gestured fiercely to his lagging companions.

"Come on!" he hissed, and hurried to the stables. They gave each other a regretful look but followed as fast as they could walk.

They found their leader walking down the length of the stable, reading stall numbers. "It's this section," he muttered, and moved down the row.

"Ah," he sighed, and moved a step closer. "Here they are. Look at these beauties! I can see why Buster's scared of 'em."

The other two men came hurrying up, and their eyes moved to the first colt in the row, a proud, high-strung yearling. It snorted at them and rolled its eyes.

"Calm down buddy," John soothed, and unlocked the stall door with shaking fingers. He dug into his jeans pocket. "Calm down, High Spade! I've got a treat for you, yes! Look at this!"

He extended a flat palm full of chopped yew leaves, and the horse danced back with its ears laid flat.

John paused long enough to look over his shoulder and hiss, "Get the other two! We got to get this done and get out of here!"

The second man seemed doubtful. He glanced at the colt in doubt as he passed. "I dunno," he mumbled. "I think you're making him mad. Look at his eyes."

"Get over there and get to work!" his companion hissed fiercely, then turned back to the horse. He unlatched the stall door and opened it slowly.

"Come on, buddy. You'd like a midnight snack, wouldn't you? Yes."

High Spade retreated to the corner of his stall and struck at the intruder with one flashing hoof. John swore and dodged to avoid it, then came on again.

"Come on, you stubborn devil! You're going to eat this and like it!"

A pair of arms suddenly clamped his arms to his side, and John yelled out and struggled as he was dragged out of the stall and pushed down onto the barn floor with his face smashed to the concrete. The gun was yanked from his hand and his arms were pulled behind his back and cuffed by a gang of unseen guards.

John yelled again and turned his head. He was just able to see his other two friends thrown up against the barn wall. They were being frisked by guards.

A male voice commanded, "Somebody check on those Spade horses." Its unseen owner turned to him and hissed,:

"What were you trying to give those horses? Speak up!"

Another voice called back: "It's some kind of leaves. Call the vet!"

Chapter Nineteen

Carson opened the door to his room at the club, tossed his keys onto the table, and shouldered out of his jacket. The moon was streaming in through the open balcony doors and painted the wooden floors with a silver block of light.

There was something about Donna that worked on him like a glass of Pappy. She relaxed him and excited him and made him feel as if he was in a pleasant, if slightly altered state.

He was still a little drunk with her. He raised his shirt collar and took a sniff. The barest breath of her cologne was still clinging to it.

She was like a beautiful apparition he'd see shimmering in a wonderful dream. He was just entangled enough to be curious about the wild story she'd told him about being born in Bahrain. Carson smiled to himself as he unbuttoned his cuffs; then he reached for his cell phone as he drifted into the bedroom. The blue screen flicked on, and he pressed a series of buttons, then mumbled:

"King of Bahrain, extended royal family."

He scanned the results as he walked to the bed and sank down onto the luxurious coverlet. He scrolled through a list of twenty brothers, then cousins, then second cousins.

Carson pulled his feet up into the bed and raised the phone up above his head. He flicked from one list to another, then modified his search.

Bahraini extended royal family + Swedish actress.

The first article that pulled up read:

Bio of Kaled bin Ibrahim Al Khalifa.

Kaled bin Ibrahim Al Khalifa was a Bahraini banking magnate and the second cousin of the King of Bahrain and a nominal member of his government, though he filled only a ceremonial role. He died of a heart ailment in 2018, and was best known for expanding the international prestige of the Bank of Bahrain, and for his controversial marriage to Swedish film star Brigitta Lindgren. The two were married in 1989 and had one daughter, Maryam bint Kaled al-Khalifa.

Kaled and Brigitta divorced in 2008. Kaled remained in Bahrain, but Brigitta returned to Sweden, where she revived her career in film with starring roles in several popular films before retiring in 2019.

Carson stared at the screen as his hands slowly drifted down to his sides. *What do you know,* he thought in amazement, then chuckled to himself.

Donna wasn't pulling my leg after all! She is a relative of the Bahraini royal family.

And it looks like her real name is Miriam.

He laughed in wonder, shook his head, then slid the phone onto the nightstand; but he'd barely shouldered out of his shirt before the phone vibrated. He raised his brows and grabbed it up again.

It was a phone call from Keeneland, and Carson's pleasant mood evaporated. His blood ran cold. The last thing he wanted was a call from Keeneland after midnight.

"Hello?"

A worried male voice barked: "Mr. Spade?"

He frowned. "Yes."

"This is Keeneland security. We're calling to inform you that there's been a breach at the stables. We captured three men who broke into your horse's stalls. They were trying to feed the horses an unknown substance."

Carson's heart all but stopped. He pressed a hand to his chest and croaked, "Are my horses all right?"

"The vet is with them now, Mr. Spade. They aren't showing immediate signs of poisoning, but you might want to come down."

"I'll be there as soon as I can," he gasped, and scrabbled for his shirt. "Have you gotten anything out of those—those—"

"The police are interrogating the suspects. You'll be able to talk to them when you get here."

"Thank you," Carson mumbled, and shouldered into his shirt. He hung up, then called the concierge desk.

"Front desk."

"This is Carson Spade. I need a car right away."

"Certainly, Mr. Spade. We'll have a driver at the front door in ten minutes."

"Thanks."

Carson tossed the phone down and grabbed for his wallet and his shoes. He had the fleeting impulse to call Buck, but on second thought, he needed to find out exactly what had happened before he got Buck, and everyone else, stirred up. Carson paused for a split-second to sit still in the dark and press a hand to his throbbing brow.

He had the terrible feeling that he already knew who was behind this latest attack, and if it was confirmed, it would probably be better not to breathe a word of it to Buck. Or at least, not until it was all over and everything was okay.

He could only hope that everything was going to be okay.

Carson sighed and closed his eyes. He wasn't a religious man, he never had been, but he'd never been more tempted to pray; and he shot a brief glance of appeal skyward.

It wasn't much; but it was as sincere a request as he was capable of making at that moment.

Carson stood up, stuffed the phone into his trouser pocket, and hurried out of the bedroom. As he blew out of the suite and down the quiet, dimly-lit upstairs club hall, he wondered how he was going to react if the horses were hurt.

Blowing up wouldn't make things better, he knew that; but if what he suspected was true, it was going to be hard to keep from ramming his fist into Buster Hogan's smug, guilty face.

By the time the club limo arrived at the Keeneland stables, it was half past three. Carson was out of the car almost before it stopped moving, and he hurried toward the stable at a trot.

It was easy to see where the action was. There were three Keeneland security cars and two police cars parked in the barn yard area, and a group of men wearing dark nylon jackets and baseball caps huddled together under a pool of light.

Carson rushed to meet them, and one of them lifted his head at his approach.

"Are you Mr. Spade?"

"That's right," Carson barked. "How are my horses?"

The man extended his hand, and Carson squelched his impatience long enough to shake it. "I'm Tom Bridgers. I'm the head of security here at Keeneland, Mr. Spade. We've had our vet check your horses, and they aren't exhibiting any signs of yew poisoning."

"Thank God for that," Carson muttered. "I want to see them."

"Certainly. The vet is still with them, and you can talk to him. Come with me."

It was an unnecessary invitation, because Carson charged ahead of him to the barn. He turned his head just enough to shoot a question over his shoulder as he walked.

"What about the men you caught? Are they still here?"

"No," the man muttered. "The police took them."

"Did they say anything? Give any clue about who they are and why they did this?"

"Not while they were with us. The police may be able to tell you more."

Carson strode into the barn and down to the section where the Spade horses had been stalled, but his horses had been moved down slightly to new stalls. Three more security guards were standing nearby, and Carson saw, with a sickening thump in his chest, that the vet was with High Spade.

He paused in the stall doorway with his hands on the jamb and demanded: "How's my horse?"

The vet, a young, dark man, had been bending down to inspect the colt's belly; but at that, he stood up and extended his hand, and Carson shook it hurriedly.

"I think we may have dodged a bullet, Mr. Spade," he replied slowly. "It looks as if the men who broke in tonight were trying to kill your horses by feeding them yew leaves, which of course are highly toxic. If your horses had ingested any of the leaves, they'd have been showing signs of poisoning long before now. It's been about three hours. They'd have been dead long ago."

Carson closed his eyes and leaned against the wall weakly. The man went on, "The colts' heart rates and breathing are normal, there's no sign of stomach distress or damage to the nervous system. No trauma or apparent injury, though I'm going to take x-rays just to be sure. The only thing they seem to have suffered is the nervousness you might expect to have hostile strangers break into their stalls."

Carson nodded mutely, his eyes still closed. He felt almost as if he'd been the one to dodge a bullet; but he gathered his wits and stood up straight.

High Spade was unusually quiet, and Carson reached out to put a hand on the colt's muzzle in wordless sympathy. The yearling closed its eyes and nickered softly, and Carson smiled.

"I know, boy," he murmured. "That was a close one."

Tom Bridgers walked up and murmured, "Keeneland will do everything possible to make sure that your horses are secure, Mr. Spade. And that the men who broke in are brought to justice."

"I appreciate it," Carson told him, and moved on to check on Seven Bells and Blue Streak. The immediate crisis was over, but it was just beginning to dawn on him that the news of the attempted poisoning was going to fly through Lexington faster than a champion horse around a racetrack. And that, while his horses might be unharmed, there would now be a question mark hanging over them in the buyers' minds.

That it might ruin their chances at the auction.

Could he convince the buyers—could he convince Bertrand Blandings—that the Seven horses were still sound, still champion material, still fit to buy?

Buster Hogan's hard, round face appeared again in Carson's mind, and he bit his mouth into an angry line. He couldn't prove it, but he was convinced that Buster was behind the attempt on their yearlings.

He'd held Buck's arms when his brother had been ready to beat Buster's eyes together; and now he was sorry he hadn't let him go.

It fell to him now to make things right; and as he ran his hands over Seven Bell's twitching neck, Carson vowed to send Buster back to Sandy Creek not just in defeat, but disgrace. He frowned into the colt's frightened eyes and fumed:

This is personal now.

Chapter Twenty

Morgan Spade grunted into his pillow as the phone at his bedside trilled. He opened one bleary eye. The red numbers on his digital clock read 4:15 in the morning.

The phone kept on ringing, and he glanced at his wife, Heather, sleeping beside him. She was deeply asleep and he wanted her to stay that way. She was pregnant and needed her rest.

He pushed up off the bed and reached for the phone with one bare arm.

"Hello?" he mumbled.

His brother Carson's voice launched right into a long, fast blur of information, and Morgan sat up slowly and rubbed his face.

"Whoa, whoa whoa," Morgan muttered. "Slow down, Carson. I'm still asleep. You're gonna have to say again."

Carson paused, then repeated: "I need your help, Morg. Something's happened up here with the yearlings."

That woke him up. He turned over and sat up. "What—what's wrong with the horses?"

"They're all right," Carson told him, "but somebody tried to poison them tonight at the Keeneland stables."

"What!"

"I'll give you three guesses who's behind it."

Morgan's brows snapped together. He growled, "Buster, I'd bet my right arm! Did they catch the snakes?"

"Yeah, they caught them. The police have them. Look, Morg, I'm calling because I need you to check Lickety Split and our other thoroughbreds. Their feed especially. We've already had one scare at our barn, and this new thing might not be limited to Keeneland. Watch out for yew leaves around the stable. That's what these guys were trying to make our colts eat."

Morgan growled, "I wish I'd been there when they tried. I would've knocked their heads together! Anybody who's ever seen a horse die of yew poisoning couldn't do it to any animal!"

"Yeah, they're scum all right," Carson agreed. "That's another thing, Morg. I need you to not breathe a word of this to Buck. We saw Buster at the Keeneland stables, and it was all I could do to keep Buck from slugging Buster then. If Buck finds out about this, he might come back."

Morgan nodded and chuckled. "Yeah, I can see that happening," he agreed. "All right, I won't tell him. He's going to be mad when he finds out we kept it from him, though."

Carson's voice sounded exasperated. "One disaster at a time! All right, I'm going back to the hotel now. I've had a long night. Thanks, Morg."

"Sure."

Morgan leaned over to hang up the phone, grabbed his keys, then slipped out of bed. He pulled on the pair of jeans he'd thrown over a chair, shouldered into a shirt, and found his boots by feel in the dark.

He glanced back over his shoulder. Heather's chest rose and fell slowly, and her eyes were closed in sleep.

He padded out of the room carrying his boots in one hand and closed the door behind him. He drifted down the hall to the big living room and sank down onto the couch.

A harvest moon sent a pale light through the big glass wall that made up one side of the room. Its radiance was so bright that he could see with it, to pull on his boots.

Morgan grunted in disgust as he replayed Carson's words in his mind. *One of these days,* he thought grimly, *one of us is going to bust Buster. I always thought it was gonna be Buck, but now I'm not so sure.*

I might take a swing at old Buster myself, after this.

Rattlesnake!

He rose to leave the apartment, but paused halfway across the room as if struck by a second thought. He walked to a seam in the paneled wall and tapped a series of spots on a small, faintly lighter square in the wood. There was a soft beep and a small opening appeared in the wall. Morgan reached in, grabbed a pistol out of the hidden gun safe, stuck it into the back of his jeans, and walked out.

He hurried down the staircase to the first floor, and past the back hall. The only light in the house at that hour was a small golden stripe underneath the kitchen door. Conchita rose early to begin breakfast, but she'd barely arrived.

Morgan slipped across the moon-washed atrium and out the massive front door of the house. Deep cold struck him like a slap across the jaw, and he grumbled to himself as he hurried across the courtyard to his jeep, a boxy shadow in the dim lamplight.

He slid into the front seat and dug his cell phone out of his jeans pocket. He called the stable number, but to his surprise, no one picked up.

Four rings. Five. Six.

Morgan tossed the phone down, cranked the jeep, flicked the lights on, and sent it charging down the long drive toward the thoroughbred stables. The yard and the grounds and the big rolling pastures that lapped up against them all looked pale and ghostly in the glare of his brights. But maybe that was because it was easy to get spooked when you'd got bad news in the wee hours of the morning. Morgan grumbled under his breath and pressed his foot on the gas.

The long, low stable complex appeared on the left side of the road a few minutes later. The blazing exterior lights were supposed to light up the grounds like a car showroom, but the whole area was pitch dark. A thrill of fear zapped up Morgan's spine, and his jeep sprayed gravel over the little lot as it slid to a stop. He jumped out and called:

"Bennie?"

He broke into a trot as he hurried across the yard to the stable doors. "Bennie, is everything okay?"

Their stable hand's trembling voice answered from inside the barn. "Rustlers, Morg! Be careful!"

The whine of a bullet punctuated his words and made Morgan duck down behind a fence rail. He drew his pistol and peered into the line of trees behind the stables, trying to find a target in the darkness.

Another bullet shattered a piece of fence not a foot away; and Morgan raised the pistol and popped off six answering shots: *pop pop pop pop pop pop.*

A horse's whinny pierced the darkness, then there was a sudden hurrying and rustling clamor under the trees, followed by the *clop* and *thump* of horses scrambling away across dark, uneven terrain.

Morgan raised his gun again, but the thought that he might hit one of their own horses in the dark made him curse and lower his hand. He could hear the triumphant rustlers driving their prize thoroughbreds away.

"Yah! Come on! Get up!"

Morgan glanced back toward the drive. The thieves had to have a trailer nearby for those horses. *Unless* they lived close enough to just drive them cross country and through a cut fence to a nearby ranch.

Morgan crouched low, his pistol at the ready, as the sound of flight burst out all around in the darkness, flapped past, and slowly faded into the distance.

Morgan spat out an exclamation and stared at the jeep; but he couldn't chase a gang of armed men across the country in a car.

He turned toward the barn and hurried to the big doors. "Bennie, are you alright in there?"

There was a long silence, and Morg yelled out again. "Bennie! Are you okay?"

To his relief, there was a heavy clang, and the big doors opened a crack. Bennie's frightened face appeared in the opening, and he waved him in.

"Get inside, hurry!" he hissed. "They might still be out there!"

Morgan laid his pistol down on a table near the door. "Are you okay, Bennie?"

The older man nodded. "Just shook up, is all. Two rustling raids in as many weeks is about as much as this old man can take. My heart is running so fast right now it could win the Kentucky Derby." He sank down into a chair and Morgan stared down at his pale face in concern.

"Take a minute to calm down, Bennie. We don't want you keeling over! What happened?"

The older man's face twisted. "The first thing I noticed was that the security lights went out. When I went to punch the alarm, it didn't work. Then there was a lot of shouting. The other stable hands, Bob and Henry, went charging out with their pistols, and I heard yelling, and gunfire, and then the sound of horses' hooves. The rustlers came riding up on horseback, a gang of 'em. They beat the barn door open and pointed their shotguns at me and told me that if I yelled or tried to stop 'em they'd shoot me!"

Fear froze Morgan's chest, and he rushed to the other side of the barn and lifted a barn lantern high.

"Bob! Henry!"

He hurried out into the darkened yard, and to his horror, there were two shapes huddled on the ground at the far edge of the anemic light. He rushed over and knelt down beside them.

"Bob!"

The young hand struggled up on one elbow and rolled dazed eyes up to his.

"Are you shot?"

The boy shook his head. "Not shot," he gasped, "but I got my head near crushed in. I popped off a shot at the rustlers when they charged us, and one of those riders clopped me across the head with a rifle butt!"

Morgan glanced at his companion. "Henry?" He crawled near and turned the boy over. To his relief, the young man was conscious.

"Henry, have you been shot?"

The boy shook his head, but he looked as if he was in shock. Morgan fumbled for his phone and called 911.

"You two just lie still," he told them, "we'll get you"—he broke off to bark, "Yes, there's been a rustling at the Seven Spades Ranch, the thoroughbred barn. Yes, this is Morgan Spade. We have two injured hands, possible shooting victims, one with a blow to the head."

"I'm sending out an ambulance and a police car now," the operator replied. "Stay on the line, Mr. Spade."

Morgan jammed the phone back into his pocket and tore open Henry's shirt. His heart gave a sickening thump to see blood on the boy's shoulder.

"Bennie!"

A minute later Bennie's drawn face appeared in the barn door.

"Grab that first aid kit off the wall and bring it out here. Hurry!"

Fifteen minutes later red and blue lights pulsed from the top of an ambulance and a police cruiser, and Morgan watched as paramedics loaded his two injured hands onto gurneys. The weird light made the scene even more garish, and when Morgan looked up and saw Buck's red truck pulling up in the drive, he felt his cup was full.

Well, so much for keeping it from Buck, he thought ruefully. *Carson's just gonna have to deal with it.*

Buck slapped the truck door closed behind him and stalked across the yard. "What's going on?"

Morgan walked out to meet him. "We got hit by rustlers," he growled. "They busted up Bob and Henry and got Lickety Split and some of our best brood mares."

"What about Bennie?"

"He's all right. Just shook up, is all."

Buck turned without another word and stormed into the barn. Morgan followed him inside as his brother went from stall to stall, checking on the sleek thoroughbreds. The remaining horses snorted and rolled their big eyes as he scanned them, but they seemed to be unhurt.

Morgan walked up to a gleaming black mare and stroked her nose. "You don't like the sound of gunfire, do you, girl? I can't say I blame you. I don't either."

Anger shook him again, and he turned to Bennie. "What about the feed?" he demanded tightly.

Bennie stared at him in surprise. "Their feed? What about it?" he replied.

"Have you seen anything different in it, leaves, trash, powder?"

The older man shook his head. "No. It's just the same."

"I want you to check it for tampering from now on," Morgan answered, and walked over to a hay bale lying in the center aisle. "Carson just called me from Kentucky. He said that somebody tried to poison our horses in the Keeneland stables."

Buck's head snapped up, and his eyes blazed in the lamplight. "This is Buster's doing," he replied in a low, throbbing voice, and its tone made the hair on the back of Morgan's neck stand up. "He tried to steal our water and failed. Now he's trying to steal our horses. He just never stops trying to put us out of business. I wish he was here right now, just him and me!"

"Law!" Bennie chimed in, and rolled shocked eyes to his. "That's just plain devilment. People are getting so snaky mean these days, ain't nothing safe. Not even a poor dumb animal!"

Morgan raked the hay bale with his fingers and frowned. "Bennie, I want you to be on the lookout for anything different or weird in the horses' feed, or in their stalls. Anywhere in this whole area." He threw the hay down and swept the barn with dark eyes. "I want you to have this whole barn floor washed down and cleaned today, and check every speck of feed that comes here."

"I'll do it."

Buck stuck his hands on his hips and swept the plundered barn with his eyes. "I'm going to bring in some extra hands to stay here all the time. It looks like somebody's bound and determined to get our horses."

He shook his head. "I'd rather not tell Carson about this right now. It might throw him off his game; but I guess it can't be helped. He'll have to know."

He turned on the words and stormed outside, and Morgan followed him. The glare of Buck's truck headlights, and the flash of the police car, washed his own jeep in lurid light.

Morgan picked up his pistol on the way out, stuck it back in his jeans, and walked out to his car. To his horror, there was a bullet hole in the windshield.

He'd come that close to getting killed.

Buck drifted over, his face pulled into a knot and his eyes fixed on the bullet hole in the wind shield.

"This has gotten way out of hand," Buck grumbled. "I'm not gonna sit by and watch our hands get beat up and our horses stolen. I'm not gonna put up with my brother almost getting shot."

Morgan shot Buck a stricken glance, and the truth of that slowly sifted down over him, made his hands go numb. He thought about Heather sleeping in their bed up at the house, about their unborn baby, about his son Kit.

The police officer walked up to them, notebook in hand. "Can one of you tell me what went on here tonight?" he asked briskly.

Buck started answering his question, but Morgan's stunned gaze moved away from them. His eyes followed the other officer as she opened a roll of yellow crime tape and began to rope off the barn area.

Lord help us, he thought numbly; and then realized that it had been a prayer.

Chapter Twenty One

Classical music was the first thing Carson registered as the gilded doors of the Continental's private ballroom swung open: Mozart, he was pretty sure of it. The small ensemble of musicians tucked into a corner of the room sent the music out to hover sweetly over the murmuring laughter of the party goers.

It was the first big gala of the sales season, the Breeders' Party, and all the big fish were there. Carson's eyes flicked over the hundreds of people in attendance, looking for Bertrand Blandings first, and Buster Hogan second.

He fully expected to find them together.

He turned to Donna with a smile. "Are you ready to watch me in action?" he teased, and she laughed Tand took the arm he offered her.

She was especially pretty that day, and Carson shot her an appreciative glance. She looked like a runway model in an off-the shoulder sheath dress of pale green silk and strappy, high heeled sandals that showed off a long, slender pair of ankles.

His eyes lingered on them for a second, then returned to the room. His gaze skimmed the heads of the crowd, snagged on something large and red, and focused on it.

He led Donna out into the room, murmuring to her under his breath as they moved.

"Do you see that elderly gent at the other side of the room—the one with the moustache and the glass of bourbon in his hand?"

"Yes," she murmured. "Bertrand Blandings."

He turned to her in surprise, and she laughed at the look on his face. "It's my job to know club members. And club prospects. I hear he's the third richest man in America."

"Fourth," Carson amended softly, with a nod. "He's my main prospect this year. My goal is to sell all three of my horses to him."

"Good hunting," she murmured, with a twinkling sidelong glance. "I hear your yearlings are Book 1 this year."

"We work hard to make sure of that," Carson replied with a smile as they moved through the crowd. "But this year, I've been thrown a curve ball. Someone tried to poison our horses last night."

The smile vanished from her face. "What!"

Carson covered her hand with his own. "They're all right, thank heavens. But do you see that man talking to Blandings? The red-faced one?"

Donna frowned slightly. "Yes."

"He's Buster Hogan, our next door neighbor and competitor. I'm convinced that he was behind it."

She turned to search his face with dismayed eyes. "Shouldn't you call the police, then?"

"Oh, I have, never fear," he replied, his eyes on Buster. "This episode isn't the first time. Someone tried to break into our barn back home a few nights before we flew the yearlings up here. Buster's hands, most likely."

Donna turned to stare at Buster in amazement. He was talking to Bertrand Blandings and tapping the old man's chest with his finger.

"But—isn't Mr. Hogan a Breeder's Association committee member? It would be risky to just walk up and accuse him of a crime. What are you going to do?" she breathed.

"Oh, nothing so crude," Carson assured her. He paused on the periphery of the little group, narrowed his eyes, and adjusted one shoulder before he moved in.

Bertrand Blandings looked up and hailed him with every evidence of relief. "Well, there you are Spade!" he called out.

"Afternoon, Mr. Blandings," Carson smiled with all his teeth and added, "Buster, Martha Sue. Allow me to introduce Donna Bouchet."

The elderly man smiled and tilted his head. "A pleasure, young lady." His eyes narrowed, and he added, "Have we met, my dear? You look familiar somehow."

Donna smiled but shook her head. "I don't think so," she murmured. "I would've remembered such a distinguished looking gentleman."

Carson looked down to hide his amusement. Donna might be sophisticated, but she had a light, playful touch with people, and he really liked that about her.

Bertrand smiled at her, then moved his eyes to Carson; and his eyes flashed over the rim of his glass.

"I hear there was a bit of a dust-up with your horses last night, Carson," he murmured, and Carson nodded.

Bad news traveled fast, all right.

"I'm afraid so," he murmured and snagged a pair of wine glasses from a passing waiter. He handed one to Donna and lifted the other to his lips. "The horses are all fine," he added, with a short, direct glance at Buster, "but three men got into the stable area and tried to poison them."

Martha Sue's mouth formed a perfect O. "Oh dear!" she fretted aloud, "That's terrible, isn't it, Buster?"

Buster shook his head and looked down into his drink. "Yeah, that's tough luck alright Carson," he commiserated. "I guess it'll be weeks before the vet can give them a clean bill of health. Too late for the sale. Better luck next year!"

"Oh, they were all examined thoroughly," Carson replied smoothly." Last night, by the Keeneland vet. He took blood tests, did x rays, everything. He said it was a close call, but that all of them are unharmed and just fine."

Buster stared at him. "Huh," he grunted and took a drink.

Carson scratched his nose and crossed his arms. "I also talked to the police this morning," he went on, and glanced at Buster's face. To his grim satisfaction, the mention of the police made Buster's red face go pale.

Blandings gave him a sympathetic look. "Did the police catch the scoundrels?"

"Oh yes. Last night," Carson replied pleasantly, and had the pleasure of seeing Buster's pallor deepen to make him look positively ill. "The police haven't gotten anything out of them yet, but I'm sure they will. You know what they say," he added, and smiled directly into Buster's frowning eyes. "There's no honor among thieves."

Buster took another drink; and Carson tilted his head and went on, "Funny thing though. The police told me that all three of them had been to this hotel the day before yesterday. They were caught on the security cameras. They visited a hotel room and stayed for about twenty minutes."

He took a long, leisurely sip of wine. "It was on the third floor. Room 315."

Martha Sue's face clouded over. "But that can't be right," she objected. "That's *our* room number!"

Carson closed his eyes in wordless gratitude that Buster had brought his wife to the party, then opened them again to enjoy the look on

Buster's face. It was roughly the same look he supposed Buster would wear if he'd swallowed a fly.

Blandings raised his brows and turned to stare at Buster. "Is that true, Hogan?"

Buster spluttered and laughed a bit too loudly. "Of course not. There must be some kind of mistake." He raised grim eyes to Carson's face. "There have been no visitors to our suite since we came here. If the camera showed that men walked in, they must've broken into our suite just like they broke into Keeneland."

Martha Sue frowned. "But—"

"Be quiet, Martha Sue!" Buster barked, and controlled himself with a visible effort.

Donna regarded Buster steadily. "You must have suffered thefts if your suite was broken into," she observed softly. "I'm so sorry."

"I haven't noticed anything gone," Martha Sue frowned, and Buster stifled an exclamation.

"My best shoes and my watch are gone," he announced. "I didn't tell you because I didn't want to worry you, Martha Sue."

"Good heavens!" she exclaimed, with a startled look. "We were robbed and I didn't even know it!"

Donna bowed her head and rubbed her nose, and Carson's eyes slid to Buster's as he replied:

"I'm sure the police will be happy to take your statement, Mrs. Hogan. They'll have a statement from the thieves to compare it to."

Blandings snorted, coughed, and took a drink; and Buster shot him a murderous glance. But Carson only smiled and raised his glass, and Donna's fingers found his and curled around them.

Chapter Twenty Two

"Do you think Mr. Blandings was convinced that your horses are all right?"

Carson turned to smile at Donna, and she smiled back over her wine glass. The party had progressed to the luncheon phase, and they were seated at an assigned table with ten other people, none of whom were the Hogans, or Bertrand Blandings.

Carson's eyes moved from her face to the chef's table in the middle of the ballroom. Its centerpiece was an ice carving of a rearing thoroughbred, and the glorious statue blocked him from seeing Blandings, or who was at Blandings' table.

"Yes," he replied at last. "If Bertrand Blandings had concerns about our yearlings' health, I believe he would've said so. But I'm going to give him time to breathe before I talk to him again. I don't believe in buttonholing prospects."

"Like Buster?" Donna replied with a smile, and he laughed and nodded.

"Yes, like Buster. But I can't afford to get complacent just because Buster's a blowhard. I don't think Blandings likes him, but he's suffering Buster because he can't afford to let personalities cloud his judgment. Blandings is a shrewd horse trader."

"I wonder what he thinks of Buster now that you're done with him?" Donna chuckled. "It was a pleasure to watch you turn what could have been a negative into a positive. Now, instead of Blandings worrying about your horses, he's wondering if Buster paid some random thugs to kill them."

"Yes, I imagine everyone here is wondering about that," Carson agreed. "And I'm not done with Buster, by the way. Still, I predict that Buster's about to lose his seat on the Breeder's Association committee."

"Well, some people are impossible. They say you can't straighten a dog's tail," Donna shrugged, and took a forkful of cucumber feta roll.

Carson shot her a quick glance. "Do they say that in Bahrain?"

Donna giggled and nodded, and Carson turned in his chair to face her.

"Satisfy my curiosity," he murmured. "Why did you tell me that the story of your childhood wasn't true?"

She raised her gold-brown eyes to his. "I might as well. No one ever believes it."

Carson held her eye. "I would have."

She tilted her head to consider him. "Maybe you would," she conceded with a smile. "You haven't had a very ordinary life either."

"And that suits me right down to the ground," he agreed as he cut another bite of duckling. "My childhood was spent in the Texas backcountry, and we didn't even have air conditioning. My grandfather was a fine man, but he lived his life disappointed that it wasn't still the 1800s. I did not share his love of the rough life. No one on earth was happier than I was when our family came into money."

Surprise dawned across Donna's face. "Oh? I thought you were always wealthy. You look as if you were."

Carson shook his head. "Oh, no. Thank you for the compliment, but we were dirt poor until my eleventh birthday. That was when they discovered oil on an old farm my grandfather owned. It turned out to be such a gusher that we're still living off the royalties. Our ranch and our thoroughbred stables bring in good money, it's true, but the oil is what really keeps us comfortable."

Donna smiled and returned to her meal. "Yes, I can certainly understand that. Like in Bahrain."

Carson turned to look at her. "I imagine Bahrain was very different to America. Wasn't it?" he asked softly.

She glanced at him quickly, then lowered her eyes. "I had a very happy childhood. I was my parents' only daughter, and very spoiled," she laughed. "I had tutors who taught me several languages. I was trained to navigate the most rarified circles. But I would've left even if I hadn't had the arranged marriage spat with my father," she added thoughtfully. "I wanted to see the world, wanted to live as many different lives as I could." She glanced up at him, and there was a flick of yearning in her eyes that captured him.

"They say that to learn another language is to have another soul," she added softly. "That's true, as far as it goes; but it's far more true, that to live a different life is to have another soul. It expands you. You see more, understand more, *feel* more." She paused and shrugged a slender shoulder. "Don't you find?"

Carson coughed and reached for his glass. "Well, I can't lay claim to speaking more than one language well, and while I get around the states fairly often, I haven't visited much of the rest of the world, if you don't count the Caribbean," he confessed. "I'm sure I'd enjoy it. I usually enjoy new places; but I'm attached to my own home." He raised his brows and laughed. "Though it sounds odd to hear myself admitting that. My family's been driving me crazy lately."

She smiled at him. "Really? How so—or is that an impertinent question?"

He shook his head. "Not impertinent at all. I complain bitterly and often," he laughed. "It's just that my eldest brothers have gotten married fairly close together, and now they're growing their families. The house is full of women and babies."

Donna burst into a soft peal of laughter that lit her eyes. "Are women tiresome to you, then?"

"Oh, women are never tiresome," he assured her, with a sharp smile. "Babies aren't, either. I love my nieces and nephews. I suppose I'm just not ready for the place to be so different, so quickly. Or at least," he mumbled into his glass, "it feels quick."

"I think I know your trouble," she told him, with a sly smile. "You don't want to be married, and you're afraid it's catching! I can't say I blame you."

It was his turn to burst out laughing, though his amusement was tinged with a bit of alarm that she'd read him so accurately, and so fast.

"Is it obvious?" he sputtered.

"Only if you look," she smiled.

A sudden fanfare from the musicians kept him from asking her more. There was a small dais at the head of the ballroom, and as they watched, the president of the Breeders' Association stepped up onto it and tested his mike.

"Well, a warm Kentucky welcome to all our members!" he smiled. "I hope you're all enjoying the party."

Scattered clapping and murmuring greeted his words, and a small group of men and women slowly joined the man on the stage.

Carson leaned toward Donna slightly to murmur, "That man in the center is Terry Jenkins. He's the president of the Breeder's Association. The others are the rest of the officers."

Donna raised an eyebrow. "I thought you told me that Buster Hogan was an officer," she whispered. "Where is he?"

The edge of Carson's mouth curled up. "I don't know," he replied in a tone of delight.

"But I can guess."

Chapter Twenty Three

"Where are you going, Buster?"

Martha Sue looked up from the table with her fork halfway to her mouth, and Buster stifled an impatient retort.

"I"m just stepping away for a minute," he told her, then leaned closer to hiss, "to find the men's room!"

"Oh. Well, hurry back, dear. You're supposed to be on stage soon, remember."

Buster rose from the table, buttoned his jacket, and threaded his way between the tables and across the crowded ballroom. He noticed the other diners were watching him go, and he could feel his face going red. Bad gossip traveled fast, and he was keenly aware that in that moment, public opinion was against him.

He swept through the ballroom doors, but he had barely gained the carpeted hall outside before two men in dark suits intercepted him.

"Mr. Hogan, we're hotel security. We're going to have to ask you to come with us."

Buster stared at them in outrage. "What in the—do you know who I am?" he demanded, and jabbed a finger back at the ballroom doors. "I'm with the Breeder's Association. I'm going on stage in a minute!" A flick of alarm tempered his rage enough for him to add, "What's this all about?"

"We're here to escort you out of the building. We need you to come with us."

Fury jumped in Buster's heart, followed quickly by fear. "I'm not going anywhere! This is an outrage. I'm going to call my lawyer and have you and the hotel management prosecuted for false arrest!"

One of the men pulled his jacket back just far enough for an I.D. badge to peek out. "The police are outside, Mr. Hogan. If you make a scene, we're going to have no choice but to call them."

"Why, the very idea!" he gasped. "As if I was some kind of bum! You're going to be hearing from my lawyer, I promise you that!"

The two men each put a hand on his arm, and Buster fairly spat in rage, but had no choice but to let himself be led away. He had to pretend he didn't know what this was about, but he knew. When that smug pretty boy, Carson Spade, had said somebody had tried to get at his horses, it had hit him like a punch to the gut, because he knew.

It was those three idiots he'd hired, trying to show him they could do the job right the second time; and if they'd talked, he was done.

He was going to jail. He might be going to jail even if they hadn't talked, because the blockheads had come to his hotel room and linked themselves to him.

"Come with us, Mr. Hogan."

Buster felt his face going red as the people milling in the hotel lobby turned to stare at him being led away. It was a moment he'd be lucky to live down, even if they couldn't pin anything on him.

In these select circles, reputation was everything.

He glanced back over his shoulder as he was hustled along. He hadn't had time to coach Martha Sue, and he could only hope the cops didn't talk to her before he did. They had to get their stories straight.

When he turned back, he was being carried through the main doors of the hotel. A police cruiser was parked outside the doors, and an officer opened the door as they approached.

"What am I being charged with?" he demanded, as he was pushed into the back seat. No one answered immediately, and fury surged up in him. He wanted to beat on the windows and yell, but he had to keep his temper under control.

He had to think. He had to be smart, or he was ruined.

The cop and the security officers talked for a while, and occasionally one glanced down at him as he fretted in the back seat. Buster's wits finally returned to him, and he reached into his jacket for his phone. He called Martha Sue's number, and to his frustration, she didn't answer.

Isn't that just like a woman, he fumed. *Gabs all day about nonsense, and won't even answer her phone when it's life and death!*

The phone rang on, and he thought: *Pick up, you ninny! Pick up the phone!*

To his relief, his wife finally picked up, and he barked: "Martha Sue, I need you to leave the party and go back to our hotel room. I don't want you to talk to anybody. I want you to call our lawyer and tell him I've been picked up by the police."

There was a long, heavy pause on the other end. "Police?" she quavered. "Buster, where are you?"

"In a police car," he snapped. "Go back up to our hotel room and stay there. Remember, don't talk to anybody, don't answer any questions unless our lawyer is there. Call him!"

Martha Sue's voice trembled on the edge of tears. "Buster, why are they taking you away?"

Buster closed his eyes. "I don't know. I'll call you when I know more. Just do what I told you."

The sound of sniffling came from the other end of the line. "I will, puddin'," she replied. "Call me!"

Buster pressed the red button and stuffed the phone back into his jacket just as the police officer climbed into the front seat. The officer turned and extended his hand.

"I'm going to need you to empty out your pockets," he commanded, and Buster's face went red again.

"I need you to tell me why I'm being hauled away, and where I'm going!' he spat.

The office gestured for the phone, and Buster swore under his breath, but dug in his pockets for his phone and keys. He slapped them into the officer's hands, and the policeman turned back.

"You're being taken down to the police station for questioning, Mr. Hogan," he drawled.

"Why?"

"It's in connection with an attempt on the Seven Spade Ranch's yearlings out at Keeneland," the officer drawled.

Buster's heart jumped into his throat, but retorted, "Well, *I* didn't do it!"

The officer turned to glance back at him. "We have three men in custody who were caught in the act trying to kill those horses," he replied, and cranked the car. "They were also seen going into your hotel room the same day."

Buster licked his lips. "I see. So I'm guilty by association!"

The officer nudged the car down the hotel drive, slowly and easily. "We'd just like to ask you a few questions, Mr. Hogan."

"I refuse to answer any questions until my lawyer's with me," Buster shot back. "Strong arm tactics won't work with me, I don't care if you are a cop. I'm one of the richest men in Texas. I have friends in high places!"

The officer turned his head just enough to glance at him over his shoulder. "Huh," he grunted. "Well, our record is unbroken then, Mr. Hogan. Everybody we talk to has friends in high places."

Buster closed his eyes and bit back the scalding explosion of profanity that was building up in him. He could feel his blood pressure soaring, but he had to play his cards smart if he was going to stay out of jail.

But that wasn't easy when his imagination was showing him Carson Spade back in that ballroom, boozing it up with that little blonde fancy piece. He clenched his teeth to imagine Carson congratulating himself. Laughing that the Spades had won the game now that *he* was in trouble with the law.

You haven't won nothing buddy boy, Buster thought grimly, *not by a long shot. Just let me get out of this and I'll teach you how this game is played.*

I'll make you sorry you ever messed with Buster Hogan!

Chapter Twenty Four

The sound of a spoon against a wine glass attracted Donna's attention to Terry Jenkins. He was standing on the little stage at the head of the ballroom. He smiled and put his hands up.

"Well, now that everybody's had a good meal, we're going to stop yakking and let the band come up on stage," Jenkins told the glittering crowd in the hotel ballroom. "We hope you stay to dance and catch up with your friends. Have a nice time, folks."

Jenkins threw up a hand in parting and led the other officers of the Breeders' Association off the stage. After they'd gone, the musicians slowly climbed up on the little stage and set up. Soon they struck up a slow, languid air.

Carson blotted his lips and turned to Donna. "Would you like to dance?" he smiled.

Donna smiled back and nodded her assent. The little dance floor was empty, and she and Carson might be the first couple on it, but she wasn't shy. She didn't care if hundreds of people were staring at them.

The only person she was going to see was him.

Donna twined her arms around Carson's neck, and his hands clasped her waist lightly as they swayed in time to the slow, dreamy music. After a fine meal they were both loose and relaxed, and a wistful smile curved Donna's lips as they moved.

It was a luxury to dance with Carson. He was a delightful partner. He was an experienced and self-assured dancer, he always knew where he was leading her, he moved smoothly and with confidence.

His touch was almost perfect. He held her respectfully, not too loose and not too tight, yet warmly enough to remind her that he found her attractive.

The only fault she found with him was that he didn't hold her close enough. She wanted to put her head on his chest, right there in front of everyone, and he seemed to read the thought off her face. Carson smiled down at her, and then, by unspoken mutual consent, he tightened her to his chest, and she snuggled close to rest her head on his shoulder as they danced.

Donna closed her eyes and let Carson rock her gently in his arms. The slow tempo of the song and the sensation of being cradled close pushed her under a sweet, sparkling wave. Carson's subtle cologne whispered scandalous things to her as she rested her head on his chest: it spoke of a beach at midnight. A roaring fireplace in a snowbound mountain cabin. She could just see it, too: Carson chasing her down a secluded stretch of sand as she laughed; or the two of them reclining on a bearskin rug with a bottle of champagne catching the light of the fire.

Donna breathed a sigh. She wasn't usually such a romantic; but for the moment at least, she was under a deep, drowsy spell, and she didn't want to wake up.

"You're as limp as a noodle," Carson whispered into her ear, and a bubble of laughter rose in her throat as she stirred.

"No, don't move. I love the way you feel in my arms," he went on, and the warmth of his breath made her neck tingle. "You're so relaxed. So easy to lead."

You have that effect on me, Carson Spade, she wanted to say. *Like a little too much champagne.*

She was dimly aware of the other dancers around them, but she kept her eyes closed and let Carson bend her this way and that as the sweet, slow, old-fashioned music cast a spell over them both.

Too much moonlight, too much wine

Too much kissin' for this heart of mine.

Tell me you need me, my sweet dove

Cause there's no such thing as too much love.

Carson turned her in his arms again, and laughed softly in her ear as she melted into him. "I could dance with you all night," he murmured. "You're as light as air."

Donna's eyelids fluttered open, and she gazed up into Carson's eyes, held them with her own. The smile slowly faded off of Carson's face as she challenged him, and they stopped swaying.

Roses and ashes, kisses and sighs
Starlight sparkling in my true love's eyes;
Ribbons and teardrops, meadows that sing
A lacy gown and a golden ring.

Carson slowly took her chin in his hand and bent down. The light faded, and Donna closed her eyes to enjoy the sensation of being kissed in the middle of a roomful of people. Her fingers curled into Carson's jacket as his lips spoke to hers: softly, sweetly, and more and more insistently.

Her brows went up and her eyes opened briefly, but slid shut again as she melted into him. His lips were speaking promises, were making her see things she couldn't utter aloud, and she was just beginning to respond when the sounds of soft laughter around them made Carson kiss her once more, and raise his head.

Donna opened her eyes. She felt half-drugged, and she shuddered to think of how she must look to the smiling witnesses dancing all around them. Mussed, most likely.

But she couldn't keep her eyes from Carson's face; and in spite of the people around them she saw the same things in them, as in her own.

Desire. Intrigue. Playfulness.

Carson smiled wryly at the other dancers, then slipped an arm around her and whispered in her ear.

"There's another party in town tomorrow night. Come with me."

She was well-pleased, but she pretended to deliberate for a few moments. She smiled up into his eyes.

"All right then, Carson," she murmured, and was quick to note the look of pleasure that flicked across his face. He smiled that sharp, crooked grin that she was beginning to love and gave her a quick peck on the cheek.

"You're my good luck charm," he whispered; and kissed her again.

Chapter Twenty Five

Buster buttoned up his jacket as he skipped down the police station steps with his attorney at his elbow. "I may not be able to sue the cops, but I want to sue that hotel's security for frog-marching me past everybody I know!" he spat. "I've never been so humiliated in my life!"

His attorney was a small, worried looking man in a gray business suit. "Look, Buster," he replied in a low voice, "I need to know the whole story here before I can defend you against any charges. Do you have any connection to the three men who tried to poison those horses?"

Buster stopped dead on the sidewalk and turned to glare at him. "How dare you ask me that question!" he raged and jabbed a trembling finger toward the police station. "Those Keystone cops asked me that a hundred times, but I *expect* to be treated like a criminal in there! I expect to feel practically mugged by *them*, but I am surprised to hear that my own lawyer doesn't believe me! What do I pay you for?"

The other man stood his ground and fixed his client with a straight, serious look. "Your story doesn't make any sense, Buster," he insisted quietly. "You're lucky that I kept you from telling it to the police. We can't deny that those men came to your room at the hotel. It's on their security video."

"Because they were breaking in!" Buster retorted. "I told you that our hotel room was robbed!"

His attorney pinched his mouth into a tight, exasperated line. "If that's true, then they didn't force the door and they entered when you and your wife were still in the suite," he replied dryly. "Your comings and goings were on the security video, too! It doesn't bode well for you, Buster, that the cops already have that video. They're building a case against you, and you're just lucky that those men they have in custody haven't said they know you."

"It's because they *don't* know me!" Buster spat.

The other man shook his head. "I can't represent you, Buster, if you refuse to tell me the whole story. I can see that there's more than you're telling me, and so can the police."

Buster swelled up like a frog. "You have a lot of gall to accuse me of lying! I don't need any lawyer who doubts my word. I want a lawyer who's working for *me*, and not the cops!"

"I'm doing my best to work for you, Buster," the attorney replied, in a tone of restrained anger. "It would help a great deal if you'd cooperate with me."

Buster watched in fury as the other man walked briskly to his car parked on the curb. The attorney climbed in, slammed the door shut, and drove away in a cloud of exhaust, leaving him stranded on the sidewalk.

Buster swore savagely, jammed his hand in his jacket for his cell phone, and flicked it on to call for a cab. His heart was pounding with rage, but his mind was whirling. He'd been lucky that those three idiots hadn't implicated him so far, no doubt because they believed his threats; but even so, the finger of suspicion was pointing at him.

He had to knock it away and get back on track, or he'd never sell his yearlings, and he needed to sell them. He was struggling financially. The Lazy H needed a quick infusion of cash, and he was counting on those horses to provide it.

The line stopped ringing, and as soon as it was picked up, he barked, "I need a cab down at the Lexington police station. Yes, the one downtown."

He hung up and stuffed the phone back into his jacket with a scowl. The news of this fiasco would be all over town by nightfall, and his instincts were telling him that if he skulked off like a guilty dog, his career as a thoroughbred breeder was over.

He had to get right back up in the saddle. To brazen it out.

Most people believed what they were told, and if he told them he was innocent loudly and often enough, he was confident he could ride out the storm.

Providing, of course, that those idiots didn't turn and rat him out to the police. There was nothing he could do to prevent that, and it made his blood pressure spike and his head pound; but he couldn't afford to indulge his temper.

He had to walk a very fine line now, or he could land up in jail. He had to put on as much of a smiling face as he could. He had to go back to all the parties and drink and dance and schmooze the buyers and act like nothing was amiss.

It was his only hope; and it still might not be enough. But he had no choice.

Buster jerked his jacket cuffs straight, scanned the busy street through narrowed eyes, and settled down to wait for the cab. He hadn't been forced to wait for a cab for years; and it didn't improve his mood.

There was one thing for sure, though: if those three chuckleheads blabbed, if they threw him under the bus to save themselves, he'd made good on his threat.

He'd see to it that it was the last thing they ever did. And he was going to settle the score with the Spades, too, before it was all over.

Because Carson Spade had made sure that old Blandings heard all about his botched attempt on the Seven horses. Carson had accused him without accusing him, and the result was that now Carson was miles ahead and he was fighting just to stay in the race. Now he was going to have to work twice as hard to catch up. To win old Blandings over.

He wasn't going to forget that. And he was going to make sure that Carson would never forget it, either.

Whatever he had to do.

Chapter Twenty Six

The Beaumont Hotel in downtown Lexington was a five-star resort that occupied a whole city block, and the antique, red-brick structure was almost 150 years old. The interior decor was an homage to Victorian elegance, with Persian carpets and crystal chandeliers and antique furniture. Its main ballroom was so opulent, with its inlaid marble floors, velvet drapes and ceiling high windows, that it looked like a movie set.

Donna found herself staring at them as Carson escorted her into the huge, glittering ballroom the next afternoon. She couldn't help noting that the luxury of her surroundings contrasted sharply to her joblessness, but she pushed that worry to the back of her mind. Carson was there by her side, his hand curled warmly around hers, she was sure to be offered dainty *hors d'oeuvres* and champagne, and for the moment at least, life was good. She and Carson might part soon—they almost certainly would—but she pushed that away, too.

She had always been one to enjoy the moment.

Carson led her to where Bertrand Blandings was chatting with some other businessmen. Blandings looked up, saw them, and acknowledged them with a wave of his hand.

"Well, Texas is represented now," Blandings smiled. "Hello Carson. Donna." He turned to the group and added, "This is Vernon Evans, the owner of the Double E Ranch in Oregon, and Denton Holt, owner of the Crazy Eight in Louisiana."

Carson smiled and extended a hand. "Good to see you again, Vernon. Denton."

The conversation flowed easily, and was light and pleasant until an angry, red-faced man and his wife arrived.

Buster Hogan.

Buster walked up and stood directly in front of the older man, leaving Carson almost no opportunity to get a word in edgewise.

"Afternoon, Mr. Blandings," Hogan smiled. "I guess we're going to see a bit of one another around town this week." He turned to introduce his smiling wife. "This is my wife, Martha Sue. Say hello to Mr. Blandings, sugar."

Martha Sue was wearing a big green hat and a matching pantsuit. She bubbled over with laughter, but the tone sounded a bit nervous to Donna's ear.

"It's nice to meet you, Mr. Blandings," Martha Sue giggled. She put a hand on her husband's arm and announced, "You men may talk about horses all you please, but this isn't all about business for Buster and me. It's our wedding anniversary this weekend!"

"Congratulations," Blandings replied, with a faint nod as he lifted his bourbon glass to his lips. Donna murmured a polite "Congratulations," and Carson raised his glass briefly.

"It's good to see a couple stay together these days," Blandings opined. "So many are splitting up. It may be old-fashioned, but I don't trust a man over thirty who isn't married. No businessman, anyway. It shows a trifling personality. A lack of stability."

Carson didn't flick an eyelash, but Donna felt, rather than saw those words punch him right in the gut. He had to be seeing his chances vaporize like a puff of smoke. Carson's fingers on hers went suddenly slack, and she shared his secret disappointment.

But Buster's eyes lit up. He put his hand on Martha Sue's shoulder and assured them all, "Well, Martha Sue and I have been married for 25 years."

Martha Sue's brow clouded over. "Twenty-six, Buster," she corrected, but her husband ignored her. Instead, he turned a smiling face to Carson.

"Carson here can't make that claim," he added slyly. "He's never been married, have you, Carson?"

Donna stared at the red-faced Buster in distaste, and then, to the apparent astonishment of everyone there, she curled her fingers tighter around Carson's and turned to smile right into Buster's eyes.

"Actually, yes. Carson and I *are* married," she announced calmly.

Carson's mouth fell slightly open, and for an instant he was too stunned to speak. But

Buster Hogan went beet red and spat: "That's a lie! Carson's the biggest playboy in the world. You never see him with the same woman two days in a row!"

He pointed a stubby finger into her face. "That woman's his wife like I'm his fairy godmother!"

Carson chuckled into his drink. "Now that's something I'd pay to see, Buster," he agreed, and the people around them joined in soft laughter; but Donna narrowed her eyes to angry slits. She pulled herself up to her full height and laid her hand on Carson's arm.

"It's true. We're married," she told them all, and stared them down defiantly; and Bertrand Blandings turned his head to glare at Buster, too.

"I must say, Hogan, it's ungentlemanly to accuse a lady," he frowned; and Buster sputtered, "But it's true! They don't even have wedding rings, look at their hands! She's just lying to you on Carson's behalf. I know him, we live next door to one another!"

The old man stiffened instantly, and Donna felt Carson's fingers tighten on hers.

"We've ordered our rings," he told Buster calmly. "They're being custom made in Switzerland."

"Bah, that's a barefaced lie!" Buster cried, and shook Martha Sue's hand off his arm.

Carson pulled his hand out of Donna's and his expression darkened. "Maybe you'd like to step outside, Buster," he replied in a low voice; and Buster's face went a shade deeper red.

"You come on, boy!" he roared, and heads turned toward them as Carson and Buster faced off. But Bertrand Blandings put down his glass and walked in between them.

"For pity's sake, calm down Hogan," he hissed. "And you, Carson, I thought you had better sense! I won't do business with either one of you if you start a brawl in this place!"

Carson stepped back immediately, but Buster clenched his fists and scowled. "This isn't over," he vowed, and pointed at Carson's nose.

"That's the first true thing you've said today, Buster," Carson agreed, and Buster glared at him, and then at Blandings, and stalked off with his worried wife trailing after him.

Carson watched him go, then sighed and turned to Donna. "Are you all right?"

She nodded, and he slipped an arm around her shoulder as he faced Bertrand Blandings. "My apologies, Bertrand," he murmured, and the old man nodded.

His eyes moved to Donna's face. "Please accept my congratulations on your marriage," he murmured. "I wish both of you every happiness."

Donna felt a wave of embarrassment slap over her, and she cast her eyes down to hide it from the older man; but Carson beamed at him.

"Thank you, Bertrand. I'm the happiest man in the world." He pulled her a bit closer to him.

The old man saluted them with his glass and drifted off, and Carson turned his head to whisper in her ear.

"Thank you, *bella*. You saved my bacon just now."

Donna glanced at him ruefully. "Maybe; but I'm afraid I created as many problems as I solved."

Carson smiled and raised his eyes to the ceiling. "Well, maybe not," he replied. "Can we go somewhere a bit more private to talk about it? I think I have a proposition for you."

She raised an eyebrow and laughed, and he smiled and shook his head as he led her away. "Oh, not that kind of proposition."

Carson piloted her through the crowd and outside into the big hotel corridor outside the ballroom. He glanced around, then pointed to a door at the end.

"Let's try the hotel library. It looks empty."

Donna frowned, but shrugged and followed him down the hall to the little room. There was a small table flanked by two leather chairs, and every wall was lined by magazines and books.

Carson sank down onto one of the chairs, reached inside his jacket, and pulled out a beautiful embossed deck of cards. Donna watched in curious silence as he pulled it out of the little box. The cards were a soft black with red and white drawings, and the suit and number of each card was embossed in gold.

Donna picked one up curiously. The card was soft to the touch, with a smooth matte finish.

It was a deck like the ones professional card players used.

"What if we make another wager?" Carson asked, and his bright blue eyes were brimful of laughter.

Donna crossed her arms and returned the card. "What kind of wager?"

Carson took it and shuffled it back into the deck. "High spade. The highest spade wins on the first draw."

"And the stakes?"

Carson's smile deepened, and his eyes challenged her. "If you win, I'll do anything you want."

"Oh come now. *Anything*?"

He lifted his chin and nodded. "Anything."

"And if you win?"

Carson shuffled the cards again. "If I win, you have to be my escort for as long as I'm in town for the auction." He glanced up at her with a mischievous twinkle. "*And* you have to pretend to be my wife at all the parties."

Donna raised her hand and wiggled her fingers. "What about the rings? Your friend is right, that story sounds odd without rings."

Carson set the deck down on the table. "He's not my friend, and he's almost never right," he sighed. "But I'm willing to take care of that objection. —Is it a bet?"

Donna rolled her eyes to the ceiling, but sighed, "It's a bet."

Carson smiled from ear to ear and leaned back in his chair. "All right, then. Ladies first," he invited, and Donna bent over to pick a card. She turned it over and slapped it down on the table.

"Two of hearts."

Carson pulled a card and threw it down beside hers. "Jack of clubs."

Donna reached down to pull another card and flicked it down. "Ten of spades."

Carson reached for his card and threw it down. "Five of diamonds."

Donna pulled a third card and smiled as she tossed it down. "Queen of spades," she smirked, and crossed her arms.

Carson shot her a worried glance, took a deep breath, and reached for a card. The frown lifted from his brow, and he threw his card down with a smile.

"King of spades."

"What!" Donna cried, and shot him a suspicious glance; but Carson clapped his hands in triumph.

"Lady Luck has spoken," he announced, and gathered up the cards. He slipped them into the little cardboard box and returned it to his jacket pocket.

"Now, we should go to the jeweler's first, and I'll buy a nice pair of rings. Then I'll just give you the credit card, and you can go buy whatever you like. Dresses, shoes."

Donna felt her face going hot. "And what's wrong with *my* clothes and *my* shoes?" she demanded.

"Nothing," Carson replied smoothly. "You're a vision in them. But I'm going for authenticity. A rich man with a new bride always showers her with outrageously expensive clothing, and that is what I want Bertrand Blandings to believe is happening with us. So you can buy the best designer labels, with my blessing."

Donna blinked at him as he rose from the chair and extended his arm. "I must be dreaming," she murmured, and Carson laughed as he led her away.

"Just be convincing, and I'll make this worth your while," he promised.

Well you'd better, Donna thought wryly as they breezed out of the room. *Because I'm risking my job and the chance of a lifetime to play this game with you, Carson Spade!*

Chapter Twenty Seven

Donna's lips parted from Carson's, and she looked up into his smiling face as they parted on her doorstep that afternoon. He brushed her cheek with his hand.

"See you tomorrow, Donna."

She watched as he turned, stuck his hands in his trouser pockets, and skipped down her front steps and away across the lawn.

Donna floated into her condo rather than walked. She wanted to laugh at herself for falling under Carson's spell, but she couldn't deny that she was slipping a bit more every day. Those clear blue eyes of his were beginning to work their way into her dreams.

And what was even more troubling, was that now she wasn't quite so eager to drop everything to fly off to India.

Not yet, at any rate. She was having too much fun.

She twirled in the foyer, dancing on air, and was on her way upstairs when the bell rang again. Her heart quickened, and she hurried to the door, thinking that it must be Carson.

She swung the door open, laughing, "Did your forget something, Car—"

But the man standing on her doorstep wasn't Carson Spade. It was Mr. Tolliver, her boss. Donna's words trailed off into silence and she tucked a stray sprig of hair behind one ear. "Mr. Tolliver!" she stammered, then gathered her wits enough to add: "I'm afraid I wasn't expecting you. Please come in."

She stood back to let him pass, and one look at his grim expression made her heart sink. *Well, looks like he's here to deliver the heave-ho speech,* she thought ruefully. *I can't say I'm surprised. I've hardly been discreet.*

Well, que sera sera.

Donna gestured to her front room. "Please, come and sit down, Tom," she invited. She pasted a smile on her face. "Can I offer you a drink, or something to eat perhaps?"

Her boss gripped the arms of a stuffed chair and sank heavily into the seat cushion. "No, thank you," he replied stiffly. "I'm afraid this is not a social call."

Donna perched on a chair arm and swung one long leg gently. "Maybe I can help you," she told him softly, and with a flick of genuine sympathy. In all the time she'd known him, her boss had never once raised his voice or been confrontational, and she could see that he was deeply uncomfortable. She decided to spare him the need to make a long speech. They both knew why he'd come.

She tilted her head to one side. "You're here to tell me I'm fired, aren't you?"

Tom sighed deeply and looked down at his hands. "I'm afraid so," he murmured. "I wish I could give you more latitude, Donna, because you're an excellent manager and a pleasure to work with. But the owners were adamant. They feel that if I make an exception for you, they won't be able to uphold the non-fraternization policy with other employees."

He waved his hand in the air impatiently. "Personally, I've always been uncomfortable with that rule," he sighed, and unbuttoned his jacket, as if it pinched him. "I think the club shouldn't get into its employees' private lives. The owners do have the right to demand professional behavior during job hours, but afterwards—I don't see it." He shook his head. "I'm sorry, Donna."

"Don't be," she smiled. "I understand. I made the decision, and I understood the likely consequences. I'll miss you and my other coworkers, and I've loved working here; but to tell you the truth, it was time. I like to change things up fairly often, and I was beginning to get a little restless."

He gave her a sympathetic look. "Well, I wish you the best of luck in whatever you choose to do," he replied. "I'll give you a glowing reference if you want one. You've kept this place running like a sewing machine, and you'll be missed."

Donna blinked back a little tear, and she smiled at him through it. "Thank you, Tom," she murmured. "You're very kind, and I appreciate it."

Her boss reached into his jacket and pulled out a thick envelope. He handed it to her.

"They're giving you a month to find another place, plus the usual severance package, with a few additions. Given the unusual circumstances."

Donna opened up the envelope and read the contents. "This is very generous, Tom," she murmured, "and I have no doubt that you were the one to suggest the extras. Thank you."

He looked up at her with an aggrieved expression in his dark eyes. "If you need a little longer than a month, just let me know," he murmured in a low tone, as if he was afraid of being overheard. "There's no rush. We can make some arrangements."

Donna looked up from the papers, then set them down and rose to walk over and press a peck to his brow. "You're a teddy bear, Tom," she told him with a little sputter of laughter.

Her former boss shook his head and stood up slowly. "I wish you and your young man every happiness," he murmured. "Whatever that looks like to you. I know that sounds ironic in these circumstances, but I mean it."

Donna smiled at him. "I know you do, Tom," and put a reassuring hand on his arm. "And you don't have to rush off. Are you sure you don't want something to eat or drink?"

"No my dear," he sighed, and patted her shoulder as he walked to the door. "I have lots of things to arrange. But if there's anything you need from me, just let me know, and I'll do my best."

Donna walked him to the door and watched wistfully as he turned on the steps to give her one last sad look.

"Good luck, Donna."

Her eyes followed him as he stumped off down the walkway, and she sighed softly as she closed the door. A little sadness swirled in her chest, as it always did when she chose to pull up stakes; but it was more than offset by a growing sense of excitement.

The lure of a new and unknown adventure just a few weeks away. It shimmered in her imagination like the portal to another world; and the mystery beyond that glittering door was most of the thrill.

She climbed the stairs slowly, riffling absently through the contents of the bulging envelope. Her former employers *had* been generous. She had a nice little stash to smooth out any bumps on the way to the next chapter.

She paused on the upper step and frowned for an instant, though. Mostly because she wasn't entirely sure what the first few lines of the next chapter described: A first class ticket and a quick flight to Bombay; or a slow, fond farewell to Kentucky horse country in the arms of Carson Spade.

Chapter Twenty Eight

"What kind of rings would you like to see, sir?"

Donna turned to Carson with a smile. He had brought her to the toniest mall in the city, and they were standing at the glittering counter of Tiffany's.

Carson put a hand to his chin and deliberated. "I want to see wedding rings," he announced decisively. "A man's and a woman's."

The clerk, a tall, thin, middle-aged man, leaned across the counter toward them. "Certainly, sir. Silver, gold, or platinum?"

Carson turned to her and looked a question, and she laughed and shrugged. "Gold, I suppose."

"Right away, madam." The clerk gave her a glance that was like a kiss on the cheek and scuttled off to find a velvet tray. Carson leaned into her shoulder slightly and murmured, "I forgot to ask what cut of diamond you'd prefer. Round, square, emerald, marquise?"

Donna gave him a sly sidelong glance and thought, *I see this isn't the first time you've bought diamonds for a woman;* but she only said, "Emerald cut, I think."

"Emerald cut it is."

Donna turned her eyes back to the glittering display of diamond jewelry in the case. She was still unsure whether this whole thing was just an outrageous practical joke. After all, what kind of man would spend the price of a car just to uphold a ridiculous, spur of the moment lie? He wasn't certain of selling his yearlings to Bertrand Blandings. And if he failed, these expensive rings would be a dead loss.

Donna swept an admiring glance over the jewelry case. Still, it appeared that Carson was going to play out the little charade, as odd as that seemed to her. She had often observed that the very rich were eccentric. Probably because they could afford to be.

But on the other hand, perhaps her handsome companion was just being true to his nature. He'd already told her that he believed he had to spend money to make money. That it was necessary to invest in business ventures.

And in spite of all the romantic trappings of love around them—the dazzling toys specially made for a man to give a woman—these rings were a business investment to Carson.

A means to an end.

She was finding that had to remind herself of that.

The clerk came back carrying a black velvet tray festooned with an array of breathtaking gold and diamond rings. Donna's eyes widened in amazement as the man set it down on the counter.

"All of these diamonds are D grade," he announced proudly. "The very best, practically colorless. A clarity rating of F. Internally flawless." He picked up an emerald-cut diamond ring and rolled it back and forth between his fingers, and the gem flashed with a thousand fiery sparks.

Donna gasped and saw her hand reaching for it even before she knew it had moved. The clerk slowly slid the ring onto her finger, and Donna turned her hand this way and that to send tiny rainbows into the air.

The clerk gave her a satisfied glance. "That is a two carat, South African stone," he informed her, as her wondering eyes gazed into its sparkling depths.

She glanced up at Carson. The look in his eyes was amused, but she could've sworn, just for an instant, that there was something deeper than laughter in them. "Well, I think we've found the lady's ring," he murmured, and reached for his wallet. He turned to look at the velvet tray and nodded toward a man's gold ring displayed there.

"I'll take that ring on the end," he announced.

The clerk evinced every sign of delight. "Excellent choice, sir. I'll measure your fingers," he replied, "and once we have the perfect fit, I'll box the rings up for you."

Donna watched in horror as Carson dug for his credit card. She put a hand on his arm and frowned into his eyes.

"Carson, you don't have to buy an expensive ring for your purposes," she whispered urgently. "The man hasn't even told you how much it costs! No one looks at jewelry that closely."

He smiled and put a hand on her shoulder, as if to comfort her, and slid the card across the counter. Donna reluctantly pulled the beautiful ring off her hand and returned it to the velvet tray, and the clerk whisked the tray and the card away.

Carson glanced at her and squeezed her arm lightly. "Don't worry," he smiled. "I told you I wanted authenticity. It's a calculated risk."

Donna shot him a glance that was probably full of the same misgivings that she felt; but one thing was crystal clear to her. Carson might or might not frequent casinos, or spend a small fortune on the turn of a card; but he was a born gambler.

"I hope it works out for you," she muttered, and suffered a flick of guilt; because it was her thoughtless lie that had put him in this awkward position.

In a strange way, she almost had an obligation to play this fake marriage charade out to the end. She had started it after all: and it was her duty to at least see that Carson didn't suffer loss because of her clumsy attempt to protect him.

Chapter Twenty Nine

Carson gave Donna a quick peck on the cheek as they walked out of the mall and was gratified to see that her expression lightened.

"You have my card. I want you to buy at least a week's worth of clothes and shoes," he told her. "Make some of it evening wear. We're going to be hitting every party in town, right up to the auction date."

A slow smile dawned across her face. "If you insist," she smiled and tapped the card against her cheek.

"Knock my eyes out," he told her, and laughed at the excited look on her face. "I mean it. Go crazy. I have to tend to some business back home, but I'll call you tomorrow morning."

"All right," she murmured. She kissed her fingertip and pressed it to his nose. "Bye, handsome."

Carson growled hungrily inside at the look in her eyes. Donna was a breathtaking woman, and he didn't want to leave her; but he had to.

"Keep that thought," he told her with a smile. "I'll call you tomorrow."

The valet pulled his rental car up to the mall entrance, and he turned to climb in. He threw up a hand in parting and pulled the car away from the mall and down the road.

Buck had left a message on his cell. He hadn't said what the trouble was, but the tone of his voice said it all. Something bad had happened back at the Seven.

It took Carson a few minutes to shake free of the pleasant intoxication of Donna's company; but at the first stoplight he pulled his phone out of his pocket and called Buck's number. To his alarm, it was picked up on the first ring. Buck's voice barked:

"Carson?"

"Yes, it's me," he murmured with a faint frown. "What's wrong? I can tell that something is. You sounded almost sick."

Buck sighed and replied, "Carson, I wish I didn't have to tell you this while you're up at Keeneland, but I have to. We got hit again. Rustlers broke into the thoroughbred barn and got Lickety Split and three of our brood mares."

Carson felt the blood draining out of his face, and he was momentarily speechless. In that stunned split-second the driver behind him honked his horn, and Carson saw that the light had changed. He blinked and nudged his car through the intersection.

"Carson, are you there?"

Carson rubbed his jaw and stammered, "I'm still here. It's just that I...have you put the police on it?"

"Of course. The sheriff's on it. The rustlers hit us in the wee hours, but the next morning we tracked them across our pastures all the way to the road. They must've had a trailer truck waiting there."

Carson was tempted to close his eyes, but he had to drive. He calculated for a minute, then replied, "All right, all those horses are micro-chipped. I have the numbers on my computer, so I'll contact the sheriff and make sure he has them. But as far as I'm concerned, it's a formality. I know who did it."

Buck's voice gathered darkness. "We all do," he growled. "It's Buster, trying to run us out of business again! He tried to starve us of water, and that didn't work, so now he's after our horses! Five'll get you ten, our horses are next door at the Lazy H right now. And when I think that Morg almost got shot trying to drive 'em off, I could knock Buster's head right off his shoulders!"

Carson looked up and had to hit the brakes hard to keep from rear-ending a gray Volvo. He pulled his hand over his face and croaked, "Is Morg okay?"

Buck's tone softened a bit. "Yes, thank the Lord! But his jeep's got a bullet hole in the windshield where they shot at him. He's lucky to be alive; but you know Morg. He took it all in stride."

A wave of relief washed over Carson, and he shook his head. "I'd have passed out," he muttered.

Buck sighed, "Well, Morg's made his peace with the Lord. He just figured that it wasn't his time."

A flick of impatience flashed through Carson at Buck's mention of God, followed by a wave of anger at Buster for confronting them all with the afterlife.

He set his mouth and replied tightly, "Send some drones over the Lazy H, Buck. See what they're doing out at their barns. I'll bet he's either got our horses now, or will have them soon."

"I'll do it," Buck replied grimly. "If we can prove that Buster did this, I'll see him in jail!"

"That's something we'd all like to see," Carson agreed. "He's in trouble already up here. They traced the three goons who tried to poison our yearlings to Buster. They were caught on hotel video going into his suite."

Buck's voice sank to an eager growl. "That's a start," he rumbled. "Make sure the police up there know about this rustling, too. If we can tie it all to Buster we might send him on a long, beautiful vacation to the gray hotel."

"I'd love to," Carson grumbled. "This is getting old. I'm tired of having to slam dunk Buster before I can do anything else."

"How's the sale of the yearlings coming?"

Carson sighed, "Well, I had to persuade Bertrand that our horses weren't damaged by the poisoning attempt. I think I succeeded, but I just found out that he distrusts single men, so I had to come up with a wife on the fly. I just finished that today."

There was a long, pregnant pause. "Come again?" Buck demanded, and Carson laughed.

"It's a long story," he chuckled. "I'm seeing a woman, and she agreed to pretend to be my wife while I'm up here. Just to level the playing field."

"Uh huh," Buck muttered. "Well, just work the phones Carson. I'll work the drones. I'll let you know if I find anything."

"Sounds good. Thanks Buck."

Carson clicked off with a frown and pulled his hand over his mouth. He'd kept himself together on the call because Buck didn't need to get more stirred up than he was; but now his own smothered anger came surging up again.

The Seven and the Lazy H had been rival ranches for years, and Buck and Buster had always hated each other. Buster's recent failed attempt to steal their water rights had only added to the feud.

But Buster had crossed a big, bright red line with this rustling. It was crime enough for Buster to steal their horses, but when his thugs shot at Morgan, the bad blood between them deepened to war. Carson fumed as he thought about Kit, about Heather and her unborn babies. One careless potshot could've turned Heather into a widow and robbed their children of a father.

Carson adjusted his shoulder. He was never going to forget this. None of them would.

But even if Buster hadn't told his hands to charge their stables with guns blazing, even if they hadn't almost shot Morgan, even if Buster hadn't made himself stink to everybody at the Seven, he'd still be going after Buster with everything he had.

Lickety Split was a beautiful horse, a champion racer and their best stud. He was worth a small fortune, and so were the stolen mares. The combined loss was north of ten million dollars; but there was more to it than that.

Their thoroughbreds were more than assets. They had personalities, they each had their own quirks.

He'd grown fond of them, and it infuriated him to think of them manhandled, driven through the brush at night, and thrown into a trailer.

Their horses were no doubt huddled in a new and strange place, surrounded by rough handlers, and terrified.

Carson pulled off the road suddenly and parked the car in a restaurant lot. He found the number for the Sandy Creek sheriff's office and closed his eyes as the phone rang.

This is the last thing I need right now, he frowned. *But I'm going to get even for Morg, and I'm getting those horses back. I'm going to sell our yearlings, and Buster Hogan's going to jail. He's gotten away with too much for too long.*

It's gloves off now.

The line suddenly picked up and a woman's flat voice intoned, "Sandy Creek Sheriff's Office."

Carson took a deep, calming breath and murmured, "Hello, Daisy. This is Carson Spade. I'd like to talk to Wilmer."

"Hey Carson," the officer replied. "I'll put you right through. He's been expecting you."

Chapter Thirty

An instant later the sheriff's gravelly voice grumbled, "Hey Carson. I hear you got hit the other night."

"Hello, Wilmer," Carson sighed. "Yes, we got hit. I'm up in Kentucky right now, and Buck just told me about it. Look Wilmer, all our stolen horses were microchipped, and I'm going to email the chip numbers to you. The chips won't help us track them, but they're proof the horses belong to the Seven. If we're quick, maybe we can get our horses back before the rustlers have a chance to dig the chips out."

Wilmer's voice sounded glum. "Well, that's a long shot, but I'll try," he grumbled. "The only way those numbers help us is if somebody scans 'em, then matches 'em up to the database."

"Every thoroughbred racehorse is microchipped," Carson replied quickly, "and everybody in the racing business knows to scan a horse before they buy it. That's why the rustlers are going to try to cut the chips out. It proves those horses are ours. But they need a vet to do that without hurting the horse. It's surgery. It has to be done under anesthesia."

"Huh," the other man grunted. "Well, I'll check with the vets around here. If somebody's brought them a thoroughbred, they'll remember it."

"Thanks Wilmer," Carson sighed. "But that's only half of it."

There was a beat of silence. "What else?"

"I'm up at Keeneland—a thoroughbred auction venue. We have three yearlings stabled there. The other night three goons broke into the stables and tried to poison them with yew leaves. Security caught them before they killed our horses, thank God." Carson paused, took a calming breath, and added, "Buster Hogan is up here, too, Wilmer. The security cameras at his hotel caught the same three mouthbreathers going into his suite."

"Well, well," the gravelly voice drawled, "ain't it a small world! Have the Lexington P.D. call me. Maybe we can make medicine."

A wan smile curved Carson's lips. "Maybe you can," he nodded. "Do you have any news about the rustlers?"

There was a heavy sigh on the other end of the line. "We tracked them cross-country to the road outside your place," he mumbled. "They had to load your horses up on a trailer parked on the side of the road. There was a big white horse trailer caught on the highway cam that night. It came up the ramp from the direction of the Seven. No tag on the trailer, driver had a baseball cap and glasses. Unidentifiable."

Carson grumbled under his breath and frowned. "Which direction?"

"North," the sheriff replied gruffly. "Away from Dallas, away from the Seven."

Carson reviewed the big ranches north of the Seven, but he didn't seriously believe any of them would receive stolen thoroughbreds. He knew, deep down, that somewhere that big white trailer had branched off the interstate, pulled off onto some forsaken country road, and met up with a waiting crew of Buster's hands. The horses had been transferred to one or more trailers and taken to different hiding places, where they'd stay until the pursuit died down and Buster was able to sell them to ignorant or unscrupulous buyers—probably through several middlemen.

But the horses hadn't been stolen primarily for sale. Buster would have a hard time unloading them to anyone in racing circles, because all thoroughbred racers were DNA tested and genetically typed. It would be next to impossible to pass off Lickety Split's foals as coming from some other sire.

The horses had been stolen to prevent the Seven's next crop of winning yearlings from Lickety Split, and to force the Seven to shell out a king's ransom to either buy a new champion stud, or rent one.

He wasn't sure he could even *do* that in time for next year's sale. The waiting list for champion studs was long.

Carson rubbed his brow and mumbled, "Driving the trailer north was a head fake, Wilmer. We all know who did this."

"You may," Wilmer reminded him, "but I don't. I know you and your brothers are mad,

Carson, and you got a right to be. But a sheriff can't guess."

"I don't, either," Carson snapped, then reined in his temper and resumed, "I believe that when we find out who did this, it'll be Buster. It's *always* Buster."

"I'd call it good odds," Wilmer agreed. "We'll see where the evidence takes us. We have a few leads. Tire tracks through a patch of mud. Some grainy clips from your security cameras. A witness who says he saw some men loading horses onto a trailer outside the Seven that night."

Carson sat up straighter. "Who?"

Wilmer's voice sounded tired. "A tourist from North Carolina who was lost and trying to get back to the interstate. Nobody who'd recognize a face."

"Oh."

"Look, Carson, you go ahead and send me those microchip numbers and share 'em with as many horse recovery outfits as you can. Maybe we'll get lucky. But don't hold your breath. It's not likely you'll ever see those horses again."

Talk to me again a month from now, Carson thought grimly; but he replied, "I'm going to hope for better anyway. Thanks, Wilmer. I'll send over the chip numbers."

"Yep. Oh, and Carson—in case anybody over there at the Seven is thinking about settling this without me—don't."

A smile curved Carson's lips. "What would I do all the way up here in Kentucky, Wilmer?" he drawled. "Of course, I can't answer for anybody else."

"You boys behave yourselves," the sheriff answered, in a worried tone.

Carson stifled a spurt of incredulous laughter. "Don't we always?" he retorted, and pressed the red button on his phone.

Chapter Thirty One

Carson returned to the Turf Club in the soft tranquility of the early evening. Golden lights filled every window of the old mansion, and its front doors were thrown open to let the last lingering breeze of a mellow autumn day waft inside.

Carson jogged up the stairs and down the quiet upper hall to his own door. He'd spent a busy, exhausting day in the city, and he was almost too washed out to eat.

He tossed his keys aside as soon as he entered the suite, then loosened his collar and unbuttoned his cuffs.

The balcony doors were thrown wide open, and a pleasant breath of evening air eddied across the room to embrace him. Purple dusk was falling over the lawn and the soft voices of other club members rose up to him in the semi-darkness as they passed below.

Carson walked over to the perfect white coverlet of his bed, sank down onto it, and reached for the dinner menu that the maid had propped up against the telephone.

He flipped it open, perused his choices, and reached for the phone.

"Hello? This is the Secretariat Suite. I'd like to order dinner in my room tonight," he murmured.

"Certainly Mr. Spade," a smiling female voice replied. "What would you like this evening?"

"I'll have the Wagyu beef, the farmhouse brown bread with truffle aioli, the roasted herbed peppers, and a glass of Cabernet Sauvignon."

"Yes, sir. It'll arrive in twenty minutes."

"Thank you."

Carson hung up and reached for his pack of cigarettes. He lit one and leaned back against his pillows with one arm behind his head.

He stared absently at the ceiling as the smoke from his cigarette curled lazily upward.

Carson took another pull on the cigarette. The best he could hope for was that one of those goons would spill his guts to the police. There was no doubt in his mind that Buster had hired them to kill their yearlings.

The three men hadn't ratted Buster out in spite of being hauled off to jail, and that told him that Buster had threatened them, and that they believed he'd follow through.

Carson exhaled smoke. He'd put in a call to the Lexington police department, and had been told that the thugs were still in jail, so he could still get to them. What he needed was to put an even greater fear into them than Buster had. A fear so intense that they'd be willing to turn on Buster and tell all they knew.

Lucky for him, that he knew just the man for that job.

Carson reached out for the phone, tapped out a number, and lifted the receiver to his ear. His call was picked up instantly.

"This is the answering service for Clemmons, Butler and Shrewsbury Law Firm."

"I'd like to send a message to Eugene," Carson replied softly. "Tell him it's from Carson Spade."

"I'll see if I can reach him, sir."

Carson leaned back into his pillow and crossed his legs. While he was waiting there came a soft knock on the suite door.

"Room service, Mr. Spade."

"Come in."

A waiter opened the door and wheeled a silver cart inside. Carson waved him into the bedroom, and the boy pushed the cart up beside his bed, unfolded a standing tray, and began to set it with napkin, silverware, wineglass and plate.

There came the sound of someone picking up the phone line, and Eugene's sharp voice greeted him from the other end.

"Well, good evening, Carson!"

"Good evening, Eugene," Carson murmured, and watched as the waiter lifted the lid off a fragrant plate of prime beef and an array of other delicacies. The waiter uncorked the wine bottle and filled his glass.

"I'm sorry to call you so late, Eugene," Carson murmured, and reached for his wallet to tip the waiter. He pressed a twenty into the boy's hand and watched as he grinned and waved before marching out of the suite again.

"I'm always here for you," Eugene murmured, though in a somewhat sleepy tone. "What can I help you with?"

Carson let the door close behind the waiter before reaching for the wine glass. "It's Buster again, Eugene."

The attorney's voice sounded surprised. "Really? I would've thought the last time would be enough. What has he done?"

"Two things," Carson told him, and took a long sip of Cabernet. "His thugs tried to poison our yearlings at the Keeneland stables a few days ago. They failed; but he sent another bunch to our stables at home and they got away with our thoroughbred stud and three of our best brood mares."

There was a thoughtful pause on the other end, then Eugene grunted: "Got anything on them?"

"Not much," Carson sighed. "But the three up here were caught by security and are sitting in the Lexington jail. They were caught on hotel cameras going into Buster Hogan's suite, though he denies knowing them."

There was a snort on the other end of the line, and Carson continued: "They haven't sold Buster out to save themselves—yet—and that must mean that they're afraid to do it. I need someone who can terrify them more than Buster did. Make them fess up."

Carson smiled over the rim of his glass. "Do we know anyone who could do that?"

Eugene replied briskly, "So you want me to represent you in your case against these three men?"

"If you'll do it. I know they were working for Buster. I just want them to admit it."

"Even if they do, the civil penalties for them would be slight at best," Eugene muttered.

"And uncertain for Buster. The horses suffered no damage?"

"No. But it wasn't because they didn't try their poor best."

"Well, Keeneland will certainly charge them with criminal trespass," Eugene muttered, "but that's a misdemeanor. Did they do any damage?"

"I understand they attacked a truck driver and a security guard to get in," Carson drawled.

"How badly were they injured?"

"I don't know."

"Well, I can use that," Eugene mumbled under his breath. "Though that would be part of Keeneland's suit, not yours. As for the theft of your horses—has anyone been caught for it?"

"Not yet. But it was Buster's crew, I'd bet my life on it. I've already talked to the sheriff, and he's not optimistic we'll get them back."

"Hmm. Well, call me if that changes. I may come up there tomorrow to see if I can talk to your three jailbirds before they fly away. What are their names?"

Carson set his wineglass down and reached for his cell phone. He flicked this thumb across it and mumbled: "Their names are...John Lambert, Ellis Campbell, and Curtis Wills."

"I'll see if they have any priors," Eugene mumbled.

"Thank you, Eugene," Carson replied in relief. "I'm sorry I called so late, but I'd like to get them while they're still a captive audience."

"Ha," Eugene grunted. "Are you still staying at the Turf Club?"

"Yes. If you tell me your flight I'll have you picked up at the airport and brought here for the weekend. You'll like this place."

"I'm sure I will," Eugene agreed. "Thank you, Carson. I'll have my secretary email you."

"See you then, Eugene. Thanks again."

"Very good."

Carson returned the phone to its cradle and leaned back into the pillow with a sigh. He reached for the wine glass and took a long, thoughtful sip.

It had been a long, tiring day, but a productive one. He'd already sunk any chances Buster might've had to get a leadership role in the Breeder's Association. No one believed Buster's ridiculous denial that the three thugs had come to his hotel room. Buster would be lucky to keep his membership.

He'd hired a detective to shadow Buster in the hope he could get video evidence of a crime. He'd called the sheriff back in Sandy Creek, and lastly, and most importantly, he'd set Eugene on Buster's hirelings.

Carson reached for the napkin, shook it out over his lap, and reached for the fork. He took a bit of the succulent beef, stuck it into his mouth, and savored its tender goodness.

He'd done all he could, for the moment, to bring justice down on Buster's guilty head; and so he was going to call it an evening.

Chapter Thirty Two

Carson stretched and sighed and snugged deep into the downy pillow. The balcony doors were still thrown open and a light, pleasant breeze flowed in through them, smelling of fresh air and dew. His busy day and luscious dinner sent him right under, and he slept heavily and dreamlessly into the night.

But sometime during the deep night, he sighed and turned toward the outer edge of the bed. His eyes flicked open, and he registered a block of white moonlight slanting across the floor. His eyes fluttered shut again and he slipped back into slumber; but this time, his dreams reflected the turmoil of wrestling with Buster Hogan, and of Morgan's brush with death.

His own voice echoed in the darkness of his mind: *It was Buster's crew, I'd bet my life on it.*

Carson frowned and muttered as the darkness in his mind vanished. He saw the Seven thoroughbred barn drowsing under the light of a big harvest moon. He heard the soft sound of a horse nickering inside, then peaceful silence as deep night settled over the countryside.

As he watched, a group of shadows emerged from the line of trees behind the barn. It was a dozen mounted riders, and the moonlight glinted off the rifles they were carrying. His heart jerked in his chest, and he muttered in his sleep as the Seven hands on guard saw them and yelled out a challenge.

Gunfire crackled, there was the sound of horses galloping, and then another gun blast. He heard Bennie's terrified yell as the riders poured through the blasted barn doors.

Get out, Carson mumbled, and his head tossed on the pillow.

To his horror, the barn doors burst open, and the rustlers galloped off with their thoroughbreds, yipping and yelling.

As he watched, approaching headlights glowed on the road and a jeep came skidding into the gravel parking lot. The door swung open and Morgan jumped out.

Morgan, he shouted, *watch out!*

Gunfire crackled from the fleeing rustlers, and one bullet hit the windshield of Morgan's jeep. Morgan crouched down behind his car and returned fire.

Carson saw himself dash to Morgan's jeep to crouch down beside his brother. *Are you okay,* he gasped, and to his relief, Morgan nodded.

Morgan stood up suddenly and popped off a series of shots: *pop pop pop pop.* Answering fire echoed from the trees, and Carson gasped as fire abruptly pierced his ribs. He tumbled backwards onto the gravel drive, and he grabbed at his chest. His lungs were on fire, and he couldn't breathe.

He rolled his eyes to see his brother's shadow bending down over him. *Carson,* he was saying, *Carson, are you hit?*

He writhed in agony and gasped for air; but he couldn't talk, couldn't breathe. His heart beat faster and faster until it trembled like a racing engine; and Morgan's face, the night sky over his head, the moon, and the world slowly faded away, then winked out.

Carson gasped and sat bolt upright in bed. He rolled wild eyes around the room and didn't recognize the strange furniture, the open balcony doors and the moonlight streaming through them. He sat there, breathing hard; then slowly the recent past came trickling back to him, and he closed his eyes in relief and slumped back against his pillow.

It was just a dream.

Carson clapped a hand to his galloping heart. The dream had been so detailed, so real. He almost felt as if he'd died and come back to life.

He lay there for a minute, then opened his eyes and stared up at the moon-mottled ceiling. He wasn't a fearful man. He was deliberate, hard-driving. He knew his business and was on top of his game.

But the nightmare still gripped him in its icy claws, because it made it real to him that some random disaster could catch him by surprise. He'd planned every detail of his business. Even the finer details of his private life.

But he'd never planned for death, never allowed himself to even think about it. He'd always pushed it away as something that didn't apply to a young, healthy man like him.

Carson rubbed his mouth and rolled his eyes around the room again. *What if I died?* he thought suddenly. *What if I got shot, or had a car accident, or had a heart attack?*

He had no plan for that. He had no grid for it, like Buck and Morgan. They had their faith to help them bear the prospect of death, but he had no such comfort.

What do I have? he wondered suddenly.

What if I died before I had a chance to enjoy the important things in life, before I had a chance to find a woman and build a family?

Carson lay there for a long moment in silence, then snorted impatiently. *This is ridiculous,* he thought suddenly, and threw himself on his side. *It's just a dream. I have every chance to live to be a hundred.*

I'm just upset about Morgan, and that's cooking in my subconscious.

He grumbled a bit to himself and closed his eyes, and his heart gradually returned to its usual strong, steady beat. He'd had a lot of stuff coming at him since he arrived in Kentucky, but he couldn't let himself get rattled in the runup to the yearling auction.

But for some reason, he couldn't get back to sleep right away, and as much as he tried to banish it, that nagging little voice echoed in his head.

How would I deal with death?

Three o'clock in the morning was no time to wrestle with his own mortality; but he had no answer to that question. And even though he pushed it to the back of his mind, that little voice whispered to him as he drifted off to sleep again.

Chapter Thirty Three

"Oh, yes, those were *made* for you," the boutique salesman nodded in approval. Donna lifted her chin and stared at her own reflection through a pair of $1,000 bejeweled sunglasses.

She felt a little guilty to burn through Carson Spade's money so fast, but he *had* told her to go crazy; and she had to assume that he knew what he was doing. She tilted her head this way and that in front of the little mirror to judge the effect.

"That oversized look is all the rage in Paris this season," the salesman added softly, and gently slid the glasses off her nose. "These glasses are made of midnight black titanium. Light and flexible and strong. And these are all

Swarovski crystals on the rims and stems. I must say, this pair gives you a very—Audrey Hepburn look."

"I'll take them," Donna told him promptly.

The man beamed at her. "I don't say this to everyone, but I think you made the right decision," he told her in a low, confidential tone. He brushed the glasses with his fingers. "This style suits your face to perfection, and the glasses are exquisitely made." He opened a pink leather case, placed the glasses inside, and carefully closed it up.

Donna watched him ruefully. She was being schmoozed, but this particular salesman did it so pleasantly and well that she couldn't cherish pique toward him.

Then too, she thought he was right, at least when he said the glasses suited her. They were the right shape for her face, even if they were shockingly overpriced.

She could add them to the list of shockingly overpriced things that she'd been buying all day—the lovely pair of Dior sheath dresses, the flirty Jimmy Choo heels, the Burberry coat for daytime and a fabulous Chanel faux-fur jacket for evening.

Donna reached for her purse and pulled out Carson's card, and the flash of light from her ring finger made the salesman's eyes widen. "*Oooh*," he marveled, and reached out to take her hand. He turned her fingers gently and smiled as the diamond flashed fire. "Someone certainly loves you!"

Donna gave him a little smile and glanced down at the ring ruefully. "Yes," she murmured, but couldn't help feeling wistful. Carson Spade didn't love her, they hadn't known one another nearly that long. To his credit, he hadn't told her that he loved her, though she was fairly certain he'd be delighted to have a short, pleasant fling before they parted ways.

It made her a bit sad that his glorious ring was just costume jewelry. A prop in the little play they were performing.

It would be wonderful to marry a handsome, charming, fun-loving fellow like Carson. Life would certainly never be dull. Carson had both the means and the temperament to make it perpetually exciting.

It was a pity she was leaving the country.

The salesman took the card and rang up the purchase. He shook out a glossy pink shopping bag, lined it artfully with tissue paper, and tucked the pink leather glasses case inside. He handed it to her with a smile.

"Is the receipt inside?" she asked, with a touch of anxiety; and he nodded.

"Of course. If you change your mind you have thirty days to bring the glasses back."

"Thank you," Donna murmured in relief. She'd made the same request at all the shops, because she was racking up a hideous bill. She considered it her duty to make sure Carson could return everything.

"Go forth and dazzle," the salesman told her, with a wave of benediction; and Donna giggled, took the bag, and waved farewell.

She strolled out into the mall, swinging her shopping bags in both hands. They were getting a bit heavy, so she decided to stop for a nice dinner at the French restaurant in the mall.

The smiling greeter led her into the dark interior of the restaurant, which was lit only by sputtering gas lamps and tabletop candles. He gave her a cozy corner booth table, and she set her bags down on one seat and slid into the other. The woman handed her a menu, clasped her hands and murmured, "What can I bring you to drink?"

"Mmm… I think a mineral water with a twist of lemon to start, and a cup of espresso with my meal." Her eyes flicked over the dinner menu. "I think I'll have the *Salmon en Papillote* with white asparagus, with a spinach salad with warm bacon dressing on the side."

"Coming right up."

Donna handed off the menu, then dug in her bag for her phone. She flicked it on, then called Carson's number.

The phone picked up, and Carson's smiling voice drawled, "Hello, beautiful lady."

Donna smiled and twirled a spoon between her fingers. "I just thought it'd be polite to tell you that I charged $20,000 to your card today. But don't worry, I kept the receipts."

Carson's soft laughter made her ear tingle. "That was considerate."

She reached for a glass of water and took a sip. "What kind of wife do you want me to be specifically?" she teased. "A socialite, a horse enthusiast, a party animal? It'll help me to get into character."

Carson's tone dropped an octave, and the sound of it made the skin on her neck prickle. "Well, we're supposed to be newlyweds," he murmured, "so it would make sense for my wife to adore me. In a publicly-appropriate way, of course, though I don't object to PDAs."

Donna laughed aloud and nodded mischievously, "I'll make a note. A few neck nibbles and hand squeezes. Maybe a little footsie under the table."

A male waiter bent down to place her mineral water on the table. Donna met his eyes and winked, and he raised an eyebrow and smiled as he withdrew.

"You're on the right track," Carson agreed. "I like your initiative."

Donna laughed again and reached for her drink. "When's our next appearance?"

"Ummm....the day after tomorrow. The Racing Alliance will be holding a party at Tavern on the Green," he murmured. "It's an indoor-outdoor affair depending on the weather, and it looks to be fair, so I'd say dress for a garden party, but bring a light jacket in case it gets cool."

"Do you want me to charm your Mr. Blandings?" she smiled. "I take it he'll be there, of course."

"Of course. And just be your usual lovely self," Carson replied smoothly, and Donna felt herself going warm with absurd pleasure in spite of herself.

"I'll pick you up Friday evening at five."

"I'll be ready. *Ciao.*"

"Ciao, bella."

Donna hung up with a soft giggle, and as she put her phone away the waitress arrived with her meal. The woman placed the plates down in front of her, and the fragrant, delicious aroma curled into the air.

"Enjoy."

Donna smiled at her and unrolled her napkin. But as she took a forkful of salmon, she was only half-experiencing the delicious taste.

She was imagining making good on her promise, and playing footsie with Carson Spade.

Chapter Thirty Four

Eugene Clemmons opened his briefcase on the plain plastic table in the visiting room of the Lexington jailhouse. A scruffy-looking, unshaven man glared at him suspiciously from the other side of a thick plexiglass window.

"Who are you?" the prisoner demanded, and Eugene looked up at him through his glasses.

"My name is Eugene Clemmons. I'm an attorney. I'm representing the man whose horses you allegedly tried to kill."

"Yeah, well I got nothing to say to you," the man scoffed, and leaned back in his chair. He waved his hand dismissively.

"Mmm," Eugene murmured and lifted a sheaf of papers from his briefcase. His eyes flicked over them. "Well, Mr. Lambert, I see that Keeneland is bringing a civil suit against you and your friends for criminal trespass. This is in addition to the state's charges of assault involving a truck driver."

The man leaned across the plastic counter and hissed, "It's a lie! My buddies and I were drunk that night, we went to Keeneland on a bet. Ellis bet me $500 that I couldn't get as far as the stables. Nobody was trying to kill any horses!"

"The state will also be charging you with animal cruelty and attempt to commit a crime," Eugene forged on. "Lastly, my client will be bringing a civil action against you to recoup the $3500 fee he incurred for vet services and diagnostic testing pursuant to the alleged attempt to poison his horses."

"I told you, it was a prank!" the man shouted, and brought his fist down on the counter. The guard standing behind him reached out and yanked him roughly back into his chair.

"That's enough out of you, Lambert."

The man shot the guard a resentful look, then turned around to glare at Eugene, who flipped a page in the sheaf of papers.

"I see here that you have some serious prior convictions, Mr. Lambert," he sighed gently. "You were recently released from Beaumont Federal Penitentiary. For...hmm...armed robbery. I see you spent ten years there." He raised his eyes. "You live in Texas, then? That's a long way from Kentucky."

The man crossed his arms and looked away, and Eugene flipped a page. "Before your incarceration in Beaumont, you spent time in various Dallas-area city and county jails for drunk and disorderly and petty theft. There are some domestic disturbance records here, as well."

"Why are you here?" the man demanded sharply. "I got nothing to say to you, so you might as well get out!"

Eugene closed up the sheaf of papers, tucked them back into his briefcase, and laced his fingers together on the plastic counter. He trained a mild look on the scowling inmate.

"If you're convicted of even some of these crimes, Mr. Lambert, you're likely going to prison again," he sighed. "I do not predict, but if I had to bet, I'd say that you're very possibly looking at another ten years. You're thirty five, isn't that right? In the prime of your life." He shook his head.

"My client is a very rich man, Mr. Lambert, but he is also a compassionate man. He has no desire to ruin another man's life, even though some might say that would be just." The look in his eyes sharpened as he met the other man's gaze.

"My client is prepared to drop his charges against you, Mr. Lambert, and even to advocate on your behalf, if you'll testify in court. If you tell the court who put you up to this."

A sly, knowing look spread across the other man's coarse features. "Oh, I get it now," he grinned. "You want me to help you bring somebody down, is that it? Well, sure, buddy. Where do I sign?"

Eugene's expression hardened. "I've spoken to the prosecuting attorney here about the charges he plans to bring against you, Mr. Lambert. He's open to the possibility of lessening their severity if you help the state. So I'm in a position to help you or to hurt you," he replied softly. "It makes no difference to me which it is, but it will make a great deal of difference to you." He tilted his head and considered the scowling inmate before him, as if he was staring at a new and revolting species of animal.

"If you tell me the truth, it's possible that you might only get a couple of years inside with good behavior. But if you lie to me, I'll see to it that you rot there."

The inmate's face twisted, and anger and fear struggled visibly in his eyes. "You're a real hot shot, are you?" he sneered.

Eugene tilted his head in acknowledgment. "I let my results do the talking, Mr. Lambert. If you're smart, you'll cut a deal with me. But if you're not, if you believe a lot of threats from a born liar, you're going down."

The man's eyes snapped up. He licked his lips. "Born liar," he echoed. "Who do you mean?"

Eugene gripped the briefcase handle and stood up. "I think you know exactly who I mean, Mr. Lambert," he drawled. "I'll let you think about my offer." He pushed a card through a small opening in the plexiglass wall. "Call me when you're ready to be smart."

The prisoner made no move to take the card, but his eyes were fixed on it as Eugene turned his back and marched out of the room.

Eugene maintained a poker face as a guard opened the door to let him out. But as soon as the thick metal door had swung shut behind him, a sneaking smile curved up one corner of his mouth, and he whistled a little tune as he strolled down the hall.

Chapter Thirty Five

"Buck, I still think you should talk to Eugene before we do this."

Luke swatted a bug off his jaw and leaned against a fence post. It was about two in the morning and black dark night, because the sky was clouded over. It was cold, what was more, and he glanced back toward the Seven ranch house longingly.

But his older brother uttered a scornful snort. "I'd be ashamed to be so chicken-hearted," he replied as he peered over the ranch fence and into the gently rolling meadows beyond.

The pastures of the ranch next door—the Lazy H.

Buck clutched a small drone and nodded toward the controls that Luke was holding. "You tell me you know how to fly this thing?"

"Yes," Luke replied uneasily. "But just because it ain't against the law to fly a drone over somebody's ranch, doesn't mean that's all there is to it. What if Buster's hands shoot it down, and find out it's ours, and sue us? It'd be embarrassing."

Buck turned to glare at him. Luke knew it was a glare even in the darkness, and he stepped back a respectful pace.

"I'll tell you what embarrasses me," Buck growled. "I get embarrassed when million-dollar horses get rustled right out of my barn. I get so embarrassed that I decide to get 'em *back*."

"Aw come on, Buck," Luke objected. "You think Buster's gonna have those horses running around in his back pasture? Buster's not *that* dumb."

"I don't put anything past him," Buck grumbled. "He's got the nerve of a circus monkey. It's just lucky for us he's got the same size of a brain. Now turn this thing on so we can get it in the air. Carson's counting on us."

Luke grumbled under his breath, but he flicked the 'on' switch on the controls. A little blue screen jumped to life between his hands.

"All right now, Buck. Put it down on the ground and step back from it."

His brother bent down and set the camera drone on the ground, then stepped back a few paces. Luke pressed another button, and the drone came to life with a soft whirring sound. It slowly rose into the air and paused ten feet above the ground, a small dark shape betrayed only by a soft, dim light.

"You see what I mean," Luke murmured, and nodded toward the hovering drone. "If it's quiet, like it is now, you can hear it. You can see the light, if it's close."

The big shadow beside him stuck its hands on its hips. "Send it over," he sighed. "I want to see that barnyard. I want to see those horse pastures."

Luke bit his mouth into a frustrated line, but sent the drone gently up into the air. "All right then," he sighed, and nudged the drone up and over the fence line.

He watched the little blue screen, and the ghostly images of the night vision video. He moved the drone westward and increased its speed as it hurried over the open meadows toward the big barn complex of the Lazy H, off to the southwest.

Buck walked over to stare at the controller over his shoulder. He pointed at a dark blob in one corner of the screen.

"What are those?"

Luke tilted the screen slightly to let him see it. "Horses out to pasture. They're not ours."

Buck peered at the screen and nodded. "No they aren't," he agreed. "I can tell the difference even on that crazy thing. They're work horses. Scruffy, too."

"Yeah," Luke sighed. "I feel sorry for their horses. Buster tends his horses just enough to stay out of trouble, but he's sloppy with 'em. One of his horses walked up to the fence line last week, and its coat was a mess. It wanted a nose rub, and I gave it one, but it was all I could do not to climb over and give it a good brushing myself, poor old thing."

He moved the controller gently, and the picture on the screen slowly shifted from blank, open pastures, then to a dark line of trees. Luke carefully sent the drone higher to sail high over the topmost branches, and then lowered it again on the other side of the tree line. Beyond, the rolling meadows were pinched into smaller fenced pastures, which in turn gave way to a huddle of small outbuildings.

"There you go," Buck muttered, "you're getting close to the barns. Try to get in low over the barn yard and the pastures around it."

Luke shook his head. "I know how to fly the dang drone, Buck," he drawled.

"Well go ahead and get it over the barn then," Buck retorted. "Let's see what they got over there."

Luke stifled an impatient reply and brought the drone down lower, slowly and gently. The outer horse pens slowly swam into view, with groups of horses standing clumped together with their heads down.

"More work horses," Buck mumbled; and as they watched, a few of them looked up and switched their tails.

Luke moved the drone up again to float over the roof of the big barn, and they both peered at the ring of pens around it. Luke made the drone drift down over the eaves on the far side. There were three horses in a pen on that side of the pen, and Luke sent the drone down to look at them.

"No," Buck sighed, "those aren't ours, either. It's a shame we can't send it down into the barn."

Luke glanced at him. "Well, technically, I could, if I can find an open door," he shrugged. "But we'd get caught sure."

Buck turned to him in the darkness. "Go ahead and try it."

"I know there's somebody in there, Buck. We're taking a chance just putting it on the roof!"

"I'll take the responsibility. Try."

Luke shook his head and muttered, "All right. Just remember what you said!"

He gently nudged the controls, and as they watched, the camera showed them the barnyard as the drone drifted down from the roof. The few horses in the pen looked up at it sleepily and watched as it turned and floated around the side of the building, searching for an open door.

Luke hissed suddenly and brought the drone to a stop. Buck frowned.

"What is it?"

"There's somebody around the side of the barn," Luke whispered, as if he was afraid the shadow would hear. "One of the hands."

Buck leaned closer. "Think he sees it?"

"I don't know."

They stood there in silent suspense and watched as the dark shadow stretched its arms, appeared to yawn, and turned to face the barn wall.

"Oh for crying out loud," Buck muttered. "He's taking a pee."

"Now's our chance," Luke breathed, and nudged the drone high above and behind the man, then around the side of the barn. "Look!" Luke hissed, "He left one of the doors open."

Buck leaned in to squint at the little screen. "Go ahead and take your shot. This may be our only chance."

Luke inhaled and barely pressed the button to send the drone down, slowly and gently, and into the barn. There were no other humans visible on the little screen, and Buck murmured, "Get in close to the stalls. It's gonna be tricky to make out details."

Luke sent the drone drifting down the center aisle of the barn, and the horses lifted their heads and pricked up their ears at the drone as it stopped and hovered there.

"That first one has a blaze," Luke murmured. "None of our yearlings do." He inched the drone down to the next stall, and the next. "No, that one's a mare...and the next one's white. That one's got a notched ear...the other two across the way are black." He sighed in disappointment. "Looks like none of them are ours."

"Turn the camera around," Buck muttered, "we don't want that guy walking in on us."

Luke gently rotated the camera lens, and to his horror, there was a shadow closing the barn door behind him.

"Quick," Buck hissed, "send the drone up into the rafters! It should be dark up there. Maybe he won't see it!"

Luke sent the drone up sharply and set it down on a cross beam in the ceiling. From that vantage point they could see the whole length of the barn, and they watched as the puzzled-looking hand walked under the drone, glanced toward the restless horses, and turned this way and that with his hands on his hips.

"He knows something happened," Luke worried aloud; but Buck murmured, "He didn't see it. If he did, he'd be grabbing for something to knock it down."

Something huge and black suddenly scrambled over the screen, and they both jumped.

"Spider," Buck grumbled, and Luke closed his eyes and mouthed silent exclamations.

The screen cleared, and they bent over it. The hand was walking from stall to stall, checking on the horses; but then he scratched his neck and sauntered back to a little office at the end of the barn.

As soon as he disappeared, Buck nudged Luke in the ribs. "Now's our chance to get the drone out."

"He closed the door," Luke muttered. "We're trapped!"

Buck rubbed his jaw with one big hand. "Ain't there any other way out?"

Luke looked up to frown at him. "Well, now's a fine time to ask!"

As they watched, another man walked into view and the first hand came walking out of the office to meet him. The two stood there talking to one another with their arms folded across their chests, and the minutes dragged on.

"Who are those two?" Buck muttered, and leaned close to look.

"Oh, who knows," Luke grumbled. "I don't keep track of Buster's hands!"

To his relief, the second man raised his hand in parting and turned to leave. They both watched as he opened the big barn door, and to Luke's joy, he left it standing ajar.

"Think you can get the drone through that little crack?" Buck worried aloud.

"Only one way to find out," Luke grunted, but Buck put a warning hand on his shoulder.

"Check for the other guy," he warned; and Luke scanned the screen.

"I don't see him," Luke murmured, and nudged the drone off the cross beam. He turned it gently toward the open door and sent it floating high through the air.

The top of the big barn door slowly floated into view. It was hanging ajar, and the opening looked barely wide enough for the drone's rotors to clear.

"It's gonna be close," Luke grumbled. "If it hits the door it's going down and we're caught."

"Just keep going," Buck told him. "You're doing good."

A sudden projectile next to the drone made them both jump. Something hit the barn wall nearby and fell, and Luke's heart jumped into his throat.

"We've been spotted," he yelped, and sent the drone toward the narrow opening as fast as he dared.

"Quick," Buck hissed, "before he closes the door!"

Luke held his breath and tried to thread the needle with a drone more than a half-mile away. The camera showed the drone squeezing through the space with no room to spare, and then the screen showed the barn yard on the outside. He breathed a sigh of relief, then sent the drone sharply into the air.

"Send it over the roof," Buck urged him, "so he won't be able to shoot it down!"

Luke sent the drone zooming over the high barn roof, then straight up into the sky as fast and as far as it would go. The barn quickly shrank below the drone, and the surrounding countryside opened up.

"Look," Buck worried, "there he is in the barn yard. Get out of there!"

Luke turned the drone back toward the Seven and opened it up. The outbuildings and surrounding pastures zoomed past far below, and soon it had left all danger of pursuit far behind; but Luke's heart sank.

"They're going to know we're onto them," Luke muttered; but Buck snorted, "That's alright with me. Let Buster be mad for a change! When you're the biggest liar and thief in Texas, you can expect attention!" He stuck his hands on his hips and was silent for a moment, as if he was trying to calm himself.

"Just get the drone back, and we'll be on our way. They may suspect, but without the drone they can't prove anything."

Buck looked down and shook his head. "Well, at least we know they're not keeping our horses at the Lazy H. I guess we need to focus our attention on the local vets. Those horses are chipped, and if Buster wants to sell 'em, he'll need to have those chips taken out."

"We need to get out of here," Luke muttered. "They might chase the drone back to us."

Buck glanced back at the jeep parked in the field behind them. "Well, just get it back, then. I'll be in the car."

He turned on the words and walked across the pasture to the jeep. Luke stood nervously at the fence, staring westward; and soon a small, faint light appeared in the sky.

"Come on baby," he breathed, "come to Poppa."

The jeep's motor cranked to life, and Luke watched in relief as the drone came zooming up to the fence line. He brought it down, slow and gentle, until it rested on the grass beside him.

"Grab it and let's go," Buck barked from the open car door. "I think I see lights out there."

Luke bent down to retrieve the drone, and as he straightened, he could see a pair of headlights off the west. They were small, but getting bigger and brighter every second.

"Come on!" Buck urged.

Luke juggled the equipment in his arms and skipped back to the jeep. He'd no sooner slid in than Buck sent the jeep curving sharply around, and they bounced over the rough ground with the lights off.

"Slow down!" Luke gasped, as he tried to hold onto the camera. "You're going to make me drop it!"

Buck glanced into the rearview mirror. "I can see 'em coming over those pastures," he muttered, as the jeep bounced onto a narrow dirt road. Buck turned the wheel and they went roaring off to safety in a cloud of dust.

Buck's big shoulder shook with silent laughter. "I'd give a hundred dollars to see Buster's face when they tell him we sent a drone right into his barn. They'll be a few guys getting their cans handed to them tomorrow morning, is my guess."

Luke clutched the camera to his chest and shot his brother a wry look. Buck turned to meet his eye, and they both suddenly broke out laughing.

Chapter Thirty Six

Donna unlocked the door of her condo and waltzed in with a half-dozen bags swinging from her hands. She set the bags down with a happy sigh, closed the door behind her, and kicked out of her shoes.

She reached into one of the bags, pulled out a glossy pink hat box, and carefully lifted the lid. She reached in and lifted a massive white party hat from the tissue paper, turned toward the hall mirror, and set it on her head.

The huge, floppy brim concealed half her face, but it was the perfect hat for a lawn party in horse country. Chic. Elegant. And the perfect match for the white off-the-shoulder Dior dress with the navy blue bell skirt.

She was still turning her head this way and that when the doorbell trilled. She frowned faintly and set the hat down.

I'm not expecting anyone, she thought in puzzlement. *Unless Carson's decided to drop by.*

She opened the door, and to her amazement, a familiar face was smiling at her.

"Tim!" she gasped, and opened her arms. Her friend walked into them and returned her hug. "What are you doing here? I thought you were on your way to New Delhi!"

"I was," he smiled, "but my plans got a bit derailed by the monsoon season. There's a ferocious storm there right now and I decided to postpone the flight for a few weeks until the weather settles."

Donna closed her mouth and laughed, "Please come in. I'm glad you arrived when you did. I just got back from an epic shopping spree."

Tim walked into the house with his hands in his pockets. "I can see that," he joked, and lifted up one end of the wide-brimmed hat. "Shades of the fabulous sixties! You haven't lost your fashion sense, I see."

"Come into the living room," she begged, and pulled him along by the hand. "What can I get you? I have a bottle of Chianti, some tea, a little coffee."

Her tall guest sauntered into her living room, hiked up the hems of his slouch trousers, and sank into one of her stuffed chairs. Donna smiled as her glance flicked over him. Tim was as rumpled and handsome as a movie director should be, with his loose, curly brown hair, deep tan, and Hawaiian shirt and cargo pants.

"A glass of wine sounds perfect."

Donna drifted into her little kitchen and he went on, "I had to fly down to Nashville to take care of some business, and thought I'd hop up here to pay a call."

Donna smiled at him through the doorway as she opened her refrigerator. "I'm so glad you did. I've missed you. How long has it been?"

"Five years," he murmured, and shot her a laughing, surprised look. "Five years." He shook his head.

Donna poured out two glasses and carried them back into the living room. She handed one to her guest and took a sip from the other as she sat down in a chair facing him.

"It seems like yesterday to me," she smiled. "You were the struggling movie producer in Paris, and I was the struggling designer at that little *atelier* on the Left Bank."

His eyes met hers over the rim of his glass. He nodded, "I still say you should've stuck it out. Your designs were inspired. And speaking of which," he added, "I have to confess that I have an ulterior motive in coming here."

"Oh dear," she teased. "I sense an intrigue."

Tim set the glass down and turned to face her with a smile. "I was hoping I could persuade you to come with me to Delhi when I go. The last time we talked you said you'd think about it. Designer for a movie. That'd look nice on a resume. Be a lot of fun, too. India is a smorgasbord for the senses. The light there is different, the colors more vibrant than anywhere else on earth."

The smile faded briefly from Donna's lips. She recovered instantly and laughed, "Of course I'd love to come with you to Delhi."

He tilted his head to one side and gazed at her quizzically. "But?"

Donna waved her glass in the air and sputtered, "It's just that—"

The front bell trilled again, and Donna turned toward it in dismay. "Oh...please excuse me, Tim."

"Certainly."

Donna shot him a smile and walked out of the room, closed the interior door behind her, and went to the front door. To her surprise, it was Carson.

"Carson," she stammered, and glanced back toward the living room. It was none of Carson's business who her other friends were, but she found that she didn't want him to know that another man was in her living room. To her embarrassment, she felt her face going hot.

Carson flashed a white smile. He was standing on her front stoop with his hands in his pockets, looking just like a magazine cover model in his casual jacket and designer slacks. "I thought I'd drop by to see what you're doing this afternoon," he smiled. "It's a perfect day for a trail ride. Would you like to go to the stables and take a short trip up into those hills?" He nodded toward the low, red and yellow-spattered mountain behind the stables.

Donna tucked a tendril of hair behind one ear and nodded. "Oh, yes, that would be wonderful," she replied.

Carson's expression brightened. "Great. No business, just a nice relaxing jaunt."

Donna glanced at him wistfully. "That sounds lovely, but I'll need a little time to get ready. I just got back from a hard day of shopping," she laughed weakly. "And that reminds me. I still have your card. I need to give it back."

Carson shrugged easily. "No rush. I'm not worried about it."

Even in her nervousness, Donna raised her brows in confusion. "You know your own business best," she marveled, "but is it really so important for me to have such expensive things?"

Carson nodded, and the light gleamed off his glossy, blue-black hair. "Yes. A billionaire's bride is always showered with extravagant clothes and jewels. If we're going to put this over you'll have to flash them. Don't be afraid to step into the part."

Donna met his eye. "I won't," she murmured, and they held that gaze a beat too long before she blushed and looked away.

"I'd like to ask you to come in, but—"

To Donna's dismay, the living room door opened in the hall behind her, and Tim came sauntering out curiously. Donna felt a wave of heat crawl up from her feet to her hair, but Carson just tilted his head and smiled.

"I'm sorry to interrupt," Tim told her apologetically, and touched her elbow lightly.

"But I have to run. I only meant to drop by for a few minutes."

"You're not leaving?" Donna replied in regret, but her old friend nodded. "I have to catch a flight to New York. Think about what I asked you." He leaned down and kissed the cheek that she offered, nodded to Carson, and walked to the foot of the steps.

Tim turned to look up at her and smiled. "It'll be just like Paris," he added, and a reluctant smile crept over Donna's lips.

"I'll call you."

"Goodbye, Tim. I'm glad you came by."

Tim raised a hand to wave at her and walked off briskly. Donna cleared her throat in embarrassment and ventured, "Won't you come in, Carson?"

Carson shrugged. "I'll let you get ready," he smiled. "And I'm sorry, I didn't mean to scare your guest away."

"Oh, you didn't," she assured him. "He was only here for a quick visit." She cleared her throat again.

Carson took a step back. "Well, I'll give you time to get ready. Does three sound about right?"

"Fine," she replied in relief.

"See you then," Carson smiled, and turned to go. Donna watched him with a knot of conflicting emotions tangled in her chest: embarrassment, impatience with herself for feeling apologetic when she didn't owe anyone an apology, a ridiculous fear that she'd offended Carson, and dismay about what that said about her feelings toward him.

She sighed, turned back inside the house, and closed the door. But as she walked upstairs to shower and dress, she felt the weight of the decision looming before her.

Would she jet off to New Delhi with Tim and have the adventure of a lifetime, or would she stay to gamble on a rich playboy she was only just getting to know?

Chapter Thirty Seven

Carson strode back across the club campus in deep thought. The sight of that tall, tan stranger coming out of Donna's house had hit him like a punch to the jaw, though of course he hadn't shown it.

It looked like he had a rival.

Carson adjusted one shoulder. *Rival* might be a strong word, but still. He and Donna were on track to something warmer than a flirtatious acquaintance, or so he thought. Of course they had no real relationship, per se. He had no claim on her aside from the charade they were playing.

But the sight of her with another man was unexpected, and he found that he was suddenly very curious about 'Tim' and what he'd meant by, "It'll be just like Paris," and "Think about what I asked you."

Surely that rumpled slob hadn't asked her to *marry* him.

Carson rubbed his jaw. During his outings with Donna, she'd never behaved like a woman contemplating marriage with another man. Unless the two of them had some kind of fight, maybe. Some women threw themselves into new flirtations when they'd just broken up with their boyfriends.

Of course Tim might merely have asked for a date, or something like it.

But Donna hadn't seemed *that* affectionate with Tim. Surely, if he was something special to her, she'd have introduced him as such.

She hadn't introduced him at all; and that told its own story. She was usually very polished and polite.

Carson walked along with his head down and his hands in his pockets as the wheels in his head turned. He didn't have the time to get sidetracked with a new romance, but he couldn't keep his mind from circling back to 'Tim.'

Who was he, or more importantly, who was he to Donna?

Carson stopped in the middle of the lawn and glanced back over his shoulder at the neat row of condos at the end of the little street.

He shook his head and started walking again. He wasn't an especially sentimental man, and he'd had many delightful dalliances with women in his life. He knew the life cycle of such attachments; or at least, he knew them from his own perspective.

He usually didn't feel much jealousy, because he saw the end from the beginning. What was the point of jealousy, when you knew going in that the relationship was a pleasant, but temporary interlude?

But to his own surprise, he was feeling jealousy bubbling in his heart now. He rubbed his chest uneasily. It had been a long time since he'd been jealous.

Still, the feeling wasn't at all strange. Donna was a very desirable woman, a woman he was more than willing to compete for. She was beautiful and intelligent. She was well-traveled and sophisticated, soft-spoken and charming. But she was different from the women he'd known before.

She was a woman who was completely at ease in her own skin.

She radiated comfort, both with herself and with him; and yet he sensed she was something of an adrenaline junkie, too. The tension between her serenity on the one hand,

and her thrill seeking on the other, was fascinating.

He found it very alluring.

Carson questioned his heart as he walked over the manicured grounds. He needed to get his head on straight, to figure out exactly what he felt for Donna before he started competing with some other guy for her.

When he considered it, he had to admit that in his subconscious, he'd started to see Donna as attached to him at the least. As *belonging* to him at the most, if he was really honest with himself.

Even though he had no grounds for that feeling. He and Donna had enjoyed a few delightful outings together, they'd kissed, they were attracted to one another, she'd agreed to help him with Bertrand Blandings.

None of that meant anything, really. They were only beginning to get acquainted.

Maybe he was taking this fake wife thing too seriously.

Yes, on second thought, he certainly was; because when he closed his eyes, he saw himself pushing Tim off a high bridge, and watching in pleasure as his rival's Hawaiian shirt flapped like big bat wings until he hit the water with his arms outstretched.

Ssplasssh.

It was childish. Absurd.

But that mental image amused him all the way up to the clubhouse porch, through the plush hall beyond, and up the stairs to his suite.

Once he got there, Carson took more than his usual care with his appearance. He took a long, hot shower, toweled off, and gave his face a light, afternoon shave to get his skin extra smooth.

He splashed on aftershave, brushed his hair, and completed a painstaking toilette before shrugging into a light cream-colored sweater, tan riding trousers, and riding boots.

He gave himself a critical look in the mirror. *You don't look very happy,* he told his reflection; but it figured. He hated to lose, and he was running behind on all fronts.

His best stud and mares had been stolen. His yearlings had almost been poisoned. He was no closer to selling them to Bertrand Blandings. And he'd just found out that his girl—or rather, his date—had a tall, tan friend that she probably liked better than him.

Better up your game, bud, he told the mirror; and he intended to.

Chapter Thirty Eight

When her bathroom clock clicked to 2:55, Donna was putting the last finishing touches on her hair. She'd pulled it to one side in a loose golden braid that curled over her left shoulder.

She stepped back and assessed herself. She didn't have a riding habit handy, or even riding trousers. She'd gone in the other direction entirely.

Extremely casual. It was a complete change from her usual preference for elegant clothes.

She looked almost like a western cowgirl in a loose white cotton shirt, braided belt, and jeans. She glanced down at her boots with a sigh. In spite of working at one of the most elite horse-racing resorts in the country, she didn't even own a proper pair of riding boots.

She hadn't ridden a horse in over a year; but she wasn't worried. It was like riding a bicycle. Once you learned, you never forgot.

Donna was in the act of snapping in a hoop earring when the doorbell rang downstairs. She hurriedly snapped in the other one, glanced at her reflection one last time, and hurried off to answer it.

The door swung open to reveal Carson Spade in a riding outfit that looked as if it had been ripped straight from the pages of GQ. Carson looked as if he should be posing in the Irish countryside with his thoroughbred mount grazing nearby.

Donna glanced down at her own clothes and suffered a flick of chagrin. "Right on time!" she smiled, and was relieved to see that Carson's manners were far too good to seem to notice the difference in their clothes.

"Are we ready?" he asked, and she nodded and closed the door behind her. Carson extended his arm like a cavalier, and she laughed as she took it.

She glanced at the curb and commented, "I see you found the golf carts."

Carson made a face and laughed. "Yes, but I've never driven one before, so I apologize in advance."

"No golf?" she asked in surprise. "Everyone else here plays that game."

"Not me," Carson replied sturdily. "Or at least, not voluntarily. Golf bores me even when I'm playing it. It's too quiet for my taste. But then again, I was raised on football, and that's a savage blood sport like bullfighting. So I suppose I can blame my environment."

"Now you're just teasing me."

"You might be right," he winked, then helped her climb into the passenger's side of the cart.

He circled the cart to slide into the driver's seat, grinned at her, and sent the cart puttering down the little walkway. It curved away from the little cluster of houses and circled the edge of a wide, lush horse pasture on the way to the club barns.

It was a cool afternoon, slightly overcast but not rainy. Donna glanced up at the trees as their cart passed under. A sudden gust of wind sent a flurry of red and gold leaves scurrying across the concrete path ahead of them. It was slightly past the peak of fall, and bare spots were beginning to pop up in the massive oaks all around them. Soon winter would strip the branches bare and turn the wind to ice; but for the moment, the weather was crisp and perfect for a fall ride.

The once-distant club barn was slowly growing larger and closer. It was a long, low wooden building built in the classic Kentucky style. It was neat as a pin, painted brown, and surrounded by miles of split-rail pasture fences.

Carson turned to look at her as he drove. "I decided to play it safe this time and reserved two mares. I hope you aren't disappointed."

"Oh not at all," she assured him, and leaned back in her seat. "Some of my best horses were mares."

"I'm glad to hear that," Carson confessed. "I didn't know how accustomed you are to riding."

Donna glanced up at him in surprise. "Oh, very. My father owned some of the finest Arabians in Bahrain. I always had a pony as a child. I don't remember when I first climbed into a saddle."

She sighed and added wistfully, "One of the hardest things about leaving home was leaving my horse behind. A beautiful white Arabian mare with a mane like silk. I named her Sharara."

"What does that mean?"

Donna stared out across the green pastures and momentarily saw her horse standing in it. "It means 'spark' in Arabic. She had that kind of personality. Always a little spark of mischief in her eye."

Carson shrugged a bit and smiled, "Well, I can't promise a mischievous Arabian with a sparkling personality. In fact, I asked specifically for fat, sluggish mares with low energy and no ambition."

Donna's gentle melancholy vanished. She burst into laughter and turned to Carson to reply, "You must've thought I was going to fall right off the horse's back!" she teased.

"I like to plan for every contingency," he grinned, and turned the golf cart into the barn yard. A uniformed stable hand was already standing in it, and he greeted them as their golf cart pulled to a stop.

"Welcome back, Mr. Spade," the man smiled, and nodded to her. "Donna."

"Hello Charles," she smiled.

He gestured toward the barn. "I'm sorry Mr. Spade, but I wasn't able to fulfill your request for mares. All of our mares are still out this afternoon. Are you all right with a pair of stallions? I ask because I don't recommend them for beginning riders. Thoroughbred stallions are full of spit and vinegar, and they can be hard to handle."

Carson turned to her and looked a question, and she rolled her eyes and nodded.

"We're good," he assured the man, who brightened visibly. "I apologize, Mr. Spade. But if you'll just wait a minute I'll bring your horses out."

The man disappeared inside the barn and Donna climbed out of the cart to join Carson. She sauntered up to him and planted her hands on her hips.

"Are you sure you're comfortable with a stallion?" she teased with a mischievous smile. "You heard what he said."

Carson slid an arm around her shoulders and pulled her to his chest playfully. "I'll do my poor best," he promised gravely.

In a few minutes the man returned, leading a pair of saddled, coal-black thoroughbreds. Donna stared at them in admiration. The stables had been managed separately from the club, and so she hadn't had occasion to visit it often, or see the club's horses close up. But now, she had to say she was impressed with the quality of their thoroughbreds. The proud black beauties standing before them were magnificent horses. Their coats were gleaming, their manes were long and wavy, and their eyes were bright and curious.

Carson turned to her with a smile. "Which one does the lady like?" he asked; and Donna pointed to the smaller of the two.

"I'll take that one."

The stable hand brought out a mounting block, and Carson held the horse's head as she climbed up into the saddle. Donna settled in and took the reins as Carson climbed up on the larger horse with a quick, practiced motion.

He took the reins and turned the horse around. "Are we ready to go?"

"Ready when you are," Donna replied in a playful tone, and Carson nodded to a narrow trail head across the barnyard.

"After you, then."

Donna asked her horse to move on, and it trotted briskly across the yard and onto the narrow trail that threaded between two huge oaks and ran under the shade of a long row of trees. The sun peeped out briefly and sent a bright beam of golden light through the leaves, painting the ground with dappled light as the falling leaves swirled around her. It disappeared just as quickly, then shone out again twice as bright, then faded behind the clouds again.

She turned in the saddle to look back, and Carson was riding behind her a dozen yards or so. He caught her eye and called, "I feel like I need to apologize for scaring your friend away this morning. I hope it wasn't an inconvenience."

"Oh no," Donna told him, and turned back around. "He only had a few minutes. He had to catch a plane."

"Hmm," Carson murmured. "Well, I'm glad then. I was afraid I arrived at a bad time."

Donna smiled a little as she replied, "Tim is an old friend. I knew him when I lived in Paris. He's a movie director."

"Interesting. What movies has he directed? Maybe I've seen one of them."

"Oh, he runs a small start-up studio," Donna replied. "He's done mostly art house movies. Some of them have won awards at Sundance and other venues, but they're not the big-budget films most people go to see." She sputtered with affectionate laughter. "He likes deep explorations of human relationships and odd, esoteric subjects. His latest movie was a documentary on the snowy owl."

There was a long, pregnant silence behind her, and Donna turned just in time to see a decidedly unimpressed look flit across Carson's face.

It disappeared just as quickly, but it looked remarkably like jealousy, and she stifled a smile as she turned back again.

"Tim's a gifted director. I think he'll be a household name one day."

"Hm."

Donna smiled up at the cloudy sky and added, "He's about to begin shooting a new film in India. He wants me to come out with him and design the costumes."

There was another long, pregnant pause behind her. "Not in the next few weeks, I hope," Carson replied brightly.

"No," Donna assured him. "A wager is a debt of honor. I'll play your wife at all the parties, just as I promised." She turned to smile at him. "And I haven't decided if I'm going to take Tim up on his offer. I'd love to see India, though."

"Yes," Carson murmured. "It'd be an exciting opportunity. I wish I could tell you what to expect, but I've never been to India. I did have a business contact once who went there, but he died. They said it was complications of malaria, poor devil."

Donna turned in the saddle to stare at him. Carson returned her gaze with an expression of bland innocence.

"What?"

The multicolored leaves whirled past them like confetti as the path left the shade of the oaks and turned to follow the course of a wide creek. Red and orange leaves floated downstream on the clear water, and their approach startled a pair of quail. Two brown shapes burst from the bushes near the creek and flapped up into the air and away.

Donna's horse snorted in fright and tried to rear, but she leaned forward, moved the reins towards its ears, and urged it forward. To her relief, it landed and danced sideways nervously, but finally resumed a wary progress down the trail.

Carson's voice called, "Are you all right?"

Donna patted her horse's neck. "I think so. This big boy looks like a bit of a scaredy cat." She leaned down again to pat the horse's quivering neck and murmured into its ear.

Carson moved his horse up beside hers on the trail. "I'll go first," he offered. Donna was tempted to roll her eyes, but laughed instead.

"If you insist."

He smiled at her over his shoulder as he passed. "I'm trying to be gallant," he teased. "This is a first. Don't discourage me."

"You're being silly again," she told him. "I've seen you be gallant at least twice."

He turned to make a face over his shoulder. "Thank you. I feel better," he nodded, and she laughed at his expression as she followed him down the narrow trail.

The trail steadily became more remote and beautiful, winding through the rolling pasturelands and the untended thickets surrounding them. They moved through stands of massive oaks still crowned with clouds of bright leaves, stretches of pine forest carpeted with fragrant needles, and were surprised by unexpected clumps of flowers and fruit: fringelike petals of bright pink asters peeping through the underbrush, and wild blackberry bushes, laden down with fruit.

Carson paused to pull a few berries off the branches and tossed them to her. Donna laughed, caught them, and leaned over the horse's neck to let it lip the tasty berries from her hand.

Donna let her eyes rest on Carson's broad, straight back as he urged his horse forward.

Her gaze lingered on his shoulders as swayed in the saddle, and on his gleaming black hair, cut in a straight, precise line across the back of his neck. She'd never seen him unshaven, or with a single hair out of place; and she was beginning to wonder what he looked like with his inky hair a bit mussed, and a twelve o'clock shadow on his jaw.

She'd never seen him flustered or out of control; and suddenly she wanted to.

The trail ahead gradually widened out, and as soon as it was broad enough, Donna clapped her knees against the stallion's flanks and sent it flying past Carson's horse to rocket far ahead. She looked back over her shoulder, hair flying, laughing, and saw him look up and send his own horse after her.

She urged her mount to a flying gallop across the flat, grassy trail as it stretched out ahead of her. Her breathless laughter trailed behind her like a bright flag, billowing out behind her like a red banner for Carson to grasp as he gave chase. They raced over the trail as it broadened out into a flower-studded meadow and disappeared into the grass; and Donna was making for the eaves of an oak grove a few hundred yards ahead when Carson's horse flashed past her like a dark blur, blocked her way, and forced her to slow the horse to a canter, then to a trot, then to a stop.

Donna slid off the horse, gasping with laughter, and leaned against its flanks to catch her breath. But when Carson climbed off his horse and came walking over, she whirled and fled to the shelter of the trees. She could hear him behind her, and she slowed just enough to reach the first oak before he caught her.

Carson's laughter mingled with hers as he grabbed her arm and turned her to face him.

Donna fell back against the trunk of the oak, brimful of laughter; and in that breathless split second, their eyes met.

The smile in Carson's clear eyes slowly faded, and when he pulled her into her arms, her own were already curling around his neck. Thunder growled in the sky over them, and a few big drops spattered on the ground around them; but as the wind freshened and played with strands of her hair, Donna was only aware that Carson Spade was kissing her like she was the last woman on earth, and that it made her feel hot and cold and reckless and coy and totally and wonderfully unprepared. She smiled under his lips, moved deeper into his arms, and walked her fingers up his neck to muss his perfect hair.

Chapter Thirty Nine

"Talk to me."

Buster Hogan held the cell phone to his ear, and his frown slowly deepened as his hand's agitated voice gabbled on the other end.

"Buster, somebody flew a drone into the barn last night."

"What?"

The voice explained, "It was early in the morning. Jubal said he saw a drone up in the dark part of the rafters. It was drifting toward the doorway, and it zoomed out before he could knock it down."

Buster pinched his mouth into a hard, angry line. "What do you mean, it got out? What do I pay you clowns for?" he burst out. "Why do you think I make you jugheads spend the night in that barn, except to *protect* it?"

The other man's voice was thick with regret. "I'm sure sorry, Buster. But we're looking for animals or rustlers. Nobody thinks that somebody's going to send a *drone*."

Buster glanced up and caught sight of Martha Sue's pudgy, worried face in the bedroom doorway of their hotel suite. She was wearing a pink housecoat and her head was covered in pink curlers. He waved her away, and she shrugged and pattered off to the bathroom.

"It's the Spades," Buster fumed. "They're looking for their horses, and they know we've got 'em. I guess they thought I was gonna keep in my barn!" he scoffed. "Where are those horses now?"

"They're safe," the hand replied in a low voice. "We got 'em all in different places, all hid away real good. They're beauties, all right. Should bring a pretty penny."

"Keep 'em there," Buster retorted. "Don't move any of them unless you think somebody spotted them. And you tell those boys that if any one of 'em breathes a word about it, I'll take care of him."

The other man's voice was cold with fear. "Yes, sir."

"Is Jubal there?"

"No, sir. Today's his day off."

"Call him and tell him not to come back. He's fired. And tell the rest of the hands that if there's another drone on the Lazy H, they shoot it down on sight!" Buster barked and jammed his thumb on the red button.

He stood there in the middle of the hotel room with his eyes closed and his mouth closed tight in frustration; but he only had a minute before the phone trilled again. Buster picked it up and barked:

"What!"

His attorney's worried voice replied, "Buster, this is Ron. I'm calling because I just found out that Lambert's cutting a plea deal. He's turning state's evidence."

Buster felt the blood draining out of his face, felt his fingers going numb.

"Do we have any reason to be worried about that, Buster?"

Buster licked his lips. "Of course not," he replied with more assurance than he felt.

His lawyer's tone was wary. "I don't know yet what he told them. But I found out that the Spade lawyer went down there to talk to him a few days ago. I don't like it, Buster."

Buster licked his lips. "Was it Eugene?"

Ron's voice was faintly puzzled. "I think they said his name was Eugene, yes."

Buster closed his eyes and cursed soundlessly. It was a moment or two before he gathered his wits; but he finally did.

"Now look, Ron," he urged, "what we need to do is tell them that the guy's a con and a liar. He's telling them what they want to hear to save his own skin."

"Are you worried about what he might be telling them, Buster?" his attorney asked softly.

Fury flared up in him. "Why would I worry about that jailbird?" he retorted. "He's got a rap sheet as long as my arm, of course he'll make something up if a lawyer dangles a plea deal in front of his nose! I want you to get everything you can on him. We have to show that he's a born liar. Which he is."

There was a heavy silence on the other end of the line. Finally the attorney sighed, "All right, Buster. I'll get his priors and hope we can build a defense on it. We'll find out soon enough what he told the authorities. But I will say this: if it involves you, you're going to need a story you can back up with evidence. I can't make bricks without straw."

"What does this have to do with bricks?" Buster retorted in frustration; but the line was dead.

He hung up with a strangled profanity and stuck his hands on his hips. It was plain to see that Lambert had sung like a bird, and even his own lawyer didn't believe his story.

But he was pretty sure that even if Lambert had implicated him, the idiot couldn't prove what he said.

He'd been careful to cover his tracks. They had no evidence of what he'd hired them to do.

But them blundering into his hotel room, and now this, was going to be real bad for his reputation; and it was gonna be hard to sell his horses to Bertrand Blandings if the old man took him for a cheat and a liar and a horse killer.

The old goat didn't even trust unmarried guys.

Buster ground his teeth and paced in frustration. That stupid idea of the old man's should've made it easy for him to beat out Carson Spade; but instead, Carson had claimed he was a married man and got away with it, and he was being cussed all across Lexington because those three jailbirds had botched a simple job.

Life wasn't fair; but if he could only prove that Carson was lying about being married, he could even the playing field.

Buster crossed his arms and chewed on his thumbnail. Carson was as slick as grease, and lightning quick. So his best bet would be to trip up that little heifer who was pretending to be his wife. If he could catch her in a lie in front of Bertrand Blandings, Carson's whole story would fall apart.

He'd be shown up as a fraud. Untrustworthy. And that added up to...no sales.

Buster's eyes narrowed in fierce glee at the mental picture of Carson Spade standing in front of a frowning Bertrand Blandings and some of the most important buyers in the country...slowly dying inside.

But the only way to make that happen was to go to the same parties, and to get that woman in front of Blandings long enough to make her admit the truth; and so he was going to see to it.

Chapter Forty

Carson barely touched the small of Donna's back to guide her from the restaurant patio toward dozens of linen-draped party tables set up on the lawn outside. As they passed, a blues trio on the patio sent its jaunty music curling over their heads.

The two of them had arrived slightly and fashionably late to the garden party. The Tavern on the Green restaurant was hosting it for The Racing Alliance, and the sunny fall afternoon provided a perfect setting. Billowing white clouds sailed past in a blue sky, and the breeze across the lawn was pleasantly cool.

The dining tables were already more than half full, and the soft sound of conversation and laughter drifted out over the grass. Uniformed waiters came shuttling past holding bottles and platters as the two of them walked out to their assigned table.

Carson's eyes flicked ahead. He'd requested and gotten two seats at Table Five, because it happened to be the table that Bertrand Blandings was assigned. He noticed that his distinguished quarry was already seated there and was talking to a handsome older woman wearing a sweeping hat, a sleek black pantsuit, and a double loop of fabulous black pearls.

Carson's eyes returned to Donna as they approached the table. He'd told her to knock his eyes out, and she'd more than complied. She was wearing a hat with a huge white brim, a pair of big designer sunglasses, an off-the-shoulder sundress with a white bodice and a dark bell skirt, and a pair of delicate high heeled sandals that made his eyes drift to her slender ankles.

She looked like an heiress fresh from the Riviera, because everything she was wearing was from an exquisitely expensive fashion house. Every time she moved her left hand, the diamond ring flashed like a falling star.

Confidence welled up in his chest. Anyone who looked at Donna's glowing face, and the elegant way she held herself, would have no trouble believing that she was his bride.

Carson moved up a pace as they arrived at the table to pull out a chair for Donna. She turned to beam at him as she sank into it, and Bertrand looked up to smile, "You look very lovely this afternoon, Mrs. Spade."

"Thank you Mr. Blandings," Donna murmured and smiled first at him, and then at Carson. "I'm very happy."

Carson sat down beside her, took her hand, and gave her fingers a brief peck to flash their wedding rings.

Bertrand looked amused. "Well, I'm glad to see that business isn't posing a hindrance to your honeymoon." He turned his glance to Carson.

"Carson, do you think that you can tear yourself away from your lovely bride long enough to let my inspection team examine your horses?"

Carson made sure to retain his hold on Donna's hand as he turned to smile, "Certainly, Bertrand. Anytime you please! Just let me know what time's convenient."

Bertrand lifted his fork to his lips and nodded. "Next week would be convenient. How about Friday?"

Carson's delighted smile went all the way down to his heart. "Perfect!" he laughed and lifted his glass to his lips. Bertrand had actually suggested the next step in the sales process without having to be massaged. He was about to close, he could practically taste it.

He was beginning to hope that Bertrand might buy all three of the Seven yearlings.

Carson sighed happily and picked up a small menu on the plate in front of him. There were four meal choices, and as he perused the list a waiter stepped up and hovered discreetly at his elbow. Carson leaned back and turned his head, and the waiter leaned down to catch his quiet words.

"I'll have the shrimp and grits with a Roquefort salad on the side," he replied. "Black coffee to drink. Donna, what do you like?"

She twirled the menu in her fingers. "I think the *foie gras* with Italian plum appetizer," she murmured, "followed by lamb with mint sauce and a glass of Riesling."

"Very good."

The waiter took their menus and disappeared, and Carson stretched an arm across the back of Donna's chair and crossed his legs. He glanced back toward the patio, and stiffened to see a familiar face staring back.

Buster and Martha Sue had arrived, and Carson steeled himself to play defense for the rest of the outing. He leaned toward Donna to whisper, "Don't look now, but Buster's here. Game on, sweetheart."

She nodded just enough to show that he heard him. Carson glanced away and wished he could've known how Buster had managed to snag a spot at their table when he hadn't been assigned one.

The next thing he heard was Buster's sly voice drawling, "Well, it's like old home week, isn't it? Hello Bertrand."

The old man stiffened and shot him a frosty glance. "Buster. Martha Sue."

To Carson's annoyance, Buster took the seat next to Donna and settled right in. "Well, I know Carson and...what's your name again, honey?"

Donna turned toward him. "You can call me Mrs. Spade," she replied coolly. Buster held her eye and shook out his napkin. "Huh," he grunted in a skeptical tone.

Carson bowed his head to hide a smile and added, "You're looking well tonight, Martha Sue."

Buster's wife pulled her chair up to the table with some difficulty and shot him a flustered, but pleased look. "Thank you, Carson! I went shopping yesterday and fell in love with this dress."

"Yellow suits you," Carson told her solemnly, and was amused to see her giggle.

One waiter stepped in to take the newcomers' menu orders, and another returned to place Carson and Donna's drinks and entrees on the table.

"Thank you," Carson murmured thankfully, and took a sip of black coffee. He had the feeling his wits could use as much sharpening as they could get.

Buster got rid of the waiter and turned his attention back to the table. His eye snapped to Donna's glittering diamond ring, and he nodded toward it. "Well, I see you got that wedding ring you ordered from Switzerland, Mrs. Spade," he drawled, with a dry emphasis on her name. "Must've been a challenge to have a wedding without your rings."

Donna lifted her wine glass to her lips and looked away in apparent boredom, and Carson stepped in. "We had substitute rings, Buster," he replied shortly, and turned back to his meal.

"Where did you have your wedding?" Buster asked in a curious tone.

Donna turned to stare at him. "We had a private ceremony at a friend's house," she drawled.

"Here in Lexington?"

She met his eye. "Yes."

"Well, well," Buster smiled. "That just goes to show you how you can be fooled. I never would've figured you to settle down, Carson. I could've sworn I saw you with a little brunette last month in Sandy Creek. Must've been a relative or something, I guess."

Carson shot him a drop-dead look, but was spared the necessity of a reply when Bertrand cleared his throat and put down his fork. "How are your horses doing, Buster?" he asked in a cool tone.

Carson noticed that Buster's eyes gleamed with avarice. "They're doing great," he replied quickly. "Best horses at the auction! You need to bring your inspection team by to check 'em out. Don't take my word for it!"

Bertrand grunted but said nothing, and Carson enjoyed a grim relish as Buster cleared his throat and shut up at last.

The meal progressed without further unpleasantness, and when it was over at last, Carson shot a quick glance at Donna. He was afraid she might be daunted or upset by Buster's rudeness, and was relieved when she caught his eye and winked.

An unexpected warmth spread across Carson's chest. Donna was polished and feminine and utterly beautiful, but he was learning that she had no trouble holding her own. She was quick-witted and unflappable.

Nothing much seemed to trouble her. Not even Buster, and for a split-second he was almost envious of her equanimity. He'd spent most of the afternoon wishing he could punch Buster in the teeth.

Donna glanced away, and Carson let his eyes rest fondly on her. She'd taken off her hat at the table, and her copper-gold hair was twisted into a sleek, elegant chignon. His eyes drifted to the nape of her smooth neck, skimmed her bare shoulder, and ran along the graceful curve of her arm.

What's the matter with me, he thought suddenly. *It's a beautiful afternoon, I have a gorgeous woman with me, and I'm wasting my time worrying about Bertrand Blandings and Buster Hogan. The blazes with them.*

The blazes with the auction. The blazes with all of it.

I'm going to spend the rest of the evening dancing with the loveliest woman in Kentucky.

He blotted his lips with his napkin, threw it down, and leaned over to whisper in Donna's ear. "There's dancing inside. Come with me."

She tilted her head slightly toward him and smiled softly. Carson smiled back and pushed his chair back.

Bertrand looked up and objected, "Leaving us so soon?"

Carson spread his hands in smiling appeal. "Can you blame me?"

Bertrand sputtered with laughter. "No, I can't, young man. You two enjoy yourselves. I'll see you at the auction."

"I'll see you there, Bertrand," Carson replied, and stood to help Donna up.

She put her hand in his and rose gracefully, and he slid an arm around her waist as they walked across the lawn to the restaurant.

She turned to whisper, "Well, how did I do? Was I a convincing Mrs. Spade?"

Carson glanced at her and was snared by those laughing golden brown eyes. His smile faded, then shone out again.

"You were perfect in the role."

He surprised a look in those lovely eyes that made him catch his breath, but just for an instant. It was a flick of wistfulness. Almost of...

He smiled again and bowed his head as they walked. No, he couldn't assume.

As they breezed through the patio the blues trio playing there poured out a wailing lament with a bawling horn, a chattering drum and a musky saxophone.

The horn slid into another long wail as they passed into the dimly-lit restaurant. A cozy dance floor was tucked just behind the open doors, and Carson pulled Donna smoothly into his arms as they stepped out onto it. He swung her around, and around again, and she laughed and moved with him as light as air.

Carson closed his eyes and turned her this way and that. She felt so slender and frail in his arms, and an unexpected wave of tenderness swept him for this delicate, knowing creature. She didn't especially need protecting, but he suddenly felt protective toward her.

"You look serious," Donna observed in a soft, amused tone. Carson opened his eyes and smiled down at her. "Seriously pleased," he amended; but to his surprise, he didn't want to tell her more.

He wasn't sure he was comfortable with how he was coming to feel toward Donna. He wanted to thank her for helping him, but they'd long since moved past that. He wanted to kiss her, but they were in public. He cleared his throat, but to his surprise, the words he was trying to say stuck in his throat. Laughter had always jumped to his lips; but he was finding that deeper words died there. He looked away.

Donna's tone was still light and affectionate. "Don't tell me you're flustered," she teased. "Do I make you nervous? No, I can't believe it."

This time he did laugh, and a wave of relief followed after. They were back in familiar territory, and he raised her arm and twirled her to the music, then pulled her back into his arms.

"Do I look nervous?" he smiled. She tilted her head to consider him as they swayed, and she arched an eyebrow.

"I recognize that look," she murmured, with a twinkle in her eye. "And you're right, it's not nerves."

Carson swung her suddenly, then led her right out of the restaurant and into a secluded garden alcove just outside. He pulled her into the little corner behind the door, tightened his arms around her, and looked down into her laughing eyes.

What they told him made him take her chin in his hands, bow his head, and kiss her. He poured in it all the things that he couldn't bring himself to say.

I want you, certainly; but more than that. He was telling her that he wanted the light in her, that twinkle that shone out of her eyes when she laughed. That he wanted her relaxed, serene silence in quiet moments, her lithe body in his arms when they danced, the wry wisdom she'd reaped from her extraordinary life.

That he wanted all of her, and not just the pleasure of an easy dalliance for a little while.

The full weight of what he was saying suddenly hit him, and he paused in doubt and gave Donna a last, light kiss. He pulled back from her and smiled crookedly into her eyes.

He was beginning to scare himself.

Her fingers brushed a sprig of hair back from his brows. 'Well," she whispered, "You certainly are going for authenticity.

"But you better kiss me again just to be safe. We never know who might be watching."

Carson grinned and bowed his head again; but to his dismay, he couldn't keep his kisses from telling his secret, and wondered if Donna could hear what they were saying.

Chapter Forty One

Carson stood in the open doorway, took a deep breath, and set his hand lightly on Donna's back. They were a bit early, but the Keeneland auction room was already half-full of buyers, sellers, and agents.

He leaned forward slightly to whisper, "Well, this is it. The first day of the auction."

Donna smiled slightly. "Scared?"

Carson nodded. "Right down to my bones," he replied, and guided her down the center aisle to their seats. The auction room was built in a circle, with a central aisle dividing the seating into curving rows of green chairs. There was a small showing ring at the front of the room and a high raised desk behind it for the auctioneers.

Carson showed Donna to their seats on the right side of the room, right next to the center aisle. As they settled in, he handed her a copy of the yearling catalog page and a flyer for the day's yearlings up for auction.

She took it and scanned it curiously. "Which horses do you have up for auction today?"

Carson leaned over to point at the list. "There's ours. Seven Bells, Blue Streak, and High Spade."

Donna looked up long enough to murmur, "I don't think I ever saw your yearlings."

"You're right. I should've taken you by the stable to have a peek," he agreed. "But then again, since the poisoning attempt the Keeneland security has clamped down on visitors."

Donna gave him a troubled look. "Your horses didn't suffer any harm, you said?"

"No, thank heavens," he sighed, and unbuttoned his jacket.

Donna glanced back over her shoulder and scanned the other attendees. "Will Buster Hogan be here today?" she murmured in a faintly worried tone.

"Probably not," he sputtered. "Buster's horses almost never make Book One. These are the finest yearlings at the auction."

Donna stared at him with a whimsical smile. "Are we preening just a tiny bit?" she teased, and Carson felt his face go warm. He glanced at her out of the corner of his eye, then admitted:

"Maybe just a *tiny* bit."

Donna glanced down at the catalog page for Carson's horse, High Spade.

Hip No. 15. Consigned by Seven Spades Ranch.

High Spade, by Lickety Split and Moonlight Sonata.

She frowned and turned to Carson to ask, "What do all these other things mean?"

Carson pointed to the page and replied, "Those brackets show High Spade's parents, grandparents and great-grandparents. The graph below shows the sire Lickety Split's racing wins and history and his foals, and the second graph shows the same for the dam, Moonlight Sonata."

"I see," Donna murmured. "Preakness winner, very impressive, three other wins. Several purse wins for Moonlight Sonata as well." She shook her head. "Wonderful bloodline."

"We make sure of that," Carson told her with a hint of pride in his voice, and Donna smiled and looked at him again; but he refused to let her tease him a second time.

She glanced over her shoulder again and turned back to murmur, "Look, there's Mr. Blandings."

They both glanced discreetly, and as they watched the elderly gentleman strolled down the center aisle and took a seat on the opposite side of the big room. There was a young man with him, and Donna leaned toward Carson and whispered, "I think the other man is his son, Trevor."

Carson shot her quizzical look, and she shrugged, "I'm paid to know these things."

A group of latecomers came streaming in through the rear doors, and as they settled in two men walked up onto the showing ring platform and took their seats behind the high desk.

Carson inhaled and reached for Donna's hand. She took it with a smile and whispered, "Steady. You look like a father at his child's school play."

Her cheek made him sputter with laughter, and he squeezed her hand as a Keeneland employee led a beautiful palomino yearling out onto the small auction stage.

The auctioneer abruptly launched the proceedings.

"This year's Keeneland Yearling Auction is under way," he announced. "We'll start with a palomino gelding from Flamingo Farms in Florida. Let's start at one hundred thousand, one hundred thousand, yes sir, two hundred thousand, can I hear two hundred thousand, thank you, we have two hundred thousand, who'll make it three?"

Carson glanced out over the auction auditorium. It was hard to follow the action.

Potential buyers bid with the slightest nod or flick of a finger, and the auctioneer's machine-gun delivery was a blur.

"Five hundred thousand, five hundred thousand, yes sir, can we have six hundred, who'll bid six hundred?"

Carson's eyes slid to Bertrand Blandings. The old man was sitting in his chair, staring at the palomino yearling in an attitude of alert attention, with both hands folded over his walking cane. To Carson's relief, he seemed to be keeping his powder dry.

Donna smiled at him. "You might as well relax," she murmured. "You've done everything you can. And," she added wryly, "this isn't even your horse."

Carson turned around impatiently and settled uncomfortably in his chair. He could sense that Donna was amused with him, but he couldn't help it. The auction was going to be torture for him until it was over, and there were five horses scheduled before his.

Five auctions between him and the results of all his hard work. Five auctions until he found out if it had paid off, or not.

He fidgeted in his chair, unable to even pretend to be cool, as the palomino was sold off, followed by a magnificent bay, two chestnuts, and a beautiful black.

To his alarm, Bertrand Blandings had bid on, and bought, the glossy black yearling, and for a breathtaking seven hundred thousand dollars.

When Seven Bells, and then Blue Streak were led up to the auction ring, Carson sat in rigid suspense. It seemed hardly ten seconds from the time the auctioneer opened the bidding, to the sound of the gavel slamming down. He didn't even see if Bertrand Blandings had bid on his horses.

But by the time High Spade was being led up to the little auction ring, it was beginning to sink into Carson's brain that his first two horses had sold for a combined three million dollars.

Donna leaned over to squeeze his arm jubilantly. "Congratulations, Carson!" she smiled.

He hardly dared to exhale. "Did Bertrand Blandings buy them?" he croaked.

Donna glanced over at the elderly man. "It happened so fast, I didn't see."

She turned around, then nodded at the show ring. "Here comes your last horse," she smiled.

Carson watched as High Spade was led out onto the small show ring. The colt's proud bearing, strutting walk and glossy bourbon-brown coat made him the handsomest of their offerings that year, and Carson held his breath as the auctioneer began.

"The presentation of High Spade from the Seven Spades Ranch in Texas, who'll start the bidding? One hundred thousand, one hundred, two hundred, two hundred, three hundred thousand, we have three hundred thousand, who'll make it four?"

Carson chewed his nails and shot a glance toward Bertrand Blandings. To his delight, the elderly man raised a finger and the auctioneer replied, "We have four hundred, four hundred thousand, five, five hundred, five hundred thousand dollars. Five, five, thank you sir, five hundred thousand dollars."

Carson leaned back in his chair and did his best to look indifferent as the auctioneer repeated, "Six hundred, six hundred, yes, six hundred thousand, seven, seven, seven. Do I hear seven hundred thousand?"

Carson glanced at Bertrand Blandings out of the corner of his eye. The older man was sitting in his chair, as still as stone.

"Seven hundred thousand," the auctioneer repeated, then resumed, "Thank you ma'am, do I hear eight? Eight hundred thousand, nine, nine, yes, one million dollars, one million. One million two hundred thousand, thank you sir, one million five, one million five."

Carson felt Donna's fingers curling around his in silent jubilation as the auctioneer continued, "One million five, yes we have one million five. Two million, do I hear two million, two million. Two million dollars, we have two million dollars. Do I hear two million five? Two million five, two million five, thank you sir, three million, three million dollars. Three million dollars, three million? Yes, sir, thank you. Three million two hundred thousand, three and a quarter million? Going once, going twice, and"—the auctioneer banged the gavel down, "High Spade to the gentleman at three million dollars."

Carson closed his eyes in overwhelming relief, and Donna hugged him joyously. "Bertrand Blandings bought High Spade," she whispered. "You did it, Carson!"

Six million dollars, he thought to himself. *It's a record for us.*

He took a deep breath, gathered his wits, and turned to a beaming Donna.

"Hope you're rested up," he told her with a smile, "because we're going to celebrate. We're going to dance the night away!"

Chapter Forty Two

Luke Spade grabbed an apple off a bowl on the kitchen table and took an absent-minded bite. The kitchen was just about the only place in the ranch house that he felt safe anymore.

Their cook Conchita was jealous of her territory, and Kate and Heather knew by now to leave the downstairs kitchen alone.

He frowned down at the apple. Those two had hunted him like a pair of bobcats after a rabbit. They wanted to get Carson fixed up with a wife; and when Carson had escaped, they'd turned on *him* instead.

They'd roped him into dinner with one of Kate's old school chums, but they didn't tell him she was there specially to meet him. He rubbed his neck. He wasn't taking anything away from the woman, she seemed like a nice person, but she sure didn't have Kate's looks. And they'd all sat around the table smiling at him, like they thought he was going to propose to her on the spot. He'd gotten out of there as soon as he could; but it had been a nasty evening.

All because Carson had set them onto *him* to save himself; and he owed Carson for that, big time.

The kitchen phone trilled, and Luke took another bite of the apple, lobbed it into the trash can with a flick of his wrist, rubbed his hands on his jeans, and went to answer it. He lifted the receiver, leaned against the kitchen cabinets, and reached for a snack cake.

"Lo?"

There was a long, heavy silence on the other end, then a trebly, elderly female voice quavered, "Is that you, Luke?"

Luke felt the blood draining from his face. He dropped the cake and straightened up like a guilty schoolboy. "...Y-yes?"

"You know who this is, don't you?" the old woman's voice teased.

Luke's heart sank into his boots. "Aunt Marlene?" he croaked.

Laughter crackled over the line. "Me and your Aunt Irene have missed you boys," she told him. "We haven't seen or even talked to you in a long time."

Luke laughed weakly. He hadn't seen them for a long time sure enough. Their widowed aunts, Marlene and Irene, were sweet old ladies, but they had been the terror of his childhood. He associated their house with stultifying boredom, horrible food, a bursting bladder, and lots of lectures about school and soap.

Buck and Morg and even Carson had been old and wary enough to disappear when their mother wanted to visit her sisters; but she'd packed up all the helpless younger children and dragged them over there with her.

Including him.

Luke closed his eyes and swallowed. His aunts' house had been an old clapboard bungalow on the outskirts of Sandy Creek. The front room had been as neat as a pin, and their mother had made them sit with her on the couch, all in a squirming row, all of them having to go and hating to ask permission, while she and her sisters had gossiped for hours about hairstyles, and purses, and how much a pound of meat cost at the grocery store.

"Are you there, Luke?"

Luke opened his eyes. "I'm here."

"Well, we just wanted to call to tell you that we love you all, and that we miss you."

Luke rubbed his hair and nodded. "We—we love you, too, Aunt Marlene."

He could see his twin aunts in his mind still, their iron-gray hair coiffed up on their heads just the same, with matching cat-eye glasses and identical cotton dresses, except that one aunt's dress was always green and the other's always blue.

He rubbed the back of his neck and glanced out at the hall. After their parents had died, Big Russ and Miss Annie had paid for their maternal aunts to move to a nice retirement home in Albuquerque; and that was where they still lived.

Marlene's reedy voice pulled his attention back to the conversation. "We called because we're coming out to Dallas in a few days, and we'd like to come by and visit you boys. We haven't seen you in so long, you're probably all grown up now!"

Luke glanced up just in time to see Jesse walking down the hall. He waved one arm and made urgent faces, and Jesse paused outside the kitchen doorway.

"That—that would be great, Aunt Marlene," he stammered, and Jesse scowled and made a 'no' face. Luke added, "Would you like to say hello to Jesse, Aunt Marlene?"

Jesse shook his head vehemently and disappeared, in spite of Luke's wild gestures beckoning him to stay.

"Is he there, that grumpy little bear?" their aunt laughed.

Luke grumbled under his breath, then replied, "He was passing by, Aunt Marlene, but I couldn't catch him."

A new thought suddenly occurred to Luke, and he blurted: "Carson isn't here either, Aunt

Marlene, but I can't count the times he's told me he wished you and Aunt Irene would drop by. Like I said, he isn't here now, but he will be when you come to visit. I know he'll be hurt if you don't stay with him in his apartment. Ask him to take you around town to see your old friends, too. He's told me many-a time that he'd like to."

"Oh, Carson always was a sweet boy," his aunt sighed.

"Yes, ma'am," Luke agreed, and swallowed a spurt of laughter. "He's a real home body now, doesn't get out much. Doesn't even have a wife, and at his age, too. It's kind of sad, when you think about it."

"Oh, dear," his aunt fretted aloud.

"Yeah, Carson grew up to be a shy one," Luke smiled, and rubbed his nose as he leaned against the counter. "Hardly knows how to talk to a woman. I've always said that he could use some help in that department, but you know he'd never listen to anything we say to him.

"Someone else might help him find a wife, though, if we could ever find somebody to take an interest in him," Luke added soulfully.

His aunt's voice sounded concerned. "Why, of course your Aunt Irene and I would be glad to help Carson if we can," she replied earnestly. "We used to know all kinds of sweet girls in Sandy Creek that were his age. We'd be glad to call some of them when we get there, to see if they're still free. Maybe we can help him."

Luke sputtered, "That's real nice of you, Aunt Marlene. Carson's too proud to ask for help, or even admit he has a problem, but when he's a happily married man, he'll be grateful, I know."

His aunt's voice was heavy with pity. "Well, don't you worry, when we come over we'll set to work on him. We'll see to it that Carson gets introduced to plenty of nice girls."

Luke shook with silent laughter. "Oh, that's extra good, Aunt Marlene," he sputtered. "I'll sure be looking forward to your visit."

"Oh, we can't wait," his aunt assured him. "You tell Buck and Morgan and all your brothers hello for us.—How are you doing, Luke? I guess you have a nice girl of your own by this time, isn't that right?"

Luke's smile faded. "Oh yeah, I sure do, Aunt Marlene," he replied stoutly. 'We're practically engaged, that's a fact!"

His aunt's voice was as comfortable as a pat on the head. "Well, I'm glad to hear it," she replied. "It's good to know we can concentrate on just one boy, instead of having to divide our time."

"That's right," Luke agreed quickly. "Well, it's sure been nice talking to you, Aunt Marlene," he added. "Tell Aunt Irene hello for us."

"I will, dear. Bye for now!"

"Bye, Aunt Marlene."

Luke hung up quickly, closed his eyes, and exhaled in relief; then a sneaking smile curled one edge of his mouth.

When their aunts came to visit, Carson was going to get his; and he was going to hang around the house just to enjoy the show. Luke reached for the snack cake, opened the wrapper, and popped it into his mouth with a long chuckle before sauntering out of the kitchen.

Chapter Forty Three

"Well, boys, I don't have much news for you," the sheriff coughed. "Nothing to hang your hat on, anyway."

Buck and Luke stood in the courtyard outside the Seven ranch house with their arms crossed. Wilmer had just arrived and was standing in the open door of his cruiser.

Buck's face creased in a frown. "Nobody's seen anything?" he asked in a puzzled tone.

"Not that I've heard," the sheriff replied heavily. "Your family did a good job of getting flyers out and reporting to all the horse recovery groups, but so far all I've got is tire prints that match half of the trailers in the county, and a lost tourist who only saw men in hats and glasses outside your ranch that night, and wouldn't have known the rustlers, anyway."

Buck stared down at the ground and kicked at a pebble. "We're offering a fifty thousand dollar reward," he sighed. "You'd think that somebody would grab that money."

Luke pulled his mouth to one side and rubbed the back of his neck. "Well, I guess the ones that know where our horses are hid, are counting on getting a lot more out of 'em," he added glumly.

The sheriff turned to gaze out over the meadows lapping up to the side of the drive. "Well, there's no official record of anybody buying horses with your chip numbers," he sighed. "Of course, the buyers might not have checked, or might not have cared if the horses were stolen."

He cleared his throat and turned back to stare at them. "I'm afraid that's all I have so far on your horses. There's something else I'd like to ask you about, though," he added.

"There's been a drone flying around this neighborhood. The Lazy H called to report one inside their horse barn. You boys wouldn't have seen a drone flying around this way, would you?"

Buck pursed his lips and crossed his arms. He looked over at Luke, and then back at the sheriff.

"Drone?" he mumbled, and rubbed his nose. "You see any drones around here, Luke?"

Luke rubbed his chin. "Drones...no, can't say that I have. Course, the Seven's a big spread. Lots of places for a drone to get lost in."

"Uh huh." The sheriff inhaled and drummed his thick fingers on the top of his car. "Well, let me know if you do. It's not a crime to fly a drone over somebody else's land," he added in a flat voice, "but it is a crime to spy on somebody with a camera. Pretty hefty fine, too, if it can be proven. Maybe even time in the pokey." He nodded to them. "Well, I'll be getting along. I'll let you know if anything changes."

"Thanks for coming out, Wilmer," Buck told him, and walked over as the sheriff slid into the car. He leaned over the door and added, "Come by and see us when you're not working."

"I'll do my best, Buck. Luke." He closed the car door, cranked the motor and slowly pulled away; and as they watched the car go, Luke leaned toward his brother and murmured, "You think he knows?"

Buck watched as the police cruiser slowly shrank to a tiny white dot. "What do you think?"

Luke turned doubtful eyes to the fast-disappearing sheriff's car. "Well, it's done now, ain't it? It's not like we're going to do it again.

"Unless we need to."

Buck shook his head. "I don't think that line cuts any ice with the law," he replied. "But if we get in trouble, I'll just throw you under the bus." He reached and pulled his younger brother into a headlock, and Luke struggled and yelled as Buck ruffled his blonde hair.

"It's called taking one for the team," Buck laughed, and let him go. "You don't mind doing a little jail time, do you, Luke?"

Luke wrestled free and aimed a sideways kick at Buck's knee. "I'm not nearly as scared of that as I am of something else," he panted, and pulled his fringe of blonde hair out of his eyes.

"Yeah, what?"

Luke turned to squint at his eldest brother. "Aunt Marlene and Irene are coming out to visit."

Buck's mouth fell open. "What?" he demanded. "When did this happen?"

Luke grimaced and rubbed the back of his neck. "Aunt Marlene called the other day and said they were coming out in a few days." He shook his head. "They seem to be worried about Carson," he added.

Buck crossed his arms. "About Carson, huh? Where would they get the idea that Carson's in trouble?"

Luke shrugged a shoulder and looked away. "Guess because he's the oldest of us that ain't married yet."

"Yeah, well," Buck chuckled, "I guess that lets you off the hook. Marlene and Irene! I used to be as scared of those old ladies as if they were a pair of bears."

"That's not far wrong," Luke mumbled, and Buck laughed and clapped him on the shoulder. "Naw, I'm looking forward to seeing 'em again. It'll be fun to introduce them to Kate. They'll flip over Molly and little Russ."

"Easy for you," Luke retorted with a grimace. "You got a wife and a little baby for them to *ooh* and *ah* over. They ain't gonna be asking *you* why you aren't settled down."

"You *are* scared of 'em, ain't you?" Buck laughed. "Well, there's an easy enough fix. Get married to that girlfriend of yours. How long have you two been dating, anyway?"

Luke coughed and blurted, "Should we be talking about my love life right now? I thought we were looking for Carson's horses."

Buck sobered instantly. "Yeah, that's the real trouble Carson's in," he muttered. "I don't know. The only thing I can think of is maybe sending our hands out to nose around the county. See what they can see. Well, that, and go to the vets around here. See if anybody's asked them to remove a chip from a horse's neck."

"Well, I'm ready," Luke told him stoutly, and jerked a thumb toward a sleek motorcycle parked in the courtyard. "Let's go."

Buck leaned back and squinted at it doubtfully. "I'm not getting on that crazy thing," he announced. "You're skinny, you can ride it, but I'd likely knock it over. If you want me to ride along, you need to get you a Harley."

"Nah," Luke grinned. "This one's faster. Quieter, too. It doesn't sound like a semi with a bad muffler."

He walked up to the bike, threw a long jeans leg over it, and plopped down into the seat.

Buck watched him strap on a helmet. "Where are you going now?"

Luke stomped down, and the motor roared to life. "Off to see what I can see," he replied, and the bike curved around and zoomed off down the drive like a rocket blasting off.

Chapter Forty Four

"Well, that's the last one." The elderly Marlene Ingram pressed the red button on her cell phone and pursed her lips primly. "I think four girls is enough, don't you dear?"

Her twin sister Irene nodded. "They're all very sweet home town girls right in Sandy Creek, and they all know Carson. If he can't find one nice girl in that group, it's his own fault, not ours."

"I think so, too," Marlene replied. "Well! That's the last bit of business. Are your bags packed?"

Her gray-haired sister glanced toward a pair of 1974-vintage orange vinyl suitcases. "I'm ready. I can't wait to see Sandy Creek again, and all the family."

"Twenty five years," Marlene sighed, and her twin sister leaned back in her chair and declared, "Law, has it been that long? It doesn't seem like it."

Marlene stood up and pressed a button on a side table. "I know. When we left Buck was just a skinny little boy, and now he's in his forties. A grown man." She sighed and shook her head.

After a few moments there was a soft knock on the door of their retirement home apartment, and Marlene stood up and went to open it. A young man stood in the doorway and mumbled, "You need help with something?"

"Yes," Marlene told him. "We need some help with our luggage. We're going out front to wait on the van to the airport."

"Yes, ma'am." The fellow walked in, took a suitcase in each hand, and strode out without any sign of effort. Marlene watched him wistfully, then turned to her sister.

"Well, come on, Irene. We don't want to miss the shuttle."

The two of them gathered up their purses, a pair of sweaters, and two umbrellas in case of rainy weather, and sallied forth to embark on their first big trip since 1993.

Irene turned to carefully lock their apartment door, then followed her sister down the quiet hall. They were wearing matching dresses and shoes, just like always, with one in blue and the other in green.

The big retirement home shuttle was already parked at the curb when they walked out the big glass doors. The young man was standing at the shuttle doors, and he extended a hand. "Your bags are in the bus, ladies. Where you off to?"

Marlene gave him her hand and stepped up into the bus carefully. "We're on a mercy mission," Irene told him. "We're going to visit our little nephews, and one of them is shy. He's having trouble finding a wife."

"We're going to fix him up with a nice girl."

The man shook his head and grinned. "Well, good luck. You ladies take care."

The two sisters walked to the center of the bus and settled in a seat in the precise middle. The bus doors closed with a *whoosh* and the driver pulled the bus around the circular drive and out into the street outside.

Irene watched the retirement home grounds slide past. "Who's going to pick us up in Dallas, sister?"

Marlene fished a handkerchief out of her big, dark bag and blotted her lipstick on its snowy surface. "Buck said he was going to come down to pick us up and drive us back home with him. Such a nice boy," she murmured, then closed the bag with a snap. "It'll be nice to see the ranch again, too."

Irene nodded. "I can't wait," she replied, and pulled a list out of her pocket. "Now here's a list of the girls we chose, and their addresses and numbers. I even added little notes to each one, to remind Carson of how he knows them. Most of them are his old school friends, but one works at the post office."

Marlene shot her an affectionate look. "You're always so thorough, dear," she replied approvingly. "I'm sure he'll be grateful."

Irene folded up the paper with a snort. "It's small wonder that Carson's having trouble finding a wife," she retorted. "His grandfather Russ was such a rough man, and after Brenda and Clayton died all their children fell into his hands. Russ Spade raised his grandsons by the hair of the head."

"I'm afraid that's true," Marlene sighed. "I tried to warn Brenda that she was making a mistake when she married into that family, but you know what young girls are when they're in love. Her in-laws lived out in the Texas backcountry and hardly even had electricity! How were her boys supposed to learn how to talk to girls when there weren't any girls within twenty miles? Poor things."

Her sister pressed a comforting hand on her arm. "Well, we're going to set that right, at least for Carson, bless his heart.

"Help is on the way."

Exactly two hours later the sisters marched down the long covered tunnel running from their plane to the airport concourse, shoulder to shoulder and clutching their handbags. When they emerged at last, they paused to scan the waiting area. A tall, broad-shouldered man with dark hair and a square jaw slowly stood up.

"Aunt Marlene? Aunt Irene?"

Marlene's mouth fell open, and Irene clapped a hand to hers. "Law, it's Buck!" Irene gasped. "Boy, I wouldn't have known you, you've grown so tall!"

Buck strode up and planted a kiss on each powdered cheek, and they took turns hugging him.

"You're the spit and image of your father," Irene marveled.

"Nonsense, look at his eyes," Marlene scoffed. "He's Brenda all over again!"

Buck beamed down at them. "It sure is good to see you two again," he sighed. "Come with me and I'll get your luggage. I have a car waiting around front. We'll be back home before you know it."

"Oh, it'll be so good to see the ranch again," Marlene told him fervently, but Buck shot her a sideways glance.

"Well, it ain't exactly the way you ladies remember," he coughed. "There's a lot happened since you left. We got a big new ranch house, and here lately me and Morg remarried."

Both of them gasped aloud, looked at one another in delight, and them at him.

"Tell us all about it!"

"How long ago?"

"Nice Texas girls, I hope?"

Buck shook his head and laughed. "I'll tell you all about it on the drive up. Me and my wife Kate have a daughter Molly, and a new baby, little Russ. And Morgan and his wife Heather are expecting triplets!"

The two elderly women uttered a soft, united squeal of joy, and the other passengers flowing

by turned their heads to glance at them as
they passed.

Chapter Forty Five

"Now Aunt Marlene, you and Aunt Irene aren't gonna spend your time here cooking. You're barely been here two days, and you're our guests. It wouldn't be right."

Buck shot them a worried smile and glanced back at the kitchen doorway, where a frowning Mexican woman was standing with her hands planted on her hips.

"Nonsense. We haven't had a proper kitchen in over twenty years," Irene retorted. "It's a pure pleasure to have a big gas range again, and it'll be fun to make a big chicken dinner to welcome Carson back home from Kentucky. You did say he was coming back home today?"

Buck nodded in nervous acknowledgement. "That's right, Aunt Irene. But there's so much to do here at the ranch, and it's such a nice day outside, it seems like a shame to be all cooped up inside. Don't it?"

"Shoo now," Marlene clucked. "We're making a big welcome home dinner tonight, and that's all there is to it. Won't it be nice to have everybody around the dinner table again, just like old times!"

"Yes ma'am," Buck stammered, and rubbed the back of his neck. He glanced back at the doorway again, but this time it was empty. He rubbed his jaw and shot them a troubled look. "Carson called us from Kentucky and said he was bringing a friend home with him," he mumbled. "A lady friend."

They both looked up from the stove. "Lady friend?"

"That's right," Buck smiled wanly. "He said her name was Donna, and that they met at his club, but that's all he said. He sold all our horses up there, so maybe she was good luck to him."

The two ladies looked at one another, and then at him. "Are you quite *sure* that's what Carson said?" Marlene pressed.

Buck looked confused. "Why yes ma'am," he answered. "I just thought I'd let you know there'll be one more at the table tonight."

"Thank you dear," Marlene replied faintly. "Now shoo, boy, and let us get our work done."

"As long as you're sure," Buck grumbled, and walked out with a nod.

Irene turned to her sister. "Now what do you suppose *that's* all about?" she demanded. "Carson can't come in here with some strange woman from who knows where, when we've already hand picked four lovely Sandy Creek girls for him!"

"There must be some mistake," Marlene told her comfortably.

Irene frowned as she dropped potatoes into a pot of water. "No dear," she replied with a troubled look. "I think I know what has happened. I'm afraid Carson has fallen into the hands of a scheming woman. You know Luke told you that Carson's as shy as a mole. He said that Carson couldn't get a woman to save his life. If Carson's taken up with one, that must mean that the woman got *him*."

Marlene pulled her mouth down like a baby. "Oh, dear."

"Yes," Irene grumbled. "Well, I'll tell you one thing. We've travelled hundreds of miles and spent a considerable amount of trouble to come out here to help Carson. And I for one am not going to let some brazen adventuress knock all that on the head." She dropped the last potato into the water with a loud *plop*.

Marlene gave her sister a pleading look. "*Adventuress* sounds a little strong, dear. I'm sure if Carson likes her, she must be a sweet girl."

"Don't be naive, Marlene," her sister admonished. "You always were too quick to take up for people. No, I'm sure of it, it only makes sense. How can she be a sweet girl when she practically had to chase Carson down, like a cougar after a deer? Poor boy—he didn't know enough about women to get away!"

"Well..."

"You remember what happened to poor Morgan with that awful woman he married," Irene nodded. "Cece, wasn't that her name? I could see what she was all the way from Arizona, just from the stories the family told me about her," she snorted. "It would be a crying shame if that happened again to another of these boys."

"Well, yes, I suppose," Marlene objected, "but we don't even know this girl. And if

Carson likes her, maybe we don't need to fix him up with anybody else."

Her sister fixed her with a scornful look. "We're not changing our plans one iota, Marlene. Now I'm willing to give this new girl a chance, but if I see that she's a huntress like Cece, I will do everything in my power to send her packing!"

"Law, sister," Marlene cried in alarm. "Let's not go too far! We came here to find Carson a woman, not to make him lose one."

Irene pinched her lips into a thin, deliberative line. "That depends on the kind of woman she is," she nodded.

"We'll have the answer soon, never fear."

Chapter Forty Six

"Well, here we are. Home sweet home."

Donna glanced up at the three-story ranch house as Carson pulled the gleaming rental car around the circular courtyard and up to the front door. The enormous house was a breathtaking fusion of glass and natural stone, elegant and earthy and modern.

It was twice and three times the size of the Turf Club mansion, and Donna turned to Carson with an arched eyebrow and a smile.

"I must say, I'm impressed. Your home is beautiful."

Carson grinned at her. "It'll be even more beautiful now that you're here," he told her gallantly, and seemed amused to see the blush that she could feel blooming over her cheeks.

"I called ahead and told my family I'd be bringing you back with me. Everybody's excited to meet you," Carson added, and reached out to give her hand a warm squeeze.

Donna returned his smile and clasped the hand he gave her, but her pleasure was wrestling with confusion. She wasn't exactly sure what Carson meant by bringing her home to meet his family. Was this a sweet nightcap to their pleasant acquaintance, a generous 'thank you' for helping him sell his fabulous horses, or did he see it as something more serious?

And more importantly—how would she respond if he did?

Those unanswered questions made the Spade family's reception of her loom much larger in her mind that it might otherwise have done; and Donna tried to calm the butterflies in her stomach as Carson opened his car door and climbed out.

She glanced up at the glass wall towering high overhead. She'd seen many fabulous mansions in her travels, starting with the one she'd grown up in; but she hadn't been prepared for how huge Carson's home was. The front gate had been massive, the driveway had seemed to roll on for miles, and he'd given her to understand that even *that* was only a small fraction of the ranch.

It was one thing to know abstractly that a man was fabulously wealthy; but it was quite another to see those numbers translated into ranch land and houses and cattle and horses and cars. Even with her experience of the world, she found it a bit intimidating.

Donna folded her hands in her lap and waited for Carson as he walked around the car to help her out. He walked up and opened her car door with a smile, and she'd only just slid one leg out when the front door of the mansion swung open, and a muscular giant came walking out. The man was quite handsome in a rough, careless way, and he grinned from ear to ear at the sight of them.

"Well Carson," he called, "we've been waiting for you! You gonna introduce me to your lady friend?"

Carson gave her his hand, and as soon as she was standing he gestured to the big man and smiled, "Donna, this is my brother Buck. Buck, this is my friend Donna Bouchet."

The big man stepped up and offered her a huge brown hand. Donna shook it limply, and found it warm and rough.

"Sure am glad to meet you, Donna. Come on inside, everybody's waiting on you two."

Carson's smile froze. "Everybody?" he echoed faintly.

The look that passed between the two brothers seemed to be an unspoken message. "Yeah," Buck coughed, and rubbed his nose. "Aunt Marlene and Irene have come to visit, and they whipped up a welcome home dinner just for you two."

Donna's eyes moved uncertainly to Carson's face. For a split-second the look on it was almost comical in its dismay, but the next instant it was gone, and the smooth, smiling Carson she knew was back again.

"Well! By all means then, let's go inside." Carson turned to offer her his arm, and she took it with a smile she hoped didn't look nervous.

Buck led them through the massive front door, and they walked through a sunny atrium into a big, airy space with a sitting area and a fireplace on the right and a huge, multi-level staircase straight ahead.

The front of the house was empty except for them, but they followed the sound of talking and laughter back behind the staircase and into a back hall.

Buck led them to the dining room door and stood back to let them pass. Carson turned to give her a reassuring smile, and he took her hand and led her inside.

Donna's heart quickened as she followed, because their entrance was greeted with cries of welcome. Every face at the big table turned toward them, and two elderly women that she took to be Carson's aunts rose from the table and rushed to throw their arms around him.

Carson released her hand to hug his aunts, but to Donna's ear, his voice sounded a bit nervous when he murmured, "Aunt Marlene, Aunt Irene! What a lovely surprise."

Donna noticed that the two women were twins wearing matching cotton dresses and sensible shoes, and that their eyes devoured Carson's face in what looked like a mixture of affection and pity.

"We whipped up a welcome home dinner for you Carson," one of them informed him.

"And we have a surprise for you after," the other added.

Carson cleared his throat, rested his hands lightly on their shoulders, and turned them to face her. "Ladies, this is my friend, Donna Bouchet. She's visiting from Kentucky."

Donna nodded and smiled politely. "It's very nice to meet you," she murmured, but she couldn't help noticing that they seemed less than excited. They two elderly women stared at her through their cat-eye glasses in what looked like dismay.

"Oh...how do you do, my dear."

There was an awkward silence, broken finally by Buck. "Well don't just stand there Carson, you and Donna come and sit down at the table. This chicken smells delicious, and we've been waiting for you."

Carson smiled at her and squired her to a seat at the far end of the table. He held the chair for her as she settled in, then sat down beside her.

A beautiful redheaded woman on her other side smiled and murmured, "I'm Kate, Buck's wife. We're so glad you could come and visit."

Donna nodded and smiled. "I'm pleased to meet you."

Kate leaned toward her slightly and whispered confidentially, "Don't let this place intimidate you. It can be a bit much at first."

Donna smiled. She did feel a bit overwhelmed, but she didn't want to admit it. She took a sip of water and murmured, "It certainly is a beautiful estate."

"I'll help you settle in after dinner," Kate offered. "The guest room's very comfortable, and if you forgot to pack anything, I'll lend you what you need."

Donna shot her a look of gratitude. "Thank you, Kate. You're very kind."

Kate took a forkful of potato salad. "I just remember my first few days here. But I got used to being pampered pretty quickly," she laughed.

Donna smiled. *That is going to be nice*, she thought to herself. *I get to be the guest for a change, and not the host.*

Carson dug into a platter of fried chicken with a pair of tongs. He glanced over at her. "Would you like some fried chicken, Donna?"

"Please," she smiled. "It smells wonderful."

Carson placed a fragrant, golden piece of fried chicken on her plate. He nodded toward the other people at the table. "Let me tell you who all these characters are," he offered. "My aunts you know, and Buck there. The ugly punk beside him is Luke, the grouchy one a chair down is Jesse."

Donna reached for a biscuit and smiled as she matched the faces and names.

"The beautiful blonde on the other side of the table is Morgan's wife Heather, and Morgan's beside her. We have two brothers Awol. Will's an Air Force pilot out at Langley in Virginia, and Chase is attending a communications conference in Los Angeles."

Donna nodded and filed the information away; and Carson's elderly aunt cleared her throat and asked:

"How did you and Donna meet, Carson?"

Carson glanced over at her mischievously and took her hand. "Well, Aunt Irene, I was just minding my own business at the club up in Lexington. I was like a little innocent deer in the forest, when Donna caught me like a big cat and dragged me away into the bushes."

The table erupted into laughter, and Donna stared at Carson in wry exasperation. "That's not the way I remember it," she objected, as he leaned over to give her a peck on the cheek.

And yet, when she glanced around the table, she couldn't help noticing that everyone seemed to think the joke hilarious, except Carson's elderly aunts.

They were staring at him with horrified expressions; and only a direct question from one of the brothers broke that look of undisguised shock.

Chapter Forty Seven

Carson leaned over and gave Donna a warm, lingering kiss on the doorway of the guest room. She closed her eyes in bliss and savored Carson's attention to detail. He was an artist when it came to love; his technique was advanced, but varied. The touch of his lips often began with pastel shades of sweet and playful, gradually deepened to tones of naughty, and melted into the midnight blues of more adult moods.

Most of his kisses were an unspoken question; and she noticed that the question was gradually intensifying.

Carson leaned back and played with a sprig of her golden hair. "I'll let you settle in for the night," he sighed, and released it. "You're bound to be a bit tired."

Donna opened her eyes and stifled a sigh of appreciation. "Not especially," she assured him with a smile, and looked up into his face with a mischievous expression. "But it is getting a bit late."

"I'll show you around the place tomorrow," Carson promised softly. "Maybe take you to lunch in town. Though," he laughed, "the only good restaurant around here burned down about a year ago. Maybe we'll find a nice quiet place."

Donna laughed with him. "That would be lovely. Good night, Carson."

He leaned in and gave her another slow, sweet kiss. "Good night, Donna," he whispered, squeezed her fingers, and stepped back into the hall. Donna stood in the doorway and gazed after him as he waved and turned to descend the stairs; and she sighed and closed the door.

She turned and glanced around her. The guest room, she had to say, was on a par with The Turf Club in elegance, and surpassed it in convenience. It was as modern as the club was antique, with bold, giant-sized paintings in vivid reds and browns, an oversized bed with an orange-red satin coverlet, and one wall made entirely of glass.

Donna meandered over to it to enjoy the breathtaking view. The world below her second-story window was bathed in the deep lavender of twilight. She could just make out what looked like a massive barn off in the middle distance, with a few homely golden lights in its windows; and beyond that, only deepening shades of night as far as she could see.

She hugged herself as she gazed out across that evening panorama. It would be so easy to slip into the fantasy, to imagine herself the real Mrs. Carson Spade. She couldn't deny that she was dreaming of that; but her heart was warning her against it.

Carson hadn't hinted even once that he was thinking of her as his real wife. And even if he did propose, she was unsure that she'd agree to be his wife. Carson was gorgeous, intelligent, wry, charming. She'd certainly be delighted at first; but what about a year later, two years, five years?

After the honeymoon glow faded, would her wandering heart whisper to her again of the beauties and the wonders she had not yet seen?

She wasn't sure that she could trust herself to settle down, after having enjoyed what the wide world had to offer.

Donna hugged herself as if she was cold. Carson wasn't likely to be able to settle down for the long term either. He was a playboy, a man of the world.

The two of them weren't suited to married life. The past, and the odds, were against them.

A gentle melancholy sifted down over Donna as she stood there at the window. She nibbled a pink forefinger, and Carson's diamond ring flashed on her hand.

Donna stared at it sadly. It was a shame, really; Carson was the first man she'd ever imagined marrying. They were alike in so many ways. They understood one another. If there was ever a man she might settle down with, Carson was that one.

But she couldn't see the future; and that made it hard to know what to do.

Donna stared up at the sky with a wistful expression. It felt a little lonely, not having anyone to ask for advice. Not that anyone else *could* answer this question for her; but it might be comforting to have a confidant.

Donna frowned faintly. She had no religious faith at all, but at that moment, she understood why some people did. It must be a comfort to ask God for advice, and to feel as though you heard from Him.

But of course that was unlikely. She glanced up at the sky again, then turned with a sigh and prepared to go to bed. If there was a God, He had more important things to do than to tell her who to marry. To create a special miracle for two wandering hearts.

She was going to have to figure it out for herself.

Chapter Forty Eight

"Well, what do you think of good old Sandy Creek?"

Donna looked up to see Carson smiling at her from across their little table. They were seated on the balcony of a tiny restaurant overlooking the main street of Sandy Creek. It was a bright, sunny day, with the town bustling past beneath them; or at least, bustling as much as possible for a place with a population of 10,000.

She raised a glass of wine to her lips. "I think it's charming," she murmured. "It's almost like a toy town spread out on a child's quilt. There is the courthouse, there is the fire station, there is the grocer's. And here and there, people going on their errands. One to the school, one to the shop."

Carson glanced down at the street. "I used to hate it here," he mumbled, and took a sip of wine. "I felt trapped. Like I was going to be stuck in the back of beyond my whole life."

Donna raised her brows in sympathy. Carson wasn't a man to confess vulnerability, and she was touched that he'd opened up to her.

"And now?" she asked gently.

His eyes returned to hers. He shrugged and set the glass down. "Oh, I don't know. I still spend as much time away as at home. But I don't hate this town anymore. I guess I got a lot of traveling out of my system. I satisfied my curiosity."

His bright blue eyes suddenly held hers, and Donna felt her mouth dropping open slightly in dismay. She coughed and looked away, and was relieved when he smiled and added, "Maybe it's because I'm on the high side of thirty. Getting sentimental in my old age."

Donna exhaled in relief. Carson had reverted to his usual wry, smiling self; and she laughed with him. "You're hardly in your dotage," she teased, and he smiled and nodded.

"Thank you."

Her lips curved up. She leaned back in her chair and gestured toward the street. "I must say, I don't think it deserves to be disliked. This is a pretty little place."

"Oh, I'll give you that," he agreed, and glanced down again. "And like I said, it's kind of grown on me.

"It took twenty years, but still."

Donna laughed at his expression, and the waitress arrived to set a platter of nachos down on the table. "You folks ready to order?" she smiled, and fished a notepad out of her apron.

Carson smiled as if to invite her to go on, and Donna murmured, "I don't understand everything on the menu," she confessed. "What are Rocky Mountain Oysters?"

The waitress stared at her in open mouthed surprise, and Carson cleared his throat and replied, "Maybe you should forget about that one. I've had the beef fajitas. They're pretty good. You might try the taco salad bowl."

Donna shot him an uncertain glance and murmured, "I think I'll have the mountain oysters. I like to try new things."

The waitress smiled and volunteered, "They ain't oysters," but Donna set her mouth and handed back the menu. "That's all right. I like to be surprised."

The waitress shrugged. "Okay." She turned to Carson. "What would you like, sir?"

Carson handed her the menu. "I'll have the beef fajita plate."

The waitress nodded. "I'll be back in a few minutes, folks."

After she left, Carson leaned back in his chair and gave her such a look of amusement that she coughed and asked, "What is that dish, really?"

Carson's eyes twinkled. "I think you should try it without knowing. After all, you like to try new things, don't you?"

She shook out her napkin a bit nervously. "Yes."

"Novelty is half the pleasure of eating out," he smiled. "And you wouldn't want to prejudice yourself without giving the dish a fair chance," he added, with a twinkling look.

Donna stared at his expression with a flick of alarm, but replied" "Just so."

She maintained an air of unconcern as she picked nachos out of a little plastic basket; but when the waitress arrived fifteen minutes later, she cast an envious glance at the plate of sizzling beef and sauteed onions that the waitress set down in front of Carson. It smelled surprisingly good.

By contrast, the plate set down in front of her was a mound of deep-fried meat nuggets served with a little dish of cocktail sauce.

"Enjoy your meal, folks."

Carson shook out his napkin and took a bite of the beef. "*Mmm*," he groaned, and rolled his eyes. "That's good."

Donna picked up her fork, stared at her own meal, and picked at it experimentally. When she looked up, Carson's laughing eyes were on her, and she took a reluctant bite.

He took a sip of wine. "Well, what's the verdict?"

Donna frowned. "It's...different," she murmured. "It has a tiny bit of a gamey taste, but it's...almost like chicken."

Carson's eyes were brimful of laughter, and he nodded toward the little dish. "Try it with the cocktail sauce," he suggested, but she blotted her lips with her napkin and shook her head.

"No, I don't think so," she murmured. "I don't think I like it."

Carson gave her a smiling glance, but the laughter had faded from his eyes. "I guess new isn't always better," he replied softly, and held her eye.

She gazed at him a beat longer than necessary, then lowered her eyes and confessed, "I'm learning that."

"I am too," Carson murmured, and this time his tone was serious. Donna's glance fluttered up to his, and her face went slightly warm.

The waitress arrived and smiled at them and clasped her hands. "How are you folks doing?"

"I'd like to reorder," Donna told her. "I didn't like these as much I thought I would."

The waitress gave her a knowing look. "Lots of people find that out," she nodded. "What would you like instead?"

Donna's glance flicked to Carson. "I'll have what he's having," she replied.

"Coming up," the waitress told her, and leaned over to take her plate.

Chapter Forty Nine

Luke Spade pulled his motorcycle into a parking place outside the feed and tack store in downtown Sandy Creek. He was there to pick up a new blanket and bridle for his horse.

Or at least, that was his story, and he was sticking to it.

He climbed off the bike, stood it up, and locked it before planting his hands on his narrow hips and surveying the town. Him and all his brothers had plastered reward posters from one end of it to the other, and he had to believe that *somebody* had seen *something*.

If that didn't flush some witnesses out of the bushes, he didn't know what would.

Luke jammed his hands into his jeans pockets and sauntered into the feed store with his head down. Maybe if he hung around and made himself available, somebody would pull him aside.

The familiar smell of the feed and seed embraced him as soon as he walked in: sawdust, tobacco, machine oil, and hot dogs. He meandered to the front counter, fished a pickle out of a big jar, and munched it while the cashier processed a customer.

The man turned to him with a smile. "Well, Luke, how's things over at the Seven? You ever get those horses back?"

Luke shook his head regretfully. "Nope. No tips at all. That big fat reward we put out's still unclaimed."

The cashier handed his customer a receipt, nodded in farewell, and then turned to Luke. He stuck his hands on his hips.

"Huh," the clerk muttered. "Guess nobody has anything to tell," he opined, and scratched his ear.

"Looks that way," Luke agreed glumly, and glanced around. The store was tolerably busy for a weekday, with ranchers and farmers milling around. Luke threw his hand up in greeting as some of them walked by; but though they greeted him, none stopped to talk.

Luke sighed and was just about to go for a hot dog inside a countertop case, when his eye grazed an odd figure half-hidden behind a shovel display.

The man was staring at him intently, and he seemed to be beckoning.

Luke frowned, but straightened up. The man glanced over his shoulder and back again, then waved him over with an urgent gesture. Luke followed him in puzzled silence, and as he walked the man turned and disappeared.

Luke drifted after him into a narrow, deserted aisle full of lawn care equipment. He walked to the dark end of the aisle and found the stranger waiting for him next to the grass seed section.

"You one of the Spades?" the man hissed.

Luke frowned and crossed his arms. "That's right."

The man looked like a ranch hand, young and lean and tan; but his eyes were strained. He licked his lips.

"Look, if I tell you something, will you forget that I said it?"

Hope jumped in Luke's heart. "I don't even know who you are, Mister," he drawled. "I couldn't tell on you if I wanted to. Which I don't."

The young man gave him a wary look. "All right then. Is that reward money still up for grabs?"

Luke tried not to let his excitement show on his face. "It sure is. If you can get our horses back, I'll give you a check right now."

The hand licked his lips and nodded. "Deal. Well, I saw a white horse trailer turn off onto a dirt trail off County Line Road. It's an abandoned farm people call the Old Folsom Place."

"I know where it is," Luke replied. He was beginning to wonder if the man was trolling him, and added, "Is that all?"

"No." The man looked back over his shoulder, then went on. "It was the Lazy H hands, and they unloaded a pair of thoroughbreds. Real pretty horses."

Luke frowned. "How do you know this?" he demanded.

The man glanced away with an embarassed look and rubbed the back of his neck. "I was out there with my girl," he mumbled. "We saw 'em come in, and unload the horses, and put 'em into an old tumbledown barn. Then most of 'em left, but some of 'em stayed behind.

They didn't see us, and we snuck out another way."

"How long ago?" Luke demanded, and the young man replied, "Not an hour ago. I came into town hoping to find one of you Spades. If you hurry they might still be out there!"

Luke leaned back and assessed the boy; then he reached into his shirt and pulled out a check book.

"Got a pen?"

The boy fumbled in his pockets, then produced a pen, and Luke pushed the checkbook up against a box and scrawled across it.

"There you go," he told the eager man, and handed him the check. "Fifty thousand dollars. Thanks for the tip."

The young fellow stared at it, as if he couldn't believe his eyes; then looked up at Luke. "Thanks, mister. Good luck."

Luke clapped his shoulder as he blew past and right out of the store. He grabbed his bike, mounted it, and backed it out of the parking space.

He kicked it to life and roared away down the street, out of town, and toward the old Folsom Place as fast as he could make the bike fly.

Fifteen minutes later, he arrived at the old abandoned farm. Luke pulled his motorcycle off the road and onto a narrow dirt track that sliced through a thick stand of pine trees. There was a locked pasture gate a few dozen yards down the track and a sign that read *No Trespassing*; but he just killed the motor, turned the bike into the brush, and walked it around the barrier.

He continued walking the bike down the narrow dirt track and scanned the woods around him as he moved. He was on private property and dangerous legal ground, but that was only a problem if he got caught.

He didn't intend to get caught.

The pine thicket began to thin out slightly, and when the track left it and stretched out into a long, flat, open stretch of meadow, turned the bike off of it and back into the cover of the trees. He pushed the bike up a gradual incline to the flat crown of a small rise. He propped the bike against a tree and pulled a small black case out of his saddlebag.

He glanced warily through the trees. There was a big flat pasture rolling away for ten acres or more to the left of the little dirt path, and there were two trucks, a horse trailer and a knot of men standing around on the far side of it.

He opened the case, pulled out a pair of high-powered binoculars and lifted them to his eyes.

The distant scene jumped into focus. Luke adjusted the lenses and the resolution sharpened. He could see that the men there were dressed like ranch hands, and while he couldn't make out faces from that distance, he recognized the trucks as being from the Lazy H. He sharpened the focus slightly.

One of the men was almost certainly Buster's top hand. Lucius always wore a brown Stetson and a black leather vest.

Luke turned the binoculars to the big white trailer. The back door was standing open, but he couldn't see any horses.

Minutes passed. The men stood there talking with their arms crossed, and nothing happened. The sudden sound of truck tires on gravel sounded loud in the silence. It made

Luke lower the binocs sharply and turn to stare up the little dirt track, but no truck showed up.

It had been someone turning onto another drive.

Luke exhaled in relief and lifted the binocs again. This time he was rewarded with the sight of a third man leading three horses out of the trailer.

Luke stiffened. The horses were thoroughbreds, he could see that even from a distance; and they looked awfully familiar. One of them was Lickety Split, he could swear it.

Luke sharpened the lens focus, but even at the best resolution, the horse was too far away; so he closed the glasses up and reached for another small plastic case.

Luke unpacked the drone and the controller. He glanced up at the sky, wondering if he could get the drone through an open spot in the trees. If he could get the drone up high enough, he could see the whole panorama a lot clearer. Maybe even get in close enough to verify the horses were theirs.

Luke set the drone carefully on the ground, then flicked on the power and pressed buttons on the controller. The drone came to life with a low hum, and the screen on the controller winked to life.

Luke glanced overhead again. The branches were too thick to launch the drone straight up through the trees, but if he launched it from the clear space above the dirt track it would still be partially hidden behind the cover of the pines.

Or at least, until it got well up into the air.

He picked the drone up and descended the little hill gingerly. When he reached the flat, open space of the road, he set the drone down, glanced up again, and stepped back.

The drone rose slowly into the air, and Luke had to be careful to avoid getting it snagged on branches; but he eased it up to the treetops, turned it toward the scene on the other side of the pasture, and flicked the camera on.

The scene jumped into sharp focus, more detailed than the binocs, and this time he saw what he was looking for. Luke's heart jerked angrily in his chest, because the largest horse was Lickety Split, there was no doubt. He had that distinctive blaze on his nose, he had three white socks, and his gleaming mane was still woven into the fancy braid that Heather had given him a week before.

He inched the drone slightly south to focus on the other horse. Luke bit his mouth into a tight line, because it was one of their prize brood mares, Moonlight Sonata. She was a solid chestnut brown with a black mane, and her tail was lopped short because she'd gotten a handful of burrs into it.

Luke glanced at the trailer. The Lazy H hands could load the stolen horses back up and have them out on the road again in minutes. If he wanted to get their thoroughbreds back, he was going to have to act fast.

Luke was just beginning to bring the drone back again when the sound of an approaching truck made him freeze. He rolled his eyes to the little dirt trail, and to his horror, a black truck was coming down it.

Luke stared at it. There was nothing he could do to hide. He was standing on the top of a low, wooded hill, and the pine trees and brush only partially screened him and his bike.

If the truck driver glanced out the side window, he was going to have to drop the drone, jump on the bike, and get out as fast as he could.

Luke glanced down at the controller screen. The hands seemed to have noticed the newcomer. They were staring back toward the trail, and Luke sent up a quick prayer that they wouldn't see his drone hovering just over the tree line.

The driver gunned the truck down the dirt track, and Luke's eyes followed the truck as it passed him, disappeared around the curve of the hill, and stopped dead just beyond.

The sound of a truck door slamming almost made Luke drop the drone controller; but he stood there, waiting, with a pounding heart.

Time seemed to drag. Luke stood still, waiting to hear a shout, or worse, the sound of a slug hitting a tree.

The sound of a distant shout made him knit his brows in confusion; but he soon saw what was happening. The newcomer was crossing the meadow on foot to talk to the other men. He was waving his arms and seemed agitated, and Luke's eyes narrowed.

It was Buster.

Luke's heartbeat quickened, this time with excitement. He'd caught Buster red-handed with their stolen thoroughbreds, and he had what he needed to prove it.

He turned the drone gently, fidgeted with the lens focus, and hit the red 'record' button. A sharp smile curved his lips as he followed Buster with the camera, capturing more video evidence every second; but after a minute or two he reeled the drone back down.

This was a golden opportunity for them to get their horses back, and he couldn't waste the chance.

Luke dug in his jeans pocket for his cell phone, and he punched Buck's number on speed dial. The phone rung once, twice, and then Buck picked up.

"Yeah."

Luke's eyes moved hungrily to the tiny figures across the pasture. "Buck, you gotta get out here," he breathed.

Buck's voice sounded confused. "Luke?"

"Yeah, it's me," he whispered. "I'm at the west gate of the old Folsom place. I just found our horses!"

Buck's voice practically jumped through the receiver. "Are you sure?"

Luke nodded. "Positive, but you gotta get here fast. There's only Buster and two of his hands out here right now, but they could take our horses out of here any minute!"

"On my way," Buck yelped, and the line went dead.

Luke almost stuck the phone back into his pocket; but on second thought, he tapped out a second number and left a hurried message on the machine.

"Carson, this is Luke. I've found our horses. Buster's here with them at the west gate of the old Folsom Place. If we hurry, we can get 'em back!"

Luke hung up, stuck the phone in his jeans pocket, and went to pick the drone up off the ground. He packed it back into the case, stuck it into his saddle bag, and watched the distant figures warily.

The cowboys were walking the horses, letting them graze and get some exercise; but then, to Luke's dismay, they led them back into the trailer again and closed it up.

It looked like they were moving out again.

Luke grumbled under his breath, then cast about him for a better place to hide. He grabbed the handlebars of the bike and moved it behind a thick clump of bushes, then crouched down behind a big rock to see what would happen.

As he watched, a white truck appeared around the curve of the hill, and he crouched lower as it crawled past.

When Luke raised his head again, the truck had gone. He turned back toward the pasture. Buster was busy hooking the horse trailer to the back of his truck.

It looked like there was a transfer going on; and that Buster wanted to be the only one who knew where the horses were going.

Come on Buck, Luke grumbled in frustration. He couldn't block Buster's truck with his bike; though he might try to follow him.

Buster walked to the truck and got in. Luke frowned, rose from his hiding place, and scrambled down the hill. He ran down the dirt trail toward the road and reached the pasture gate.

The old gate was rusted and sagging, but the chain and the lock were new—probably added to it by the Lazy H hands. They'd left the gate unlocked in anticipation of Buster's departure; but Luke hurriedly grabbed the sagging gate and pulled it wide open.

In a few minutes, that little dirt pig trail was going to be crammed with trucks and cars.

Luke glanced down the road, but he couldn't see if his brothers were coming. The road was heavily screened by a line of pines.

He glanced back down the trail. If Buster caught him now, he was going to have to fight for his life, because Buster was a wild man on his best day, and there was nothing more dangerous than a busted crook.

There was no sign of him so far; but that could change any minute. Luke skipped back, then turned and plunged into a dense thicket of pine trees to wait for his brothers.

The minutes passed, and Luke squinted at the road, and then back down the trail.

Come on, Buck, he thought impatiently. *Where are you?*

He stuck his hands on his hips and paced back and forth, and back again a few times; and when the distant whine of an approaching truck wafted to his ear, a wide smile split his brown face.

A few moments later Buck's red truck veered into the little dirt road and pulled up to him. The window glided down and Buck leaned over to bark: "Down this road?"

Luke nodded, and had to move quick to keep Buck from charging ahead without him. He jumped for the running board on the truck and yelped, "Let me in first!"

Buck stopped the truck just long enough to let him clamber into the passenger's seat, and he'd no sooner closed the door than three other trucks turned onto the dirt road behind them: Morgan's, Jesse's, and Hank's.

Buck gave him a dark look and jammed his big boot on the gas. The truck went hurtling down the rough track, speeding them toward the fight that had been building up between Buck and Buster for years. Luke shot his eldest brother an awed glance. Buck had the brawn to lift up the truck and throw it at Buster, and he was mad enough to do it.

They bounced down the track to the point where his bike was hidden, and Luke pointed at a pasture gate in the fence beside the road. "There's the pasture gate," he announced. "There he is, out beside the trailer!"

Buck jammed on the brakes and was out of the truck almost before it came to a stop. Luke jumped out and scrambled at his heels across the pasture as his other brothers and Hank pulled up behind. He could hear truck doors slamming as they came charging up behind them.

Buster had unlocked the trailer doors again, and was fiddling with one of the wheels when he looked up. He crouched there, staring, for a split-second; then he straightened up and went running for the truck.

Buck went flying across the pasture to catch him, and their paths converged just outside the truck door. Buster snatched for the truck handle, but Buck caught him first.

Luke stopped, panting, as he saw Buster go flying through the air and land face first in the pasture grass. He shook his head and glared at them from the ground.

"All you big heroes gonna gang up on me?" he yelled. "Well, come on, then. I'll take all of you!"

Buck took no more notice of him, but turned his back and went stomping to the trailer. He yanked the doors open and clambered up inside.

There was a long, pregnant silence; and then Buck's furious voice called out, "Luke, come and unhitch this trailer. We're taking it and our horses home right now!"

Hank and Morgan came running up, followed by a huffing Jesse. Morgan stood in front of Buster's truck door with his arms crossed, and Luke glanced up and saw why. There was a rifle rack in the cab of Buster's truck, and they all knew he was capable of using it.

Buck's scowling face appeared in the back of the trailer, and he climbed down and stalked over to where Buster was pulling himself up off the grass. Buck grabbed him by the collar. Buster's face twisted, and he balled a fist and sent it right into Buck's midsection. Buck gasped, then pulled his fist back and sent it square into Buster's jaw. Buster's head snapped around and he staggered sideways.

"You thieving rattlesnake!" Buck roared, and pulled his fist back again; but Jesse grunted, "Hold up, Buck. Here comes Carson.

"He's got a better right to slug Buster than you."

They all turned to look back toward the dirt road. A silver Jaguar was parked behind the row of trucks, and Carson was marching toward them across the pasture.

They all turned to look at Buck. He bit his lip and shot Buster a hungry glare, but he lowered his hands and stepped back.

Chapter Fifty

Carson slammed the car door and charged toward his brothers across the pasture grass. Carson shot his older brother a look that said *Back off, Buster's mine.*

Buck gave Buster a fuming look, but stepped back and let him take over.

"I always knew you stole our horses," Carson shouted at the red-faced Buster. "I knew you tried to poison our colts, too. How does it feel to lose twice, you jackass?"

Buster held his eye and came walking toward him. "What did you call me, you little punk?"

Carson ground his teeth and clenched his fists as he came on. "You heard me!" he shouted. "Throw down, you coward. I've been wanting to put my fist in your teeth for years!"

Buster stuck his hands on his hips, laughed, and tilted his head to one side. "Think you can do it, pretty boy? You come on."

Carson shouldered out of his jacket, tossed it down on the grass, and rolled up his long shirt sleeves. His brothers stepped back as Carson and Buster squared off in the grassy meadow.

"Get him Carson."

"Come on, buddy."

"Kick his can."

Carson glanced over his shoulder for a split second at his ring of smiling brothers.

The next thing he knew, something smashed his jaw like a horse's hooves and he was suddenly lying face down in the grass with his hair in his eyes. A chorus of protest circled overhead.

"Low down snake!"

"Figures you'd hit a man when he ain't looking, Buster."

Carson looked up through his hair just in time to see Buster shake his fist and bawl, "He wants it, he's gonna get it! Any of you wants it, you just step up. I'll bust all of you—one at a time or all together!"

Carson shook his head to clear the lights out of it and moved his jaw gingerly to verify that it wasn't broken. He tested his teeth with his tongue, then pushed his hands against the ground and climbed back up to his feet, slowly and painfully. He put a hand to his jaw and slid it back and forth, then glared at Buster's bright eyes and gloating smile and put his fists up again.

"Come on, Carson."

"Jab him!"

Buster's fist came at him again, and Carson dodged just enough to avoid getting his jaw smashed a second time. He turned and nailed Buster in the ear as he leaned too far forward, then danced back to avoid a wild haymaker.

"That's the style!"

"You're doing good."

Carson shook out his right hand, because every bone in it was screaming in pain. It reminded him of why he thought fighting wasn't very bright; but sometimes a man had to do it anyway.

Buster tilted his head sharply, then shook it off and waded in again.

Carson stared at him in amazement. The hardest punch he could throw to the side of Buster's head hadn't even sent him down. *Just how hard is your head, Buster,* he thought in awe, and raised his fists again.

"Look out Carson!"

Carson gasped as Buster's fist hit him in the gut like a sledge hammer. He staggered backwards with his arms clamped over his stomach, wobbled, and fell back onto the seat of his Ralph Lauren trousers.

He sat on the ground with a hand to his stomach, gasping, and as he looked up Buster came charging in to kick him. But Buck's big shadow suddenly moved between him and Buster.

"You try to kick him when he's down, I'll nail you," Buck warned with his fists clenched; and to Carson's relief, Buster backed off and wiped his sweaty brow with the back of his arm.

Buck turned to give him a hand, and Carson grabbed it as he staggered up to his feet. He shook his head.

"Maybe I...should've given this...more thought," he panted.

Buck leaned in and murmured, "You think about those scars on our stolen thoroughbreds. Think about what would've happened to our colts if Buster had fed them that poison. How they would've died in a strange place all alone."

Carson stood there bent over, with his hands on his knees; but a slow fire built up in his heart. He'd only seen a horse die of poisoning once. It was more than enough reason to smash Buster's jaw; but he had others.

Every dirty trick Buster had played on him flicked through his mind, and not just at Keeneland this year: last year, and the year before that. His frown deepened as he saw Buster trying to make him look bad in front of Donna, calling him a liar. Hinting that Donna was only the latest woman in his life, that she was nothing to him. Trying to make her feel like a fool for seeing him.

Trying to break them up, really.

Carson staggered upright and wiped his mouth with the back of his hand.

"Get out of my way," he mumbled; and Buck slapped his shoulder and stepped back.

Carson fixed Buster with an ice-cold glare through narrowed eyes and lifted his fists. "Come on, Buster," he panted. "You've been asking for this a long time."

Fierce amusement lit Buster eyes as he strutted up. He threw his arms wide open. "Hit me then, pretty boy," he mocked. "You go around with your nose stuck up in the air, like you're too good for the rest of the world. But you can't back it up, can you? Can you?"

Carson pulled his fist back, and Buster raised his elbow easily to block a straight-arm jab to the teeth. But instead, Carson threw a lightning-fast uppercut that snapped Buster's jaw to the sky and sent him into the grass.

His brothers watched silently as Buster fell backwards like a tree. Carson wiped his mouth, stepped back a few paces, and waited for Buster to recover.

"You come on," Carson gasped.

Buster was lying stretched out on the grass, and he lifted his head and gave them all a wild look. He pulled himself up to a sitting position, then scrambled to his feet. He rubbed his nose and put up his fists.

He jabbed at Carson, jabbed again, and then swung a wild roundhouse punch. Carson blocked it and counter punched with every ounce of his remaining strength. Buster's round head snapped back, and he yelled and went down again.

Carson stared down at him. When Buster groaned and rolled over on his face, Carson slowly lowered his hands, turned his back, and went to pick up his jacket. As he stooped down to get it, his brothers slapped him on the back and followed him with their eyes as he walked out to his car.

Carson glanced back only once, as he opened the car door. He saw Buck reach down, lift Buster by his shirt, and propel him toward his truck.

"You'll be hearing from me!" Buster yelled as he was pushed along. "This means war!"

Buck tossed him up against the truck and balled his fists on his hips. "No, it just means that the worst fighter in our family kicked your can, Buster," he drawled, and threw one of Buster's shoes after him.

Carson rubbed his jaw ruefully and slid into the car. A strange mix of feelings swirled in his chest as he cranked the Jaguar and pulled off the grass. Every part of his body was screaming in pain and he was disgusted that he'd had to descend to a fist fight with Buster.

But he felt a sneaking pride that he'd won it, too.

Or at least, he was happy that he'd kept Buster from kicking his teeth in. Considering Buster's readiness to kick his teeth in, that much was always a win.

Still, he would've preferred a smarter, less violent victory. Carson glanced in the mirror and groaned to see that he had a swollen jaw and the beginnings of a black eye.

When you had a beautiful woman staying at your home, a woman you cared for and wanted to impress, it was the worst possible time to turn up with a busted face; but he couldn't help it. The best he could hope for, was that he could play it for sympathy.

Although Donna was less likely to weep over him, than to smile and shake her head and dab his face with a handkerchief; but he'd take it.

Chapter Fifty One

"I have to go into town this afternoon on business, but I'll be back in an hour or so," Carson murmured. "You can take a dip in the pool if you like."

Donna gave him a look that she hoped was more confident than it felt. They had just finished a large and very satisfying family breakfast in the dining room; but Donna was secretly relieved that Carson had shown her to a quiet corner of the house after. The Spade men were boisterous table companions, but they'd scattered after breakfast to tend to business.

All the women were still there.

Donna sighed. Carson's sisters-in-law were friendly, but his aunts gave her skin a warning prickle. A nice swim would be a tactful way of avoiding their well-meaning questions, but it would be a cold day for a swim. Donna glanced over his shoulder at the gray, threatening clouds through the big plate glass window of the atrium.

"It's too cool out today," she thought aloud.

"Oh, we heat the pool in the fall," Carson assured her. "We have a sauna out there, too, for drying off after."

Donna raised an eyebrow and reconsidered. She counted a Swedish sauna one of the necessities of life; and she hadn't had a really fine steam bath in months.

"You've convinced me," she told him, and he laughed and gave her a peck on the brow.

"Enjoy yourself. I'll be back soon."

Donna followed him with her eyes as he walked across the atrium and out of the house; then she rose with a sigh and made her way up the stairs to the guest room. She had hardly reached the third step, though, when a reedy voice called to her from the hall behind the stairs.

She paused with her hand on the rail and looked down. One of Carson's aunts—she guessed Irene—was beckoning to her.

"Come and talk to us, my dear," the elderly woman called. "We've hardly had a chance to meet you yet."

Donna mustered a smile, but an internal alarm was buzzing in her chest. She was pretty good at reading people, and the keen glint in Irene's eyes told her that trouble might be brewing.

Still, she couldn't politely refuse, and the woman *was* Carson's aunt; so Donna acquiesced as graciously as she could.

"That's right," the older woman smiled, "come into the tv room and let's visit for a while."

Donna followed Irene reluctantly. There was a row of black leather recliners facing a wall-wide home theater screen, and Marlene was already sitting in one of the chairs. A larger-than-life game show host was smiling with all his teeth, and as Donna entered he cried, "That's right! Candace moves into first place!"

Irene waved him away and scolded, "Turn that thing off, sister. We've hardly had a chance to talk to Carson's lady friend since she got here."

Donna's eyes slid to Marlene's face. To her alarm, the other elderly woman looked genuinely worried as she fumbled to turn off the remote.

Donna sank down into a chair, clasped her hands in her lap, and decided to take control of the conversation.

"I understand that you ladies used to live here," she smiled, and Irene's sharp glance returned to her face.

"Oh, yes!" Marlene smiled, "We lived in a little house on the outskirts of town. Such a cozy little place. I still miss it, don't you, sister?"

"Yes," Irene replied shortly, and pivoted to: "We saw all of our sister's children grow up right here in Sandy Creek. We're very fond of our little nephews. We want to see them make the right choices in life."

The taste of disaster curled in Donna's mouth like smoke, but she parried faintly: "Of course. You must be very proud of them."

"Oh we are," Marlene assured her, but Irene pressed in. She sat down in a recliner next to Donna and turned to give her a serious look.

"I have a little confession to make, dear," she began primly. "I wanted to visit with you because I wanted to ask a few little questions. Nothing very serious.”

Donna paused, took a deep breath, and weighed her options. If she left immediately, Carson’s aunts could truthfully say that she was rude to them; but if she stayed, the conversation might go sharply south.

Still, she couldn’t be sure of that; and she decided to stay and hope that she was wrong.

“Oh?” Donna replied lightly, and mustered a smile. “What kind of questions?”

Marlene shot her sister a troubled look. “Now sister...”

Irene ignored her and plowed ahead. “Well, to start with, Donna—you say you met Carson at a resort up in Kentucky?”

“That’s right,” Donna replied less graciously, but she managed to maintain a polite expression.

“*Mmm.* How long have you worked there?”

The demanding tone in Irene's voice made Donna stiffen, and she struggled with herself over her reply. "A few years," she replied coolly. "I manage the club house and most of the resort property."

Irene nodded, with her eyes cast down. "I see. Are you from Kentucky originally?"

Donna felt a wave of heat working up from her feet, and she glanced at the doorway. "No. I was born in Bahrain."

The two older women gave her a blank look. "Is that in America?" Irene queried.

"No," Donna replied coldly.

Irene glanced at her face and shrugged. "Well, I'm sorry if I seem a little nosey," she giggled. "But we have to be careful. Morgan married a woman a few years back who completely ruined his life. She was a horrible, horrible woman who spent all his money and...well, she did *other things,* too," Irene nodded, and her voice sank to a confidential whisper. "Ran around with *all sorts* of other men. So you understand, we have to be careful about the friends we make in our family.

"Because of our wealth, you know."

Donna gasped, stood abruptly, and swept out of the room with a burning face and without a word of reply. She paid no attention to Marlene's voice calling after her as she hurried to the stairs.

Her whole heart was throbbing with shock and anger, and she half-ran up the stairs to the solitude of the guest room for fear of what she might say or do.

She reached her room, pushed the door open, and kicked it shut behind her.

"Oh!"

Donna balled her hands into fists and squeezed her eyes shut; but her anger at

Irene's outrageous rudeness collapsed almost instantly into despair, and then into tears.

She put a hand to her mouth and paced the room; but slowly, the terrible truth dawned on her.

Those two old women had no doubt only said what the rest of them were thinking: Carson had met some scheming, foreign gold digger up in Kentucky. She'd got her hooks in him, and she wasn't going to let go of her helpless victim unless she was pushed out.

They didn't like her, they didn't want her, and she certainly wasn't going to stay where she wasn't wanted.

Donna whirled on the thought, yanked her suitcase out of the closet, and threw it on the bed. She stalked to the chest of drawers and began tossing her clothes into it, and the diamond on her hand flashed like fire.

She paused for an instant to stare at it, then stomped out of the room and across the hall to Carson's apartment door. She pulled the ring off her hand, crouched down, and slid it under his door before stomping back to the guest room to call a cab to the airport.

Chapter Fifty Two

Carson pulled up to the house, killed the motor, and pushed the car door open. He dragged his aching body out of the Jaguar slowly and stiffly, and grimaced with every step up to the front door.

May I be struck by lightning, he thought ruefully, *if I ever let myself get sucked into a fistfight again.*

When he opened the door the house inside looked empty, but that suited him right down to the ground. He didn't want Donna to see him looking like he'd been dragged behind a trash truck; and so he ducked into the side room to the left of the atrium. There was a little service elevator there, and it would whisk him to the second floor with no one the wiser.

Or at least, that was what he hoped. He needed a wash and a brush, an ice pack, and a chance to practice a convincing moan, before he saw Donna.

The little elevator doors closed behind him, and Carson leaned against the wall as it glided skywards. His jaw was throbbing, he probably needed to have his teeth x-rayed, and his right eye was almost completely swollen shut.

When he squinted down at his clothes, he noticed that his shirt had been yanked out of his pants and ripped up the left seam; that three buttons had been torn off of it; and both his shirt and his trousers were grimed with dirt and grass stains.

When he pulled up his trouser leg, he discovered that his left calf was scratched and caked with dried blood, and he hadn't even noticed it.

The elevator chimed softly and opened up, and Carson pushed off the wall and slouched wearily to his own apartment door. He unlocked it, dragged in, and closed it softly behind him.

To his surprise, there was something on the carpet just inside the door. He bent down slowly and painfully to pick it up. It was Donna's diamond wedding ring.

Carson frowned down at it, but he was too beat up and exhausted to guess why Donna had given back the ring. He'd ask her after he'd got a nice hot shower and shave. He slipped the ring into his trouser pocket.

"Siri, turn on the hall lights."

A soft female voice murmured, "Lights on."

A soft line of spot lights lit his hallway like the lights on an airport runway, and Carson slipped out of his shoes and padded down it.

"Siri, turn on the bathroom shower."

"Cool, warm, toasty, or devil's griddle?"

"Devil's griddle," he mumbled, and was reaching up to shoulder out of his shirt when a soft knock at the door made him frown and pause.

There was a moment of silence, then the soft knock pecked at his door again. "Carson," a trembling voice called, "it's Aunt Marlene. Are you in there?"

Carson glanced up at the ceiling, mouthed silent words, and then replied: "Coming."

He tucked his shirt in, twitched it as straight as he could, and walked back to the door.

When he opened it, his elderly aunt raised a contrite face to his. She looked as if she was about to confess a crime, but then she noticed his bruised and swollen face. She gasped and put a hand to her mouth, but Carson reached out to pull her inside. "Don't worry, it isn't serious," he told her with more assurance than he felt. "Come in and sit down, auntie."

She shot him a doubtful glance, but allowed herself to be shepherded to his sunken living room and shown to a sleek leather recliner.

She glanced up at him as she sank down into it. "Carson, I want you to know that I didn't agree with what my sister did. And that she just wanted the best for you. She didn't mean any harm really, it just kind of...happened."

A warning prickle of alarm danced up Carson's spine, and he watched his aunt's face warily as he sank down into a chair opposite her.

"I'm afraid I don't follow, auntie," he murmured, and reached for a pillow to put behind his throbbing skull.

Marlene wrung her hands and glanced at him unhappily. "Well, it's just that we were so keen to see you settle down with a nice girl," she told him. "Especially after I talked to your brother Luke. Now you mustn't be angry that Luke tattled on you, Carson, but he said that you were having trouble getting a…a wife. Not in any mischievous way. No, he just wanted your happiness."

Carson raised an eyebrow and pulled his mouth slightly to one side. "I see."

Marlene nodded and plunged ahead. "So my sister and I promised him that we'd do our best to fix you up with some nice Sandy Creek girls. We knew just about everybody when we lived here, it wasn't hard to find any number of them."

Carson stared at her in growing misgiving. "Where's Donna?" he asked suddenly.

His aunt raised unhappy eyes to his face. "That's just it, Carson. We put so much work into lining up some sweet girls for you, that I think my sister was a little disappointed when you came here with a young lady of your own." She shook her head in gentle melancholy.

Carson stared at her, then closed his eyes and asked gently: "Aunt Marlene, *what happened*?"

"Well," she dithered, "this afternoon all the men folk left the house, and Kate went to check on the baby, and Heather said she needed to lie down and rest. And it was just... my sister and me and...Donna."

Carson's mouth dropped open slightly as she hurried to add, "Now you mustn't be angry, Carson, but my sister said some unfortunate things to your lady friend."

"Like...what?" Carson asked warily. His heart rate gradually accelerated from mild exasperation to genuine alarm.

Marlene waved her hand in the air regretfully. "Sister asked Donna where she was from, and Donna told her she was born in some outlandish place, I can't remember the name. And she asked why, and... and my sister said that the family...had to be careful about their associations, because of their wealth, you know."

Carson felt the blood draining from his face. "What!"

Marlene's eyes jumped to his. "I know, dear, but do try to understand! Irene thought she was looking out for you. She just wanted to make sure that the young lady wasn't going to be like Cece, you know."

Carson rose slowly in horror. "I hope you didn't tell her that!"

"Well..."

Carson put a hand to his mouth and struggled to control his temper. "Where's Donna?"

"She's gone. She was upset, I'm afraid."

Carson looked down at her over his hands and demanded: "How long ago?"

"Oh, she just left, dear. I think she called a cab."

Carson's heart jerked with something like panic. He put a hand to his mouth, wondering if he could get to Lexington before Donna disappeared to...who knew where.

His elderly aunt's trembling voice broke his musings. "Are...are you cross with us, dear?"

Carson forced his lips to smile, and he reached down and patted her hand. "I think it was unfortunate," he told her evenly, "but don't worry about it. I have to go out now, but you're welcome to stay here and make yourself at home."

Marlene's eyes shone. "That's very sweet of you, dear," she quavered; but Carson only patted her shoulder on the way out of the room.

He had only a few minutes to splash his face in cold water and throw on some decent clothes, because he had to get to Lexington as fast as he could. If Donna got there before him, she might disappear.

He might never see her again.

He opened the door to his bathroom suite to be engulfed by a wall of steam. He grabbed a washcloth, dunked it in cold water, and swiped his face once before turning to leave.

"Siri, turn off the shower."

"Shower off."

He blew through the hall and burst into his bedroom. He blew past the big glass wall overlooking the pool, opened his closet, threw a shirt and pair of pants out onto the bed, and began shrugging out of his shirt.

"Siri, call the DFW ticket office. I want a flight to Lexington today as soon as possible."

"Calling."

There was a long, pregnant pause as he threw on his clothes, and presently the smooth female voice murmured, "Reservation made, Skyland Airlines, coach, four thirty boarding."

Carson glanced at the clock. It was a quarter to four. He had just enough time to get to the airport if he gunned it.

His hand drifted down from his collar for a moment as it occurred to him: he hadn't even stopped to question himself.

If there was ever any doubt in his heart that he loved Donna, it was gone. When he thought about his life now, he pictured her calm, smiling face by his side.

Her soothing hand on his arm.

The thought that she might not be there after all spurred him to throw on his clothes in record time and exit the apartment a mere five minutes later. He skipped down the stairs and charged through the house so fast that he raised a breeze; and he'd hardly slid back into the Jaguar before the motor growled to life and the car scratched off down the drive.

Carson reached for his cell phone and commanded: "Call Donna."

The screen jumped to life, and the ringing phone droned on and on without an answer. Carson bit his lip and glanced out over the green blur rushing past.

She was mad, and she had a right to be: but he couldn't let her run away before he had a chance to tell her he loved her.

The possibility that he might arrive too late made him jam his foot on the pedal and roar down the long, straight drive on the way out to the road.

Chapter Fifty Three

Donna unlocked the condo door with a rattle, threw it open, swept through, and kicked it shut behind her. She'd been holding back tears for the whole flight from Texas, and now that she was alone the flood gates opened.

She bowed her head, squeezed her eyes shut, and clapped a hand to her mouth as her shoulders shook. She'd never been so humiliated in her life, and her face was still burning.

Her horrible encounter with Carson's aunts had confirmed her worst fears: that his aunts were just old enough to blurt out what everyone else had been thinking. That their smiles and friendliness were just an act.

That they were suspicious of her, and maybe even hostile, because she was a foreigner. That none of them liked her or wanted her to join their family.

That they might even believe that she was after their money.

Donna's shoulders heaved again, and she wept into her hands. As far as she'd traveled, and as many people as she'd met, she'd never been treated with so much disrespect; and she was shocked by how much it hurt.

She was a woman of the world and she'd developed a fairly thick skin. She knew she'd get over it eventually; but she didn't want to see Carson or any of his family ever again.

It was plain she was never going to fit in with them.

Donna kicked off her shoes, ran upstairs, swept into her bedroom and sank down onto the mattress. She was still weeping when her bedside phone rang. She spat out an angry exclamation, thinking that it was Carson, and didn't answer it. But when the voicemail picked up, she heard a different voice.

"Hi Donna, this is Tim. I'm just calling to see if you've made up your mind about the job on the picture. It's getting close to crunch time, so I need to hear from you."

Donna wiped her eyes and leaned over to grab for the phone. She picked up the receiver.

"Tim?"

Her friend's voice sounded relieved. "Oh, Donna, I'm glad I caught you! I've been trying to reach you for days."

A wave of embarrassment slapped over Donna, and she tucked a skein of shining hair behind one ear. "I'm sorry, Tim, I've been out of town."

"Well, I was just calling to see if you want to take the job," Tim replied simply. Donna closed her eyes, and shame washed over her again. She felt bad suddenly for poor Tim. She'd kept him dangling while she jetted off to Texas to cavort with a billionaire; and yet Tim had waited patiently for her to make up her mind.

She should've flown to India a long time ago.

"Thank you for being so patient, Tim," she replied softly. "I'd be delighted to take the job. It'll be amazing."

Tim's tone brightened. "Excellent! I've booked twenty seats on a flight to New Delhi tomorrow evening. Can you get to La Guardia by then? I'll reimburse you for the ticket."

Donna's mood hardened. "Yes, I can be there by tomorrow. I'll book a flight tonight."

"Great! We'll be in Terminal B, Gate Forty." His tone deepened to affection. "It'll be great to work with you again, Donna," he murmured. "I'm really looking forward to it."

Donna smiled wanly. "So am I, Tim."

"I'll see you tomorrow then," he replied, and there was a smile in his voice. "Feel free to call me if you need anything."

"I will. Goodbye, Tim."

Donna set the receiver back into the cradle softly and stared at it for a long moment; then she got up, wiped her eyes, and went to the closet to pull out her suitcases. She tossed them down on the bed, flipped them open, and started throwing clothes in.

The phone rang again, and Donna glanced at the little blue display. The caller ID showed that it was Carson.

Donna frowned and let the phone trill. It was useless to talk to Carson when it was clear that they weren't going to work out. Carson lived in the same house with the rest of his family, and if she made up with him and went back there, the rest of her life would be just as painful and humiliating as her encounter with his aunts.

Nothing he could say would change that.

The voicemail clicked on, and she paused and frowned at the wall as Carson's voice reached out to her.

"Donna, if you're there, please pick up," he was pleading. "I'm sorry about what my aunts did to you. What can I say, they're almost ninety. Please don't take it to heart."

Yes, Donna thought angrily, *they're ninety, and that's why I do take it to heart. They've lost their filter.*

The young and the old tell you the truth.

The edges of Carson's voice were tinged with desperation. "Donna, *please* talk to me."

The phone beeped and his voice was cut off. Donna wiped an eye and went on packing. Her heart was screaming at her to pick up the phone, but she wasn't going to do it.

She was going to pack and turn in the condo key at the front desk. She was going to fly to New York to meet Tim, then go to New Delhi and never look back.

She was going to forget she ever knew a man named Carson Spade, or that she once thought she was in love with him.

She returned to packing her clothes, and she worked doggedly for a few minutes; but to her irritation, her heart wouldn't be still. It insisted on showing her every detail of her lovely days with Carson.

A tee shirt fell from her hands as her memory showed her Carson's startling blue eyes smiling down at her. She saw him sitting at that window table in the restaurant the first day he arrived at the club, saw how the light traced his straight, strong profile, how it slid off his raven black hair. She almost caught a ghostly tinge of the heavenly cologne he'd been wearing.

Her heart reminded her of the way he'd looked that first night, when he'd called her to his room. She saw him buttoning up his shirt sleeve as he walked toward her. She saw the twinkle in his eye as he asked her out, knowing full well that she wasn't allowed to say yes.

But she did say yes.

For an instant she wavered, and glanced back at the phone; then her expression crumpled up and she turned back to packing on the verge of tears.

She had never felt so crushed in her life, or so angry with herself for feeling that way.

You're hardly a child, she told herself sternly. *You've never let anyone's opinion bother you. Why do you care now?*

The phone rang again, and Donna turned to glare at it for an instant before stomping over to snatch up the receiver. Carson's anxious voice was already talking as soon as she pressed it to her ear.

"Donna, don't hang up," he pleaded, and she pressed her mouth into a hard, tight line as he talked on.

"I'm getting a flight to Lexington right now. I need to talk to you. Please don't run away!"

"You needn't bother," she replied angrily. "Thank you for the invitation to your home, it was very polite, but I always meant to go to India."

"*India?*"

Her anger faded a bit, and a touch of wistfulness crept into her voice as she added, "It was nice knowing you, Carson. Really. I wish you every success."

She was tempted to slam the phone down, but saw her hand place the receiver gently back onto the cradle.

But if she expected to feel better after giving Carson Spade his last toodle-oo, she was disappointed. Her heart sank into her heels instantly; and though her pride was intact, it was pretty much the only thing that was.

Namaste, she whispered; and then closed her eyes as a cold tear trickled down her cheek.

Chapter Fifty Four

Donna slung her bag over her shoulder, fished her keys out of it, and picked up the handle of her suitcase. She had a six o' clock flight to New York and an overnight reservation at the Hilton near La Guardia. She'd be having dinner in New York that night.

She glanced back over her shoulder at the bright, elegant condo and felt a flick of nostalgia for the pleasant years she'd spent in bluegrass country; but she couldn't afford to indulge that feeling. She'd finally pulled herself together, and she didn't want to go under again.

She took a deep breath, took the doorknob, and pulled it open; but to her shock, there was a ragged figure on the other side of it. She stepped back in alarm, but on second glance, it was a familiar, if battered face.

"Carson!"

She dropped the suitcase handle, and all the angry words that jumped to her lips died there. Carson's face was swollen and bruised, and he was listing slightly to one side.

She threw the bag down and opened the door wide. "Carson, what happened?"

He shrugged and smiled crookedly. "I had a disagreement with Buster Hogan."

Donna's eyes flicked over his discolored, swollen jaw and his puffy eye. She put a hand to her mouth and yelped, "Are you all right?"

"Fine," he assured her stoutly. "Really, it's nothing that a few days won't mend."

She stared at him in frowning worry but only murmured, "Come in."

Carson's eyes flicked to her suitcase, but he closed the door behind him and turned to her.

He took her gently by the shoulders and looked down into her face as well as he could.

"Donna, I came to apologize," he croaked. "I found out what happened at the ranch and I'm sorry my aunts were so rude to you. It was unforgivable, but please believe me that no one else shares their feelings. My family is wild about you."

"I know I am."

Her anger came surging back, but Carson's soft lover's tone made it hard to stay mad. She looked away. "Come and sit down, Carson," she murmured.

"Not before I tell you what else I came to say," he replied softly. Donna, you—you can't leave," he told her earnestly. "You'll break my heart if you do. The reason I invited you to my home is because I've...I've fallen in love with you."

Donna raised her eyes to his, but her tears made it hard to see him. Carson put his hand under her chin and whispered, "Surely you guessed it? It's true, darling." His voice softened to velvet, and he pulled her down onto a settee beside him. "You're not like any woman I've ever met. You're soft and sweet and wise and elegant. You're beautiful and witty and I adore you."

Donna frowned fiercely and blinked back her tears. She looked up at him and replied, "Does your family adore me, Carson? Your aunts certainly don't. They told me right to my face that they thought I was a fortune hunter! Is that what the rest of them think?"

"No, no," he laughed, and cupped her face in his hands. "My family loves you. My aunts are...well, they've always been different," he confessed ruefully. "No one pays any attention to them, honestly. And they don't live with us, they're just visiting. They'll be back in New Mexico in a few days."

Donna searched his eyes, and to her irritation, what she saw in them threatened to break her fragile self-control. Carson caressed her cheek and whispered, "Tell me you love me, Donna."

The tenderness in his voice melted her heart. Donna tried to hold back her feelings, but a lonely tear escaped down her cheek. Carson crooned, "What did I say to make you cry? I'm sorry. See, I'll kiss those tears away."

Donna bowed her head and felt the touch of his lips on her lashes, feather light: one kiss, two.

"See?" he whispered. "Say you love me, Donna."

She shook her head impatiently. She couldn't let Carson seduce her, he was too good at it, she couldn't let his charms keep her from going to India and the chance of a lifetime; but she felt her resolve sliding away like sand.

"I…"

His tone was gently reproachful. "Are you going to play with my poor heart?" he whispered. "Tell me you love me."

Donna's frown deepened as she struggled with herself, but it was no use. She loved Carson with all her soul, and she couldn't hide it.

"Oh, you know I do!" she told him almost angrily; but delight dawned over his face and spread out into a beautiful smile.

"Good," he whispered. "I take it you won't mind if I kiss you, then."

Donna opened her mouth, but her last objection was stopped by a soft, sweet lover's kiss, a kiss that soothed and electrified her and convinced her of his love where words might have failed.

Carson's lips wandered down to her jaw, and then her neck. Donna closed her eyes and raised her chin and let him nibble her ear, and then press his lips to it.

"Marry me, *bella*. Come back home."

Donna's eyes flew open and she pressed her hands against his chest. She searched his eyes wordlessly as he reached into his shirt pocket and pulled out the glittering diamond ring that she'd pushed under his apartment door.

A ghost of a smile played over Carson's face as he held it just above her hand.

"As far as I'm concerned, this is real."

Donna lowered her eyes to stare at the elegant square diamond flashing fire on her hand; but only for a moment. She raised them again to Carson's face.

A little voice in her ear was urging her to give it back, to grab her luggage and flee. To keep moving, to fly to India and enjoy a brand new adventure in a magical place.

But another, deeper voice was telling her that this time was different.

Carson's eyes held hers. "Marry me, Donna."

Donna reached out slowly, took the diamond ring from Carson's fingers, and slowly slid it over her finger; then raised her face to be kissed again.

Chapter Fifty Five

"I now pronounce you man and wife. You may kiss the bride."

Donna turned toward her new husband and closed her eyes to receive his kiss. She put a hand up to his hair and tried to communicate what she felt, that mere words could never convey.

The portly justice of the peace, and the two female clerks who had acted as their witnesses, smiled and clapped quietly. One of them produced a handful of rice and tossed it over their heads.

"Congratulations," the judge smiled. "Every happiness to you children."

Donna parted from Carson's lips reluctantly and smiled up into his eyes. The look in them was indescribably tender, and confirmed what she already knew: that Carson's glib banter and careless manner concealed a man who felt deeply.

A man who was capable of sublime love.

Carson turned to the beaming judge. "Thank you for marrying us on such short notice," he murmured. "We appreciate your kindness."

"I make time for love when I can," the judge chuckled. "Best of luck."

Donna tucked her hand around Carson's elbow and he slid an arm around her waist as they walked out of the judge's chambers at the county courthouse.

They walked arm in arm through the tiled halls, out the doors, and down the steps of the white stone courthouse. It was a cold, gray, blustery day, and the wind whipped at Donna's hair and sent tendrils floating around her ears as Carson hailed a cab to the curb.

A stretch limo pulled up, and Donna laughed incredulously as Carson opened the door for her to slide in. She settled in and turned toward Carson as he clambered in beside her.

The limo driver looked back over his shoulder. "Where to, Mr. Spade?"

Carson stretched an arm across the car seat and answered without taking his eyes off her face. "Louisville."

The driver raised an eyebrow. "That's almost eighty miles away, sir."

Carson's only answer was to reach for the bottle of champagne that was chilling in a silver bucket. He popped the cork with a rush of bubbles and poured a glass for himself and her.

The driver shrugged and turned back around, and Donna took a champagne glass from her groom's hand. They touched the glasses together with a faint *ting,* and Donna lifted the glass to her lips with a smile.

It took the limo a little over an hour to reach Louisville, and Donna watched in puzzlement as the driver took the limo right downtown, and all the way out to the city's riverfront. She turned to Carson and looked a question, and he pulled her to his chest and answered it.

"It's a surprise," he murmured.

Their limo slowly inched down the street to the wharf, then turned again onto a street facing the riverfront. There were all sorts of boats tied up at the dock, and many more riding the current of the broad Ohio River: flat barges, tugs, pleasure craft and excursion vessels.

The driver brought the limo to a stop, climbed out, and came around the car to open the door for them. Carson climbed out, then held out his hand to help her follow.

Donna looked up at him with a mixture of pleasure and confusion. "Are we going to fish for our dinner?" she laughed.

Carson's fingers curled around hers. "Come and see," he smiled, and refused to tell her more; but as he led her down the riverfront road, it soon became apparent what he had planned. A magnificent red-and-white steamboat sat parked at the dock, a sugared confection of white gingerbread trim, licorice-colored smoke stacks, and a candy-red paddle wheel.

"It's huge," Donna murmured, with her eyes on the steamboat's five decks and innumerable staterooms.

Carson squeezed her hand. "It's where we're spending our honeymoon," he told her with a grin.

Donna's eyes zoomed to his face. "Oh, Carson, it's beautiful!" she gasped; and he laughed and slipped an arm around her shoulder.

Donn's eyes moved back to the steamboat, and she objected, "But what about our luggage? I didn't bring anything with me."

"There's plenty of everything on the boat," Carson reassured her. "All kinds of shops. You can buy whatever you need. We'll send for our things later."

Donna turned to stare into his face. She hadn't known such serene freedom since her early childhood in her father's house, and after all the ups and downs of her travels it felt...*wonderful.*

The wind gusted suddenly, and big drops of rain began to spatter the street. Donna giggled softly, and the two of them ran the rest of the way to the line kiosk at the end of the street.

When they walked up the gangway and entered the boat, a smiling young man in a spotless white cap and uniform smiled, "Welcome to the *Crystal Queen!*" He leaned over to scan the tickets Carson showed him. "I see you folks have a suite on the top deck. I'll show you to your rooms."

He gestured down the hall ahead, and Donna squelched a smile of glee. She hadn't felt such pleasant expectations since she was a child; and she was not disappointed.

The little hall opened out into a vast, magnificent rotunda whose central point was a grand antique staircase of polished wood, and a dazzling antebellum chandelier high over its graceful sweep. Donna's eye followed it up to the ceiling, which had been painted to look like a blue sky with white clouds.

The rotunda floor was covered in plush red carpet and Victorian furniture. Stained glass was everywhere, brass railings and knobs were everywhere, and Donna's eyes wandered over the scene in awe. The *Crystal Queen* made The Turf Club look like the cotton-gowned poor relation of a grand Southern lady decked out in silks and lace.

"Carson, it's beautiful," she breathed.

His eyes wandered up to the ceiling high above them. "Yes, it is," he sighed. "I've always wanted to ride one of these and never got around to it. I had no idea they were so…" He gestured wordlessly.

Their guide turned to them with a smile. "This is the grand staircase," he told them with a touch of pride, "but it's a long walk up to your deck, so we'll take the elevators. If you'll follow me."

The three of them set off across the vast, open space, swimming through other guests, costumed actors in antebellum top hats, suits, and hoop gowns, and smartly-uniformed line employees.

Their guide led them around and behind the sweeping staircase to a bank of old-fashioned open elevators. The cars were little more than intricately-wrought metal cages, and they reminded Donna of *fin de siecle* elevators she'd seen in the Left Bank in Paris.

The employee pulled the cage door aside for them. "Your suite is on the promenade deck, bow end. You have the luxury suite with the exclusive veranda, Suite 500."

Donna stepped inside the little elevator in growing excitement. She felt almost like a child on holiday, and couldn't help laughing at herself; but this time, the tingle she usually relished at the start of a new adventure was racing up and down her spine and out into all the little tributaries of her nervous system.

The line attendant pressed a brass button, and the car moved smoothly upwards. They watched as the huge rotunda room swiftly sank below their feet and disappeared.

The elevator door finally opened onto a covered promenade with a panoramic view of the river and the clouded sky. The breeze freshened and ruffled Carson's dark fringe of hair and Donna's skirt hem as they stepped out into the rain-scented air.

The attendant led them down the open promenade deck, all the way up to the bow of the boat, and paused outside a large suite facing directly over the proud bow of the ship. Its huge windows had an almost unrestricted view of the river ahead; and a cozy private balcony was attached to the side of it, with side walls and a low wooden rail in front for privacy.

The uniformed employee unlocked the glass doors of the suite and stepped aside for them to enter. He handed the keys and a plastic card to Carson as he passed.

"Is there anything I can get for you?" he asked; and Donna closed her eyes in bliss to hear those words come from someone *else's* lips.

"Not a thing in this world," Carson smiled. He reached into his pocket to slip the man a tip, then reached for a *Do Not Disturb* sign and hung it on the outer doorknob.

The young man smiled, tipped his cap, and walked off briskly; and Carson closed the door behind them. He lowered the blinds over the big door and windows.

Donna sank down on the white quilt over the big, downy bed. She kicked her slender feet to dislodge her pumps and made a wry face.

"How can we go to dinner tonight when we don't have anything to wear except our wedding clothes?" She shot him a mischievous look. "It's my honeymoon, and I don't even have a negligee!"

She watched as Carson walked over, sat down on the bed beside her, and loosened his tie. He turned to give her a serious look.

"Well," he sighed and took her hand, "for one thing, we're having dinner brought up to our suite tonight. And as far as I'm concerned, the only thing you need to wear tonight is a smile."

Donna sputtered out a delighted giggle as Carson slipped a hand around her waist and leaned in for a kiss; and she was still laughing

when he listed sideways onto the bed and
pulled her down after him.

Chapter Fifty Six

A few nights later, Donna drifted out to their stateroom balcony in the purple midnight. A light breeze ruffled her sheer peignoir and played with a tendril of her golden hair. She could hear the paddle wheel churning softly from the distant stern of the ship. That, and the soft splash of river water against the hull were the only sounds at that quiet hour.

She glanced back over her shoulder into the bedroom. She could just see Carson's bare foot sticking out from under the corner of the bed covers. He was fast asleep, but she had never felt more vibrantly awake.

She set her hands lightly on the rail and watched as the tiny lights of some small town faded into darkness around the bend of the river; and she raised her eyes to the lights that mirrored them in the inky sky above. Her little slice of the world felt soft and sleepy and secret that night.

As if no one saw her, out on that secluded stretch of river at midnight, except God.

Donna smiled to herself. She wasn't a religious woman, but she felt a need to thank someone or something at that moment.

Maybe God, she didn't know; but she smiled up into the infinite darkness. *If You're up there*, she prayed, *I just wanted to say thank you.*

She glanced back at the bedroom behind her. Carson's soft, regular breathing was just audible, and her smile deepened.

I never thought I could be this content. I really think I could settle down with this man for the rest of my life.

It's a God-level miracle.

She stared up at the glittering, infinitely distant stars, and it suddenly occurred to her that if God had created the blue waters of Bahrain, the fog-drenched rivers of England, the dusty outback of Australia, and the million bustling lives crossing and recrossing each other in New York, He was at the least wildly creative. He must be much bigger than she had ever been taught, and probably much different.

She gazed up at the sky. *I don't know Your name,* she prayed whimsically, *or what You are; but thank you.*

Maybe I will learn Your name some day. Until then, I will call You 'The God of those who wander, and of those who come home.'

I was one, and now I'm the other; I think because of You.

She stood at the rail in the cool silence, with her hair and robe fluttering in the breeze, for a few moments more; then she turned back into the stateroom and glided softly to the bed. She shrugged out of her robe, turned the covers back and slipped under them.

She turned toward Carson. His head was turned away, but she caressed his dark hair with a lazy forefinger, and was surprised when he turned toward her.

"I thought you were asleep," she murmured.

His eyes and his voice was heavy. "I was. But I'm glad I woke up."

He reached for her, and Donna nestled in his arms, pressed her cheek to his chest, and closed her eyes. She suffered a sudden flick of guilt, perhaps from having thought about God, and a frown flitted over her face.

"My real name is Maryam," she confessed.

"I know."

She opened her eyes in surprise and looked up at him. Carson rubbed his face with one hand and nodded, "I looked it up. I was curious. Why did you change your name? Maryam's pretty."

Donna's frown faded, and she closed her eyes again. "I wanted a Western life, so I chose a Western name." She shrugged a slender shoulder.

Carson tightened her to his chest. "Well, a rose by any other name would smell as sweet," he murmured sleepily. "I'll love you by any name you like."

Donna opened her eyes and smiled up at him. Her heart felt swollen with warmth and was so full of love that one more kiss, one more whisper, would burst it.

And yet she reached up to brush Carson's hair back from his brow, kissed him, and prepared to let it burst.

Carson smiled sleepily under her lips and kissed her back. He tangled his hands in her long hair and slowly drifted from her lips, to her jaw, to her neck. Donna closed her eyes and arched her neck as his lips wandered to her ear.

Carson was a magical lover, and Donna smiled and prepared to enjoy the second demonstration of it that night. His kisses pushed her under his spell like a drowsy wave. But even so, a small sliver of her mind remained her own to wonder:

We're a perfect match, you and I. How did we find each other, out of all the people in the world?

This, too, is a miracle.

Donna twined her hands in his hair and tangled her fingers in its silky darkness. She closed her eyes as Carson tightened her to his chest and felt herself slipping down to that drowsy place between utter relaxation and mad excitement.

That enchanted place that only she and Carson shared; a secret that only the smiling moon witnessed.

Carson whispered into her ear, so low that she lost most of it; but her ear was quick to catch the most important part. She heard his *I love you* crystal clear; and she smiled and turned to whisper her soft reply into his chest.

Chapter Fifty Seven

Six months later

"Say hello to Casey, and Bart, and Poppy."

Carson leaned over the hospital bed to peer down at the three pink, wrinkled, and very serious faces in his sister-in-law's arms. He laughed at their frowns and extended a finger. To his surprise, Casey took it in his tiny hand.

"He's going to have great hands for riding," Morgan murmured, as he gazed down in love at his little son. "Look at that grip!"

Heather leaned down weakly and kissed her little daughter's cheek. Her blonde hair was splayed out over her pillow, and she looked exhausted; but the beatific smile on her face lit up her eyes and made her face glow in spite of it.

"They're beautiful babies," Donna said softly, and brushed a feather-light caress over Bart's baby fluff. "This one looks like he might be a blonde."

Carson watched Donna's face out of the corner of his eye. Donna's eyes were alight with tenderness and warmth as she cooed over the new arrivals. Of course, everyone else was wearing that expression; but still.

He glanced at her again. He and Donna had decided not to try for a family right away. Maybe not at all. Children weren't right for every couple.

But as he gazed down at his newest niece and nephews, Carson wondered if he and Donna might one day change their thinking about babies, as they had about marriage.

A wry smile curved his lips. It was a funny world.

The two of them said their goodbyes soon after. They wanted to give Heather a chance to rest; and as they were leaving Donna sighed and took his arm.

"You can stop looking at me out of the corner of your eye," she teased. "I'm not pregnant."

Carson chuckled and shook his head. Donna was developing a frightening ability to read his mind.

"I'm not worried about it," he shrugged, and to his surprise, it was true. They weren't planning on a child, but if one came along, it was meant to be. He was beginning to believe in things that were meant to be. He glanced at Donna's delicate profile and took her arm.

He walked her out to the front entrance of the hospital, and they waited for a valet to bring the Jaguar around. Carson checked his watch as he helped Donna into the car. He had an appointment that afternoon, and he couldn't miss it.

Or more accurately, he wouldn't miss it for the world.

He had to testify at Buster Hogan's criminal trial; and he was looking forward to it. Eugene had assured them all that Buster was likely going to jail for at least five years, and possibly more, for stealing their thoroughbreds. Eugene had also opined that Buster had another six months coming for attempting to poison their colts at Keeneland, and that wasn't counting the charges he was facing in Kentucky for assault and trespassing.

Carson sighed happily. At long last, Buster was going to get his; and the knowledge that he wouldn't have to deal with him at next year's yearling auction put a spring into Carson's step as he slid into the driver's seat and pulled the car away.

It was shaping up to be an outstanding day, full of good news and happiness, and there was only one more thing needed to make it perfect. To put a shiny red cherry on the top.

Carson pulled to a stop at a red light, reached for his cell phone, and flicked it on. The screen jumped to life, and soon displayed the message he'd spent an hour drafting. He smiled down at it, then pressed the 'send' button.

Donna turned to look at him, and her clear brow clouded over slightly. "You look like you just did something really bad," she observed in amusement. "Do I want to know what it was?"

Carson glanced at her, then stuffed the phone back into his pocket. "I'm surprised at you, Donna," he told her in a tone of wounded innocence. "You should have more faith in your husband. Haven't I been a model of virtue?"

The smile faded from her eyes, and she reached for his hand. "Yes, you have," she agreed softly. "I take it back."

Carson nodded at her, as if the compliment was his due; but he had to work to smother a chuckle.

It had been a good six months since Luke had set his great-aunts on him. Six months since Luke had inadvertently almost destroyed his relationship with Donna.

Six months for Luke to get nice and comfortable and assume that he'd forgotten all about it. And since revenge was a dish that was best served cold, he'd waited until now to serve it.

A slow smile curved Carson's lips. He imagined Luke's face when he found out he'd posted a truly memorable lonely hearts ad to a dating website. One that requested 'alpha females only,' and added that he'd been 'a very bad boy.'

Carson rubbed his nose to hide his smile. It would only be days, perhaps hours, before Luke was inundated with replies from that website's more exotic denizens. It was a shame he couldn't read them himself. Knowing how horrified Luke would be, they'd be hysterically funny; but if he was lucky, Luke would quote a few when he showed up to yell at him.

He glanced over to find Donna's eyes on him. "You *have* done something bad," she murmured with a smile. "I've never seen you look more pleased with yourself. What is it?"

"Oh, just a bit of housekeeping," he told her comfortably. "Settling an overdue account."

She crossed her arms and gave him a wry look. "*Hm.* Something to do with one of your brothers, I'd say. You play pranks on each other like ten year olds."

Carson turned to look at her, then pulled the Jaguar off the road. Donna watched him in frowning puzzlement.

"A ten year old, am I?" he teased, and unbuckled his seat belt. He leaned over, grabbed her in his arms, and buried his face in her neck.

"I'll show you a ten year old," he growled as she wriggled in his arms and shrieked with laughter.

Chapter Fifty Eight

Luke sauntered out of the county courthouse with the rest of his brothers. Him and Carson had just testified against Buster Hogan, and it was pretty clear that Buster was on his way to prison.

They were all in the mood for a celebration.

Buck clapped him on the shoulder as they descended the marble steps. "Why don't we all go down to Dallas for dinner? Hey Carson, what's that restaurant you go to on the top of a building, the one with the great view of town?"

"Elevation," Carson told him. "They have a great chef there."

"Yeah, what say we all go?" Buck asked, with a big, toothy smile. Luke had to cover his mouth to keep from laughing, because after their day in court Buck was as happy as a dog in the kitchen. He was grinning from ear to ear.

"I'd like to, Buck, but I can't," Luke replied. "I got a date with Trina."

"Why don't you bring her with you?" Buck suggested, but Luke shook his head. "Nah, I better not. Trina's been kinda touchy lately. Don't wanna set her off."

"Listen to him," Jesse grumbled. "Ain't even married yet, and he's already henpecked."

Buck stuck his hands on his hips and squinted at him. "When *are* you gonna marry that girl, Luke?" he demanded. "You been going with her for five years!"

Luke waved the question away and ducked out. "You guys have fun. I'll see you at the house later."

He threw up a hand in farewell and walked out to the curb in front of the courthouse. His bike was parked there, and he sank down onto the seat and cranked the motor.

He pulled out into the street and headed out toward the interstate. Trina lived in Green Oak, a town a few miles away. It was a real short hop on the four lane.

It took him about twenty minutes to reach the little town. Trina lived in a little white bungalow facing the train tracks. The house had always reminded him of Trina. It was small and cute.

He slowed down to turn into the little gravel driveway that ran beside her house. He was as familiar with her house as he was with his own, and he parked the bike on the grass in the back and skipped to the back door.

He rapped lightly on the door and waited. Trina didn't answer right away, but she was probably just putting the finishing touches on their dinner. He assumed she'd invited him over for dinner. She cooked dinner for him all the time.

When she still didn't answer, he rapped on the door again and stuck his face to the glass pane in the door. "Trina, it's Luke," he called. "Open the door!"

After a few more moments she appeared in the hall, and he pulled his face back from the window and waited for her to open the door.

"Come inside, Luke," she told him. Her voice was firm and steady, but her eyes looked puffy and a little red.

Luke frowned as he stepped inside. "You okay, Trina?" he worried aloud.

She turned to push him lightly toward the living room. "Come and sit down, Luke," she told him. "I need to talk to you."

Luke drifted into the living room in confusion. He sank down into his favorite chair, a big overstuffed recliner, and got comfortable.

Trina sank into the chair facing his and clasped her hands in her lap. She was a cute little girl, with a short, curly bob of brown hair, big blue eyes, and freckles spattered across her nose. She was near thirty, but she looked almost like a teenager.

She had a high, squeaky little voice, too; or at least, usually. But Luke noticed, with some alarm, that her voice sounded a bit thick and stuffy now.

"Is something bothering you, honey bun?" He asked in some concern; and to his dismay, tears welled up in her eyes. She nodded, looked away, and rubbed her nose.

"Yes, Luke. Something is bothering me," she sniffed.

Luke sat up and leaned forward in his chair. "Well, you just tell me what it is, and I'll fix it for you," he offered.

Her eyes moved to his, and the look in them was reproachful. "All right," she replied evenly. "I'm upset because we've been seeing each other for five long years, Luke, and you haven't asked me to marry you!"

Surprise slapped a blank across his face. "*Marry* you?" he yelped.

Her face contracted into a frown. "Yes, marry me! I'm not getting any younger, and you aren't either." She shook her head bitterly. "I've waited and waited for you, Luke, but if you're not willing to marry me after five years, I don't think you ever will!"

Luke gestured helplessly. "What brought this on?" he demanded. "Just last week we went out and had a lot of fun at the county fair. You weren't unhappy then!"

Trina's blue eyes flashed. "Well, I am now!" she snapped. "Do you know what today is?"

Luke stared at her warily. He had the feeling it was a trick question, but he couldn't for the life of him figure what she was driving at. He shook his head slowly.

"It's the anniversary of our first date!" she complained. "And I'm not surprised you don't remember it. It just isn't important to you. You take me for granted!"

"That's not true," Luke objected and reached out for her, but she slapped his hands away. "No, you stay where you are! I didn't ask you over here for that. I asked you here because I wanted to ask you a question.

"Are you going to marry me, or not?"

Luke's mouth dropped open in shock. "*Marry* you? M-marriage is a big step, Trina," he stammered, and her face twisted in anger. She grabbed a handkerchief from a side table and pressed it to her eyes.

"You don't love me!" she sobbed, and Luke ran his hand through his hair in dismay.

"That's not true, Trina," he pleaded, but she shook her head.

"It is true! If you're not willing to marry me after five years, it means—you, don't, love, me, enough, to, commit," she sobbed.

"Baby, please listen to me," Luke began, but Trina's face suddenly hardened. She glared at him over her tissue.

"You can't commit to *anything*, Luke," she told him angrily. "You've never worked at a job longer than six months. You don't finish projects. You're a drifter.

"Well, I'm tired of drifting. If you won't marry me, then I can't go on seeing you," she sniffed.

Luke stood up in alarm. "*What?* Now wait honey, you're just upset about me forgetting our anniversary. You don't mean that," he pleaded. "Just give me ten minutes, and I'll go get you some flowers."

Trina set her mouth. "No, Luke," she wept, "I don't want flowers. I want a ring. If you won't marry me, then I'm moving on."

Luke stared at the room around him, as if he was wondering if it was real. "Trina, baby—"

She slowly stood up and stared at him with her chin raised. "I'm sorry, Luke. But I can't waste any more time on a man who isn't serious about me.

"I don't want to see you any more," she added, and twisted the tissue between her hands. "In fact, I've taken a job in Oklahoma. I'm moving right out of Texas. I'm going to make a brand new start."

Luke's hands flapped in the air. It was the only comment his stunned brain was capable of at the moment, and as he stared, Trina marched out of the room and came back a moment later carrying a box.

"Here. These are the things you've left over here. I think I got them all."

She pushed the box into his unwilling arms, and he stared down at it in shock. "I can't believe this," he muttered. "No court, no lawyer, no jury. I'm guilty and getting the death sentence!"

"You're getting dumped," Trina retorted, and pointed to the door. "Goodbye, Luke."

Luke took the box and drifted out of the house in shock. He saw himself stumble to the bike, empty his things into his saddle bag, get on the bike, and ride away.

But none of it felt real, and as he rode, the only thing that his disbelieving brain could grasp was that Trina had drop-kicked him out of her life.

All over a missed anniversary. It had to have been that.

He wasn't a drifter. He hadn't seen anybody but Trina for five solid years.

Maybe she was right about him not staying in a job long. He got bored easily. And maybe she was right about him not following through on projects. Like the hunting cabin he'd started to build and was still half-finished two years later.

The longer he drove, and the longer he thought, Luke's mood darkened from hurt to self-doubt.

Maybe Trina was right, period.

But he was too shook up to do much soul searching. The only thing he wanted at the moment was to find some quiet place to lick his wounds.

So he turned the bike off onto a narrow side road, instead of back toward Sandy Creek. He was going to get lost for a while to process what had just happened.

And then, maybe, he'd figure out how to patch up his broken heart.

Enjoy the next book in the series:

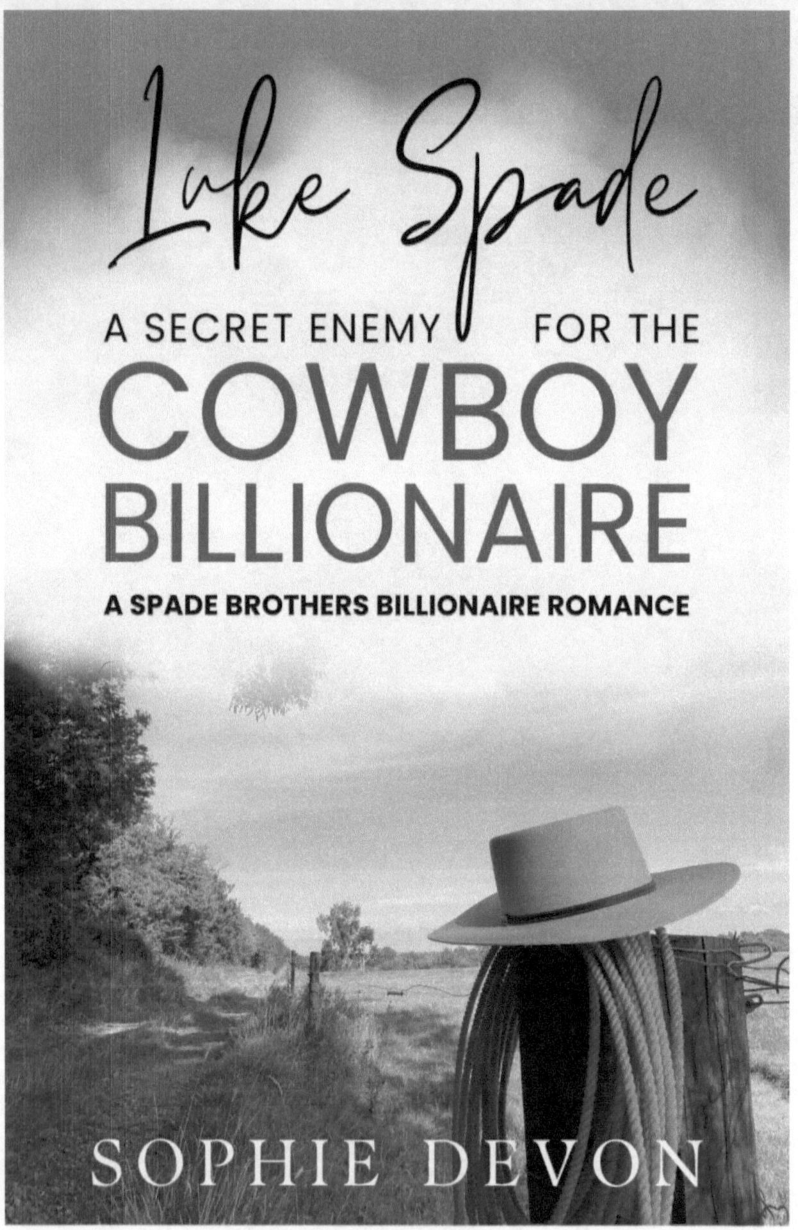

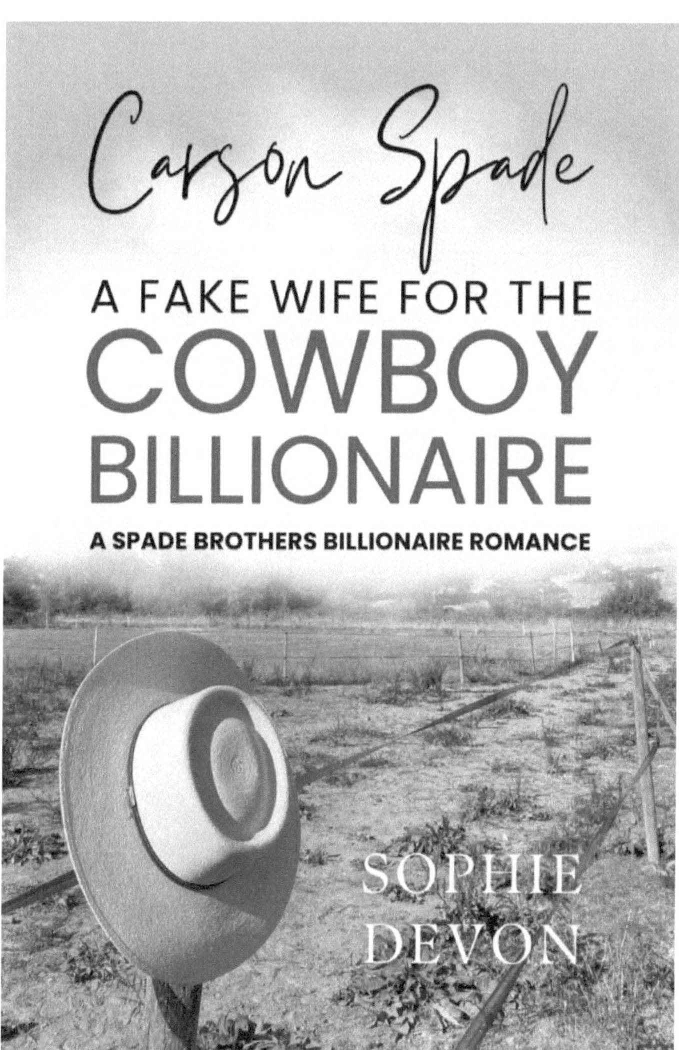
Carson Spade
A FAKE WIFE FOR THE
COWBOY
BILLIONAIRE
A SPADE BROTHERS BILLIONAIRE ROMANCE
SOPHIE
DEVON

www.ingramcontent.com/pod-product-compliance
Lightning Source LLC
Chambersburg PA
CBHW061607210726
48287CB00001B/24